Praise for
Amanda McCabe

"McCabe sweeps readers into the world of the Elizabethan theater, delighting us with a lively tale and artfully drawing on the era's backdrop of bawdy plays, wild actors and thrilling adventure."
—*RT Book Reviews* on *The Taming of the Rogue*

"Including a darling little girl, meddling relatives and a bit of suspense, McCabe's story charms readers."
—*RT Book Reviews* on *Running from Scandal*

"McCabe highlights an unusual and fascinating piece of history whilst never losing sight of the romance or adventure."
—*RT Book Reviews* on *The Demure Miss Manning*

Alys started to put on her courtly smile, prepared to meet another of Ellen's peacock friends—and her smile froze before it could form.

It had not been an illusion, a fleeting trick of her tired mind. It *was* him, Juan. Right there before her, when she had been so sure she would never see him again, *could* never see him again. She shivered and fell back a step, suddenly feeling so very cold.

He did not quite look like her Juan, bearded and ragged from the sea. He was just as tall, but his shoulders were broader, and he wore no beard to hide the elegant angles of his sculpted face, his high cheekbones and sharp jawline, his sensual lips. He wore courtly clothes of purple velvet trimmed with silver, a high, narrow ruff at his throat. But his eyes—those brilliant summer-green eyes she had once so cherished—widened when his glance fell on her.

Amanda McCabe

—

The Queen's Christmas Summons

HARLEQUIN®HISTORICAL

Recycling programs
for this product may
not exist in your area.

ISBN-13: 978-0-373-29906-5

The Queen's Christmas Summons

Copyright © 2016 by Ammanda McCabe

Printed in U.S.A.

Amanda McCabe wrote her first romance at the age of sixteen—a vast epic, starring all her friends as the characters, written secretly during algebra class. She's never since used algebra, but her books have been nominated for many awards, including a RITA® Award, an RT Reviewers' Choice Best Book Award, a Booksellers' Best Award, a National Readers' Choice Award and a Holt Medallion. She lives in Oklahoma with her husband, one dog and one cat.

Books by Amanda McCabe

Harlequin Historical and Harlequin Historical *Undone!* ebooks

Bancrofts of Barton Park

The Runaway Countess
Running from Scandal
Running into Temptation (Undone!)

Linked by Character

The Winter Queen
Tarnished Rose of the Court

Stand-Alone Novels

Betrayed by His Kiss
The Demure Miss Manning
The Queen's Christmas Summons

More Harlequin Historical *Undone!* ebooks by Amanda McCabe

Girl in the Beaded Mask
Unlacing the Lady in Waiting
One Wicked Christmas
An Improper Duchess
A Very Tudor Christmas

Visit the Author Profile page at Harlequin.com for more titles.

For Kyle, for 3 lovely years—so far

Prologue

Richmond Palace—1576

'You must stay right here, Alys, and not move. Do you understand?'

Lady Alys Drury stared up at her father. Usually, around her, he was always smiling, always gentle, but today he looked most stern. In fact, she did *not* understand. In all her eight years, her father had never seemed so grave. The man who was always laughing and boisterous, ready to sweep her up in his arms and twirl her around, could not be seen. Ever since they journeyed here, to this strange place, a royal palace, her parents had been silent.

After long days on a boat and more hours on bumpy horseback, riding pillion with her mother, they had arrived *here*. Alys wasn't sure what was happening, but she knew she did not like this place, with its soaring towers and many windows, which seemed to conceal hundreds of eyes looking down at her.

'Yes, Papa, I understand,' she answered. 'Will we be able to go home soon?'

He gave her a strained smile. 'God willing, my little butterfly.' He quickly kissed her brow and turned to hurry away up a flight of stone steps. He vanished through a doorway, guarded by men in green velvet embroidered with sparkling gold and bearing swords. Alys was left alone in the sunny, strange garden.

She turned in a slow circle, taking in her fantastical surroundings. It was like something in the fairy stories her nursemaid liked to tell, with tall hedge walls surrounding secret outdoor chambers and strictly square beds of flowers and herbs.

And the garden was not the only strange thing about the day. Alys's new gown, a stiff creation of tawny-and-black satin, rustled around her every time she moved and the halo-shaped headdress on her long, dark hair pinched.

She kicked at the gravelled pathway with her new black-leather shoe. She wished so much she was at home, where she could run free, and where her parents did not speak in angry whispers and worried murmurs.

She tipped back her head to watch as a flock of birds soared into the cloudy sky. It was a warm day, if overcast and grey, and if she was at home she could climb trees or run along the cliffs. How she missed all that.

A burst of laughter caught her attention and she whirled around to see a group of boys a bit older than herself running across a meadow just beyond the formal knot garden. They wore just shirts and breeches, and kicked a large brown-leather ball between them.

Alys longed to move closer, to see what game they played. It didn't look like any she had seen before. She glanced back at the doorway where her father vanished, but he hadn't returned. Surely she could be gone for just a moment?

She lifted the hem of her skirt and crept nearer to the game, watching as the boys kicked it between themselves. As an only child, with no brothers to play with, the games of other children fascinated her.

One of the boys was taller than the others, with overly long dark hair flopping across his brow as he ran. He moved more easily, more gracefully than the boys around him. Alys was so fascinated by him that she didn't see the ball flying towards her. It hit her hard on the brow, knocking her new headdress askew and pushing her back. For an instant, there was only cold shock, then a rush of pain. Tears sprang to her eyes as she pressed her hand to her throbbing head.

'Watch where you're going, then!' one of the boys shouted. He was a thin child, freckled, not at all like the tall one, and he pushed her as he snatched back the ball. 'Stupid girls, they have no place here. Go back to your needlework!'

Alys struggled not to cry, both at the pain in her brow and at his cruel words. 'I am *not* a stupid girl! You—you hedgepig.'

'What did you call me, wench?' The boy took a menacing step towards her.

'Enough!' The tall boy stepped forward to pull her would-be attacker back. He shoved the mean boy away and turned to Alys with a gentle smile. She noticed his eyes were green, an extraordinary pale green sea-colour she had never seen before. 'You are the one at fault here, George. Do not be ungallant. Apologise to the lady.'

'Lady?' George sneered. 'She is obviously no more a lady than you are a true gentleman, Huntley. With your drunken father…'

The tall boy grew obviously angry at those words, a

red flush spreading on his high, sharp cheekbones. His hands curled into fists—and then he stepped back, his hand loosening, a smile touching his lips. Alys forgot her pain as she watched him in fascination.

'It seems you must be the one who took a blow to the head, George,' Huntley said. 'You are clearly out of your wits. Now, apologise.'

'Nay, I shall not...' George gasped as Huntley suddenly reached out, quick as a snake striking, and seized his arm. It looked like a most effortless movement, but George turned pale. 'Forgive me, my lady.'

'That is better.' Huntley pushed the bully away and turned away from him without another glance. He came to Alys and held out his hand.

He smiled gently and Alys was dazzled by it.

'My lady,' he said. 'Let me assist you to return to the palace.'

'Th...thank you,' she whispered. She took his arm, just like a grown-up lady, and walked with him back to the steps.

'Are you badly hurt?' he asked softly.

Alys suddenly realised her head did still hurt. She had quite forgotten everything else when she saw him. It was most strange. 'Just a bit of a headache. My mother will have herbs for it in her medicine chest.'

'Where is your mother? I'll take you to her.'

Alys shook her head. Her mother had stayed at the inn, pleading illness, so her father had taken Alys away with him. She didn't know how to get back to the inn at all. 'She is in the village. My father...'

'Has he come here to see the Queen?'

The Queen? No wonder this place was so grand, if it was a queen's home. But why was her father to see her?

She felt more confused than ever. 'I was not supposed to move from the steps until he returns. I'll be in such trouble!'

'Nay, I will stay with you, my lady, and explain to your father when he returns.'

Alys studied him doubtfully. 'Surely you have more important things you must be doing.'

His smile widened. 'Nothing more important, I promise you.'

He led her back to the top of the stone steps where her father left her and helped her sit down. He sat beside her and gently examined her forehead. 'It is rather darkening, I'm afraid. I hope your mother has an herb to cure bruising.'

'Oh, no!' She clapped her hand over her brow, feeling herself blush hotly that he should see her like that. 'She does have ointments for such, but it must be hideous.'

He smiled, his lovely green eyes crinkling at the corners. 'It is a badge of honour from battle. You are fortunate to have a caring mother.'

'Does your mother not have medicines for you when you're ill?' Alys asked, thinking of all her mother's potions and creams that soothed fevers and pains, just as her own cool hands did when Alys was fretful.

He looked away. 'My mother died long ago.'

'Oh! I am sorry,' she cried, feeling such pain for him not to have a mother. 'But have you a father? Siblings?' She remembered the vile George's taunt, of Huntley's 'drunken father', and wished she had not said anything.

'I seldom see my father. My godfather arranges for my education. No siblings. What of you, my lady?'

'I have no siblings, either. I wish I did. It gets very quiet at home sometimes.'

'Is that why you came to look at our game?'

'Aye. It sounded very merry. I wondered what it was.'

'Have you never played at football?'

'I've never even heard of it. I have seen tennis, but few other ball games.'

'It's the most wonderful game! You start like this...' He leaped up to demonstrate, running back and forth as he told her of scoring and penalties. He threw up his arms in imagined triumph as he explained how the game was won.

Caught up in his enthusiasm, Alys clapped her hands and laughed. He gave her a bow.

'How marvellous,' she said. 'I do wish I had someone at home to play such games with like that.'

'What do you play at home, then?' he asked. He tossed her the ball. She instinctively caught it and threw it back.

'I read, mostly, and walk. I have a doll and I tell her things sometimes. There isn't much I can do alone, I'm afraid.'

'I quite understand. Before I went to school, I was often alone myself.' His expression looked wistful, as if his thoughts were far away, and Alys found herself intensely curious about him, who he was and what he did.

'Alys! What are you doing?' she heard her father shout.

She spun around and saw him hurrying towards her, frowning fearsomely. 'Papa! I am sorry, I just...'

'I fear your daughter took a bit of a fall here, my lord,' her new friend said, stepping close to her side. She felt safer with him there. 'I saw her, and I...'

'And he came to help me, most gallantly,' Alys said.

Her father's frown softened. 'Did you indeed? Good lad. I owe you many thanks.'

'Your daughter is a fine lady indeed, my lord,' Huntley said. 'I am glad to have met her today.'

Her father softened even more and reached into his purse to offer the boy a coin. Huntley shook his head and her father said, 'My thanks again. We bid you good day, lad, and good fortune to you.' He swung Alys up into his arms and walked away from the grand palace.

Alys glanced back over her shoulder for one last glimpse of her friend. He smiled at her and waved, and she waved back until he was out of sight. She thought surely she would never forget him, her new friend and gallant rescuer.

Chapter One

Dunboyton Castle, Galway, Ireland—1578

'And this one, *niña querida*? What is this one? What does it do?'

Lady Alys Drury, aged ten and a half and now expected to learn to run a household, leaned close to the tray her mother held out and inhaled deeply, closing her eyes. Despite the icy wind that beat at the stout stone walls of Dunboyton, she could smell green sunshine from the dried herbs. Flowers and trees and clover, all the things she loved about summer.

But not as much as she loved her mother and their days here in the stillroom, the long, narrow chamber hung with bundles of herbs and with bottles of oils and pots of balms lining the shelves. It was always warm there, always bright and full of wonderful smells. A sanctuary in the constant rush and noise of the castle corridors, which were the realm of her father and his men.

Here in the stillroom, it was just Alys and her mother. For all her ten years, for as long as she could remember, this had been her favourite place. She could imagine nowhere finer.

She inhaled again, pushing a loose lock of her brown hair back from her brow. She caught a hint of something else beneath the green—a bit of sweet wine, mayhap?

'*Querida?*' her mother urged.

Alys opened her eyes and glanced up into her mother's face. Elena Drury's dark eyes crinkled at the edges as she smiled. She wore black and white, starkly tailored and elegant, as she often did, to remind her of the fashions of her Spanish homeland, but there was nothing dark or dour about her merry smile.

'Is it—is it lemon balm, *mi madre*?' Alys said.

'Very good, Alys!' her mother said, clapping her hands. '*Sí*, it is *melissa officinalis*. An excellent aid for melancholy, when the grey winter has gone on too long.'

Alys giggled. 'But it is always grey here, Madre!' Every day seemed grey, not like the sunlit memories of her one day at a royal court. Sometimes she was sure that had all been a dream, especially the handsome boy she had seen that day. This was the only reality now.

Her mother laughed, too, and carefully stirred the dried lemon balm into a boiling pot of water. 'Only here in Galway. In some places, it is warm and sunny all the time.'

'Such as where you were born?' Alys had heard the tales many times, but she always longed to hear them again. The white walls of Granada, where her mother was born, the red-tiled roofs baking in the sun, the sound of guitar music and singing on the warm breeze.

Elena smiled sadly. 'Such as where I was born, in Granada. There is no place like it, *querida*.'

Alys glanced out the narrow window of the stillroom. The rain had turned to icy sleet, which hit the old glass like the patter of needles as the wind howled out its mournful cries. 'Why would your mother leave such a place?'

'Because she loved my father and followed him to England when his work brought him here. It was her duty to be by his side.'

'As it is yours to be with Father?'

'Of course. A wife must always be a good helpmeet to her husband. It is her first duty in life.'

'And because you love him.' This was another tale she had heard often. The tale of how her father had seen her mother, the most beautiful woman in the world, at a banquet and would marry no other, even against the wishes of his family. Alys knew her parents had not regretted choosing each other; she had often caught them secretly kissing, seen them laughing together, their heads bent close.

Her mother laughed and tucked Alys's wayward lock of hair back into her little cap. 'And that, too, though you are much too young to think of such things yet.'

'Will I have a husband as kind as Father?'

Her mother's smile faded and she bent her head over the tea she stirred. Her veil fell forward to hide her expression. 'There are few men like your father, I fear, and you are only ten. You needn't think about it for so long. Marriages are made for many reasons—family security, wealth, land, even affection sometimes. But I promise, no matter who you marry, he will be a good man, a strong one. You will not be here in Ireland for ever.'

Alys had heard such things so often. Ireland was not really their home; her father only did his duty here to the Queen for a time. One day they would have a real home, in England, and she would have a place at court. Perhaps she would even serve the Queen herself, and marry a man handsome and strong. But she could conceive of little beyond Dunboyton's walls, the cliffs and wild sea that surrounded them. There had only been that one small glimpse of the royal court, the boys playing at football, and then it was gone.

'Now, *querida*, what is this one?' her mother asked as she held out a small bottle.

Alys smelled a green sharpness, something like citrus beneath. 'Marjoram!'

'Exactly. To spice your father's wine tonight and help with his stomach troubles.'

'Is Father ill?'

Elena's smile flickered. 'Not at all. Too many rich sauces with his meat, I have warned him over and over. Ah, well. Here, *niña*, I have something for you.'

Alys jumped up on her stool, clapping her hands in delight. 'A present, Madre?'

'*Sí,* a rare one.' She reached into one of her carved boxes, all of them darkened with age and infused with the scent of all the herbs they had held over the years. Her mother removed a tiny muslin-wrapped bundle. She laid it carefully on Alys's trembling palm.

Alys unwrapped it to find a few tiny, perfect curls of bright yellow candied lemon peels. The yellow was sun-brilliant, sprinkled with sugar like snowflakes. 'Candied lemon!'

Her favourite treat. It tasted just like the sunshine Alys always longed for. She couldn't resist; she popped a piece on to her tongue and let it melt into sticky sweetness.

Her mother laughed. 'My darling daughter, always so impetuous! My brother could only send a few things

from Spain this time.' She gave a sigh as she poured off
the new tisane of lemon balm. 'The weather has kept so
many of the ships away.'

Alys glanced at the icy window again. It was true,
there had been few ships in port of late. Usually they
saw many arrivals from Spain and the Low Countries,
bringing rare luxuries and even rarer news of home to
her mother.

There was the sudden heavy tread of boots up the
winding stairs to the stillroom. The door opened and
Alys's father, Sir William Drury, stood there. He was
a tall man, broad of shoulder, with light brown hair
trimmed short in the new fashion and a short beard. But
of late, there were more flecks of grey in his beard than
usual, more of a stoop to his shoulders. Alys remembered
what her mother had said about his stomach troubles.

But he always smiled when he saw them, as he did
now, a wide, bright grin.

'Father!' Alys cried happily and jumped up to run
to him. He hugged her close, as he always did, but she
sensed that he was somehow distant from her, distracted.

Alys drew back and peered up at him. She had to look
far, for he was so very much taller than she. He did smile,
but his eyes looked sad. He held something in his hand,
half-hidden behind his back.

'William,' she heard her mother say. There was a soft
rustle of silk, the touch of her mother's hand on her shoulder. 'The letter…'

'Aye, Elena,' he answered, his voice tired. ''Tis from
London.'

'Alys,' her mother said gently. 'Why don't you go to
the kitchen and see if our dinner will soon be ready? Give
this to the cooks for the stew.'

She pressed a sachet of dried parsley and rosemary into Alys's hand and gently urged her through the door.

Bewildered, Alys glanced back before the door could close behind her. Her father went to the window, staring out at the rain beyond with his back to her, his hand clasped before him. Her mother went to him, leaning against his shoulder. Alys dared to hold the door open a mere inch, lingering so she could find out what was happening. Otherwise they would never tell her at all.

'There is still no place for you at court?' Alys heard her mother say. Elena's voice was still soft, kind, but it sounded as if she might start to cry.

'Nay, not yet, or so my uncle writes. I am needed here for a time longer, considering the uprisings have just been put down. Here! In this godforsaken place where I can do nothing!' His fist came down on the table with a sudden crash, rattling the bottles.

'Because of me,' her mother whispered. '*Madre de Dios*, but if not for me, for us, you would have your rightful place.'

'Elena, you and Alys are everything to me. You would be a grace to the royal court, to anywhere you chose to be. They are fools they cannot see that.'

'Because I am a Lorca-Ramirez. I should not have married you, *mi corazón*. I have brought you nothing. If you had a proper English wife—if I was gone…'

'Nay, Elena, you must never say that. You are all to me. I would rather be here at the end of the world with you and Alys than be a king in a London palace.'

Alys peeked carefully through the crack in the door and watched as her father took her mother tightly into his arms as she sobbed on his shoulder. Her father's expression when he thought his wife could not see was fierce, furious.

Alys tiptoed down the stillroom stairs, careful to make no sound. She felt somehow cold and fearful. Her father was almost never angry, yet there was something about that moment, the look on his face, the sadness that hung so heavy about her mother, that made her want to run away.

Yet she also wanted to run *to* her parents, to wrap her arms around them and banish anything that would dare hurt them.

She made her way to the bustling kitchen to leave the herbs with the cook, hurrying around the soldiers who cleaned their swords by the fire, the maids who scurried around with pots and bowls. *London*. It was there that lurked whatever had angered her father. She knew where London was, of course, far away over the sea in England. It was home, or so her father sometimes said, but she couldn't quite fathom it.

When he showed her drawings of London, pointing out churches and bridges and palaces, she was amazed by the thought of so many people in such grand dwellings. The largest place she knew was Galway City. When she went to market there with her mother, Father said London was like twenty Galways.

London was also where Queen Elizabeth lived. The Queen, who was so grand and glittering and beautiful, who held all of England safe in her jewelled hand. Was it the Queen who angered him now? Who slighted her mother?

Her fists clenched in anger at the thought of it as Alys stomped across the kitchen. How dared the Queen, how dared anyone, do such a thing to her parents? It was not fair. She didn't care where she lived, whether Galway or London, but she did care if her father was denied his true place.

'How now, Lady Alys, and what has you in such a temper?' one of the cooks called out. 'Have the fairies stolen away your sugar and left salt instead?'

Alys had to laugh at the teasing. 'Nay, I merely came to give you some of my mother's herbs. 'Tis the cold day has me in a mood, I think.'

'It's never cold down here with all these fires. Here, I need a spot of mint from the garden and I think a hardy bunch still has some green near the wall. Will you fetch it for me? Some fresh air might do you some good, my lady.'

Alys nodded, glad of an errand, and quickly found her cloak before she slipped out into the walled kitchen garden.

The wind was chilly as she made her way to the covered herb beds at the back of the garden, but she didn't care. It brought with it the salt tang of the sea and whenever she felt sad or confused the sea would calm her again.

She climbed up to the top of the stone wall and perched there for a glimpse of the sea. The outbuildings of the castle, the dairy and butcher's shop and stables, blocked most of the view of the cliffs, but she could see a sliver of the grey waves beyond.

That sea could take *her* to London, she thought, and she would fix whatever there had hurt her family. She would tell the Queen all about it herself. And maybe, just maybe, she would see that handsome boy again…

'Alys! You will catch the ague out here,' she heard her father shout.

She glanced back to see him striding down the garden path, no cloak or hat against the cold wind, though he seemed not to notice. His attention was only on her.

'Father, how far is London?'

He scowled. 'Oh, so you heard that, did you? It is much farther than you could fly, my little butterfly.' He lifted her down from the wall, spinning her around to make her giggle before he braced her against his shoulder. 'Mayhap one day you *will* go there and see it for yourself.'

'Will I see the Queen?'

'Only if she is very lucky.'

'But what if she does not want to see me? Because I am yours and Mother's?'

Her father hugged her tightly. 'You must not think such things, Alys. You are a Drury. Your great-grandmother served Elizabeth of York, and your grandmother served Katherine of Aragon. Our family goes back hundreds of years and your mother's even more. The Lorca-Ramirez are a ducal family and there are no dukes at all in England now. You would be the grandest lady at court.'

Alys wasn't so sure of that. Her mother and nursemaid were always telling her no lady would climb walls and swim in the sea as she did. But London—it sounded most intriguing. And if she truly was a lady and served the Queen well, the Drurys would have their due at long last.

She glanced back at the roiling sea as her father carried her into the house. One day, yes, that sea would take her to England and she would see its splendours for herself.

'That lying whore! She has been dead for years and still she dares to thwart me.' A crash exploded through the house as Edward Huntley threw his pottery plate against the fireplace and it shattered. It was followed by a splintering sound, as if a footstool was kicked to pieces.

John Huntley heard a maidservant shriek and he was sure she must be new to the household. Everyone else was accustomed to his father's rages and went about their business with their heads down.

John himself would scarcely have noticed at all, especially as he was hidden in his small attic space high above the ancient great hall of Huntleyburg Abbey. It was the one place where his father could never find him, as no one else but the ghosts of the old banished monks seemed to know it was there. When he was forced to return to Huntleyburg at his school's recess, he would spend his days outdoors hunting and his evenings in this hiding place, studying his Latin and Greek in the attic eyrie. Making plans for the wondrous day he would be free of his father at last.

He was nearly fourteen now. Surely that day would be soon.

Edward let out another great bellow. John wouldn't have listened to the rantings at all, except that something unusual had happened that morning. A visitor had arrived at Huntleyburg.

And not just any visitor. John's godfather, Sir Matthew Morgan, had galloped up the drive unannounced soon after breakfast, when John's father was just beginning the day's drinking of strong claret. When John heard of Sir Matthew's arrival, he started to run down the stairs. It had been months since he heard from Sir Matthew, who was his father's cousin but had a very different life from the Huntleys, a life at the royal court.

Yet something had held him back, some tension in the air as the servants rushed to attend on Sir Matthew. John had always been able to sense tiny shifts in the mood of the people around him, sense when secrets were being held. Secrets could so seldom be kept from him. His father used to rage that John was an unnatural child, that he inherited some Spanish witchcraft from his cursed mother and would try to beat it out of him. Until John learned to hide it.

It was secrets he felt hanging in the air that morning. Secrets that made him wait and watch, which seemed the better course for the moment. A fight always went better when he had gathered as much information as possible. Why *was* Sir Matthew there? He had only been at the Abbey for an hour and he already had John's father cursing his mother's memory.

And it had to be his mother Edward was shouting about now. Maria-Caterina was always The Spanish Whore to her husband, even though she had been dead for twelve years.

John glanced at the portrait hung in the shadowed corner of his hiding place. A lovely lady with red-gold hair glimpsed under a lacy mantilla, her hands folded against the stiff white-and-silver skirt of her satin gown, her green eyes smiling down at him. On her finger was a gold ring: the same one John now wore on his littlest finger.

One side of the canvas was slashed, the frame cracked, from one of Edward's rages, but John had saved her and brought her to safety. He only wished he could have done the same in real life. To honour her, he tried to help those more helpless any time he could. As he had with that tiny, pretty girl once, when she was hit in the head with the football. He sometimes wondered where she was now.

He heard the echo of voices, the calm, slow tones of his godfather, a sob from his father. If Edward had already turned to tears from rage, John thought it was time for him to appear.

He unfolded his long legs from the bench and made his way out of the attic, ducking his head beneath the old rafters. He had had a growth spurt in his last term at school and soon he would need a larger hiding place. But soon, very soon by the grace of his mother's saints, he would be gone from the Abbey for good.

He made his way down the ladder that led into the great hall. It had been a grand space when his great-grandfather bought the property from King Henry, bright with painted murals and with rich carpets and tapestries to warm the lofty walls and vaulted ceilings, but all of that had been gone for years. Now, it was a faded, dusty, empty room.

At the far end of the hall, his father sat slumped in his chair by the fire. He had spilled wine on his old fur-trimmed robe and his long, grey-flecked dark hair and beard were tangled. The shattered pottery remains were scattered on the floor, amid splashes of blood-red wine, but no one ventured near to clean it up.

Sir Matthew stood a few feet away, his arms crossed over his chest as he dispassionately surveyed the scene. Unlike Edward, he was still lean and fit, his sombre dark grey travelling clothes not elaborate, but perfectly cut from the finest wool and velvet. With his sword strapped to his side, he looked ready to ride out and fight for his Queen at any moment, despite his age.

What had brought such a man to such a pitiful place as Huntleyburg?

Sir Matthew glanced up and saw John there in the shadows. 'Ah, John, my dear lad, there you are. 'Tis most splendid to see you again. How you have grown!'

Before John could answer, his father turned his bleary gaze to him, his face twisted in fury. 'She has cursed me again,' he shouted. 'You and your mother have ruined my life! I am still not allowed at court.'

Sir Matthew pressed Edward back into his chair with a firm yet unobtrusive hand to his shoulder. 'You know the reason you are not allowed at court has nothing to do with Maria-Caterina. In fact, she is the only reason your whole roof did not come crashing down on your head years ago.'

John looked up at the great hall's ceiling, at the ancient, stained rafters patched with newer plaster. It was true his mother had been an heiress. But that money was long gone now.

'She cursed me,' Edward said pitifully. 'She said the monks who once lived here would take their rightful home back and I would have naught.'

Sir Matthew gave him a distasteful glance. He poured out another goblet of wine and pressed it into Edward's hand, smiling grimly as he gulped it down.

'We have more serious matters to discuss now, Edward,' Sir Matthew said. 'Maria-Caterina is long gone and you have tossed away any chance you may have had. But it is not too late for John.'

'John? What can he possibly do?' Edward said contemptuously, without even looking at his son.

'He can do much indeed. I hear from your tutors that you are most adept, John, especially at languages,' Sir Matthew said, turning away from Edward and beckoning John closer. 'That you should be sent to Cambridge next term. Do you enjoy your studies?'

Somewhere deep inside of John, in a spot he had thought long numbed, hope stirred. 'Very much, my lord.

I know my Greek and Latin quite well now, as well as French and Spanish, and some Italian.'

'And your skills with the bow and the sword? How are they?'

John thought of the stag he had brought down for the supper table, one clean arrow shot. 'Not bad, I think. You can ask the sword master at my school, I work with him every week.'

'Hmm.' Sir Matthew studied John closely, tapping his fingers against his sleeve. 'And you are handsome, too.'

'He gets it from his cursed mother,' Edward muttered. 'Those eyes…'

Sir Matthew peered closer. 'Aye, you do have a dark Spanish look about you, John.' He poured out even more wine and handed it to Edward without another glance. 'Come, John, let us walk outside for a time. I haven't long before I must ride back.'

John followed his godfather into the abbey garden. Like the house, they had once been a grand showplace, filled with the colour and scent of rare roses, the splash of fountains. Now it was brown and dead. But John felt more hope than he had in a long while. School had been an escape from home, a place where he knew he had to work hard. Was that hard work finally going to reward him? And with what?

'You said I might be able to do much indeed, my lord,' he said, trying not to appear too eager. To seem sophisticated enough for Cambridge and a career beyond. Maybe even something at court. 'I hope that may be true. I wish to serve the Queen in any way I am able.' And maybe to redeem the Huntley name, as well, if it was not lost for good. To bring honour to his family again would mean his life had a meaning.

Sir Matthew smiled. 'Most admirable, John. The Queen is in great need of talented and loyal men like you, now more than ever. I fear dark days lie ahead for England.'

Darker days than now, with Spain and France crowding close on all sides, and Mary of Scotland lurking in the background at every moment? 'My lord?'

'The Queen has always had many enemies, but now they will grow ever bolder. I hope to raise a regiment to take to the Low Countries soon.'

'Truly?' John said in growing excitement. To be a soldier, to win glory on the battlefield—sure that would save the name of Huntley. 'Might there be a place for me in your household there, my lord?'

Sir Matthew's smile turned wry. 'Perhaps one day, John. But you must finish your studies first. A mind like yours, adept at languages, will be of great use to you.'

John hid his flash of disappointment. 'What sort of place might there be for me, then?'

'Perhaps...' Sir Matthew seemed to hesitate before he said, 'Perhaps you have heard of my friend Sir Francis Walsingham?'

Of course John had heard of Walsingham. He was the Queen's most trusted secretary, the keeper of many secrets, many dangers. 'Aye, I know of him.'

'He recently asked me about your progress. If matters do come to war with Spain, a man with connections and skills such as yours would be most valuable.'

John's thoughts raced, a dizzying tidal pool of what a man like Walsingham might ask of him. 'Because I am half-Spanish?'

'That, of course, and because of your intelligence. Your—intuition, perhaps. I noticed it in you when you were a boy, that watchfulness, that—that *knowledge*. It is still there. Properly honed and directed, it will take you far.'

'You think there will be danger from Spain soon? Is that why you are going to the Low Countries to fight them there?'

'There will always be danger from Spain, my dear lad. Who knows what will happen in a few years, when you have finished your studies? Now, why don't you tell me more of your schooling? What have you learned of mathematics there, of astronomy?'

John walked with Sir Matthew around the gardens back to the drive at the front of the house, where a servant waited with his horse. He told him about his schooling and asked a few questions about court, which Sir Matthew answered lightly.

'Keep up with your studies, John, and do not worry about your father. I will see he comes to no harm,' Sir Matthew said as he swung himself up into his saddle. 'I must go now, but you will think about what I have said?'

'Of course, my lord.' John was sure he would think of little else. He bowed, and watched his godfather gallop away.

John looked back at the house. In the fading sunlight, Huntleyburg Abbey looked better than usual, its patches and cracks disguised. He would so love to restore it, to see its beauty come back to life, but he had never known how he would do that. Mayhap he could do it with secrets—Walsingham's secrets, England's secrets. But what would that be like? What path would his life follow? He wasn't sure.

But he knew that if it took spy craft, working in the shadows, living half a life to restore the Huntley name his father had so squandered, he would do it. He would do anything, make any sacrifice, to bring back their honour. He vowed it then and there, to himself and his family. That would be his life.

Chapter Two

Galway—early summer 1588

Alys, carrying a basket of linen to the laundry above the kitchens of Dunboyton Castle, heard an all-too-familiar sound floating up the stone stairs—the wailing sobs of some of the younger maidservants. Their panic had been hanging like a dark cloud over Dunboyton for days.

Not that she could blame them. She herself felt constantly as if she walked the sharp edge of a sword, about to fall one way or the other, but always caught in the horrible uncertainty of the middle. They said the Spanish Armada had left its port in Lisbon and was on its way to England, to conquer the island nation and all her holdings, including Ireland. Hundreds of ships, filled with thousands of men, coming to wage war.

She wished she could somehow banish the rumours that flew like dark ghosts down the castle corridors. It made her want to scream out in frustration.

Yet she could not. She was the lady of the castle now, as she had been in the nine years since her mother had died. She had to set an example of calm and fortitude.

She stepped into the laundry, and put down her basket with the others. She saw that the day's work was not even half-finished, with linens left to boil unsupervised in the cauldrons, the air filled with lavender-scented steam so thick she could barely see through it.

'Oh, my lady!' one of the maids, young Molly, wailed when she saw Alys. 'They do say that when the Spanish come, we will all be horribly tortured! That in their ships they carry whips and nooses, and brands to mark all the babies.'

'I did hear that, too,' another maid said, her voice full of doomed resignation. 'That all the older children will be killed and the babies marked so after all might know their shame of being conquered.'

'Don't be silly,' the old head laundress said heartily. 'We will all be run through with swords and tossed over the walls into the sea before we can be branded.'

'They say the Dutch in Leiden burned their own city to the ground before they let it fall into Spanish hands,' another said. 'We shall have to do the same.'

'Enough!' Alys said sternly. If she heard once more about the rumoured cruelties of the Spanish, people who were nowhere near Ireland, she would scream. What would her mother have said about it all? 'If they are sailing at all, they are headed to England, not here, and they shall be turned back before they even get near. We are in no danger.'

'Then why are all the soldiers marching into Fort Hill?' Molly asked. 'And why is Sir Richard Bingham riding out from Galway City to inspect the fortifications?'

Alys wished she knew that herself. Bingham had a cruel reputation after so bloodily putting down the chieftains' rebellions years before; having him roaming the countryside could mean nothing good. But she couldn't let the maids see that. 'We are in more danger of a short-age of clean linen than anything else,' she said, tossing a pile of laundry at Molly. 'We must finish the day's work now, Armada or not.'

The maids all grumbled but set about their scrubbing and stirring. As Alys turned to leave, she heard the whis-pers rustle up again. *Whips and brands...*

The stone walls felt as if they were pressing down on her. The fear and uncertainty all around her for so many days was making her feel ill. She—who prided herself on a sturdy spirit and practicality! A person had to be sturdy to live in such a place as Dunboyton. The cold winds that always swept off the sea, the monotony of seeing the same faces every day, the strangeness of the land itself, it had all surely driven many people mad.

Alys didn't mind the life of Dunboyton now. Even if she sometimes dreamed of seeing other lands, the sparkle of a royal court or the sunshine of her mother's Granada, she knew she had to be content with her father and her duties at the castle. It was her life and dreaming could not change it.

But now—now she felt as if she was caught in a con-fusing, upside-down nightmare she couldn't wake from at all.

She had other tasks waiting, but she had to get away for just a few moments, to breathe some fresh air and clear away the miasma of fear the maids' gossip had woven. She snatched a woollen cloak from the hook by the kitchen door and made her way outside.

A cold wind whipped around the castle walls, catch-ing at her hair and her skirts. She hurried through the kitchen garden and scrambled over the rough stone wall into the wilder fields beyond, as she had done so often ever since she was a child. After her mother died, she would often escape for long rambles along the shore and up to the ruins of the abbey, and she would see no one at all for hours.

That was not true today. She followed the narrow path that led down from Dunboyton's perch on the cliffs down to the bay. The spots that were usually deserted were today filled with people, hurrying on errands that she couldn't identify, but which they seemed to think were quite vital. Soldiers both from her father's castle regiment and sent from Galway City and the fort swarmed in a mass of blue-and-grey wool over the rocky beach.

Alys paused halfway along the path to peer down at them as they marched back and forth. Everyone said the Spanish were sweeping ever closer to England in their invincible ships and would never come this far north, but obviously precautions were still being taken, enough to frighten the maids. They said the Spanish had come here before, to try to help the chieftains defeat the English rulers, but they had been driven away then. Why would now be any different?

Whips and brands...hangings. Alys shivered and pulled her cloak closer around her. She remembered her mother's tales of Spain, the way the candied lemons and oranges sent from her uncles in Andalusia would melt on her tongue like sunshine, and she could not reconcile the two images at all. Could the same people who had produced her lovely, gentle mother be so barbarous? And if so, what lay deep inside herself?

Her father was banished from the royal court, sent to be governor in this distant place because of her mother's birthplace. What would happen to them now?

'Alys!' she heard her father call. 'It is much too cold today for you to be here.'

She turned to see him hurrying up the pathway, the wind catching at his cloak and cap, a spyglass in his hand. He looked so much older suddenly, his beard turned grey, lines etched on his face, as if this new worry had aged him.

'I won't stay out long,' she said. 'I just couldn't listen to the maids a moment longer.'

He nodded grimly. 'I can imagine. Spreading panic now will help no one.'

'Is there any word yet from England?'

'Only that the ships have been gathering in Portsmouth and Plymouth, and militias organised along the coast. Nothing established as of yet. There have been no signal fires from Dublin.'

Alys gestured towards the activity on the beach. 'Bingham is taking no chances, I see.'

'Aye, the man does love a fight. He has been idle too long, since the rebellions were put down. I fear he will be in for a sharp disappointment when no Spaniard shows up for battle.'

Or if England was overrun and conquered before Ireland even had a chance to fight. But she could not say that aloud. She would start to wail like the maids.

Alys borrowed her father's spyglass and used it to scan the horizon. The water was dark grey, choppy as the wind whipped up, and she could see no vessels but a few local fishing boats. It had been thus for weeks, the weather unseasonably cold, storm-ridden and unpredictable. This was usually the best time of the year to set sail, but not now. The Spanish would be foolhardy to try to land in such an inhospitable place, for so many reasons.

But faint hearts had not conquered the New World, or overrun and mastered the Low Countries. Anything could happen in such a world.

'They say Medina-Sidonia is ordered to bring Parma's land forces from the coast of the Netherlands to overrun England,' her father said. 'Why would they come here?'

'They won't,' Alys said with more confidence than she felt. 'This shall be a tale you tell your grandchildren by the fire one day, Father. The salvation of England by a great miracle.' She handed him the spyglass and took his arm to go back up the path towards the castle.

'If I have a grandchild,' he said in a teasing grumble. They had bantered about such things many times before, his need for a grandchild to dandle on his lap. 'I fear there are no proper gentlemen for you to marry here, my Alys, unless you take one of Bingham's men down there.'

Alys glanced back at the soldiers, all of them alike in their helmets. 'Nay, I thank you. If that is my choice, I shall end a spinster, keeping house here for you.'

Her father frowned. 'My poor Alys. 'Tis true no one here is worthy of you. If you could but go to court…'

Alys had heard such things before, but she had long ago given up hope of such a grand adventure. 'I admit I should like the fine gowns I would have to wear at court and learning the newest dances and songs, but I fear I should be the veriest country mouse and bring shame to you,' she said lightly. 'Besides, surely I am safer here.'

He patted her hand. 'For now, mayhap. But not for ever.'

They made their way back into the castle, into the midst of the bustle and noise of everyday life. Nothing ever seemed to change at Dunboyton. Yet she could still hear the clang of battle preparations just outside her door.

Chapter Three

Lisbon—April 1588

'King Philip will hear Mass at St Paul's by October, I vow,' Lord Westmoreland, an English Catholic exile who had lived under King Philip's sponsorship for many months, declared stoutly. He waved towards the grand procession making its way past his rented window, through the old, winding cobblestone streets of Lisbon. 'And I have been promised the return of my estates as soon as he does.'

His friend and fellow English exile Lord Paget gave a wry smile. 'He will have to get there first.' And that was the challenge. The Armada was now assembled, hundreds of ships strong, but after much delay, bad weather, spoiled provisions and a rash of desertions.

'How can you doubt he will? Look at the might of his kingdom!' Lord Westmoreland cried.

John Huntley joined the others in peering out Lord Westmoreland's window. It was an impressive sight, he had to admit. King Philip's commander of his great Armada, the mighty Duke of Medina-Sidonia, rode at the head of a great procession from the royal palace to the cathedral, resplendent in a polished silver breastplate etched with his family seal and a blue-satin cloak lined with glossy sable. Beside him rode the Cardinal Archduke, his robes as red as blood against the whitewashed houses, and behind them was a long, winding train of sparkling nobility, riding four abreast. The colours of their family banners snapped in the wind, golds and reds and blues. The sun gleamed on polished armour and turned the bright satins and silks into a rippling rainbow.

There followed ladies in brocade litters, peering shyly from beneath their cobweb-fine mantillas at the crowds, and then humble priests and friars on foot. Their black-and-brown robes were a sombre note, one lost in the waves of cheers from the Spanish crowds. The conquered Portuguese stayed behind their window shutters.

Just out of sight, the ships moored in the Tagus River let off a deafening volley from their guns. The last time Spanish ships had sailed up that river, it had been to conquer and subjugate Portugal. Now they sailed out to overrun new lands, to make all the world Spanish.

But John knew there was more, much more, behind this glittering display of power. The Armada had been delayed for so long, their supplies ran desperately short even now, before leaving port. Sailors had been deserting and Spanish gangs roamed the streets of Lisbon, pressing men to replace them.

He had to find out more of the truth of the Armada's situation, the certainty of her plans, so he could pass on the word before they sailed out of Lisbon. After that, unless they found a friendly port, he could send no more messages until he arrived in England, one way or another. All the long months of careful planning, all the puzzle pieces he had been painstakingly sliding into place, would have to be carried to their endgame now.

England's future, the lives of its people, were at stake.

'What think you, Master Kelsey?' Lord Westmoreland asked John, using the pseudonym that had been his for years, ever since he 'deserted' the Queen's armies in Antwerp and carried information to the Spanish. It had followed him now to Lisbon and beyond. 'Shall we regain our English estates and see the people returned to the true church before year's end?'

'I pray so, my lord,' John answered. 'With God's will, we cannot be thwarted. I long for my own home again, as we all do, after the injustices the false Queen has inflicted on my family. My Spanish mother would rejoice if she could see this day.'

'Well said, Master Kelsey,' Lord Paget said. 'We will bring honour and justice back to our homeland at last.'

'And we shall avenge the sacrifice of Queen Mary of Scotland,' Lord Percy said. He spoke softly, but everyone gathered around him looked at him in surprise. Percy obviously burned with zeal for his cause, praying in the church of the Ascension near his home for hours at a time, but he seldom spoke.

'Aye, the poor, martyred Queen,' Westmoreland said uncertainly.

'She was the first of us to truly witness the great cruelty of the heretic Elizabeth,' Percy said. 'The tears of Catholic widows, the poor children torn from their families and raised to damnation in the false church. I know how they suffer; I have seen their words in my letters from England.'

John wished he, too, could see those letters; the information they would contain about traitors to England, the aid they gave to the Queen's enemies, would be invaluable. Who knew what their true plans were once they landed in England? But thus far, though Westmoreland was careless with his words and his correspondence, Percy was not.

John laid a gentle hand on Percy's tense shoulder. The gold ring that had once been his mother's, the ring he never took off, gleamed. 'You shall see your family again soon.'

Percy glanced at John, a wild, desperate light in his eyes. 'I pray so. *You* will help us, Master Kelsey. You understand and you shall be there when the ships land while we wait and pray here.'

Aye, John thought, he did understand. Though not in the way poor Percy thought. He knew that England had to remain free of Spain at all costs, that the cruelty and bloodshed he had seen in the Low Countries could not be carried to English shores.

'We should leave soon, gentlemen,' Westmoreland said. 'We must take our places in the cathedral to see the Duke take up the sacred standard.'

A murmur went through the crowd, wine goblets were drained and everyone took up their fine cloaks and plumed caps.

'I must join you later,' John said. 'I have an appointment first.'

'With a fair lady of Lisbon, I dare say!' Paget said with a hearty laugh.

John did not deny it, only grinned and shook his head, and took their ribald teasing. A sacred day for them it might be, but they would never eschew gossip about pretty women. He made his way out of the house and through a winding maze of the steep, old streets with their uneven cobbles and close-packed white houses. The crowd had dispersed as the procession made its way to the cathedral and most of the houses were shuttered again, as if nothing had happened.

He could hear the toll of the church bells in the distance, could smell the bitter whiff of smoke from the ships' guns lingering in the air, but there were none to block his path. No one seemed to pay him any attention at all as he passed, despite the richness of his black-velvet mantel embroidered with gold and silver and his fine red-satin doublet.

Nonetheless, he took a most circuitous path, careful to be sure he was not trailed. He had been trained to be most observant for many years, ever since his godfather introduced him to Walsingham and his shadowy world. He had learned code-breaking along with languages at Cambridge, along with swordplay, firearms and the surreptitious use of needle-thin Italian daggers. He had honed those skills fighting in the Low Countries, then making his way at the Spanish court under Westmoreland's patronage. He was never followed—unless he meant to be.

Now, all those years of work were coming to fruition. The danger England had long feared from Spain was imminent, ready to sail at any moment. He had to be doubly careful now.

There was a sudden soft burst of laughter and his hand went automatically to the hilt of his dagger, but when he peered around the corner of a narrow alleyway he saw it was only a young couple, wrapped in each other's arms, their heads bent close together. The girl whispered something that made the man smile and their lips met in a gentle kiss.

John moved on, pushing down a most unwelcome feeling that rose up inside of him unbidden—a cold pang of loneliness. There was no time for such things in his life, no place for tenderness.

After the Armada was defeated and England was safe, after his task was done—mayhap then there could be such moments…

John gave a rueful laugh at himself. After that, if he even survived, which was unlikely, there would be another task, and another. Maybe one day he could restore Huntleyburg, even find a wife, but not for a long time. By then, he would be a veritable greybeard and beyond any mortal help from any lady. His father's bitter ghost would have taken him over. But he could redeem his family's honour, restore their good name and that had to be enough.

He finally found his destination, a public house at the crest of a steep lane. Its doorway and grimy windows looked over the red-tile roofs to the forest of ships' masts that crowded the river port. It was an impressive sight— or would be if anyone in the dim, low-ceilinged, smoke-stained public room looked outside. It was not crowded, but there were enough people at the scarred tables for the middle of a day and they mostly seemed slumped in drunken stupors on their benches. The room had the sour smell of cheap ale and the illness that came from drinking too much of such ale.

John found his contact in a small private chamber beyond the main room, hidden behind a warren of narrow corridors. Its one window looked out on to an alleyway, perfect for an escape if needed. The man was small and nondescript, clad in plain brown wool with a black cap pulled over his wispy brown hair. He was someone that no one would look at twice on the street—his real strength. John hadn't seen him since Antwerp.

'The day draws nigh at last,' he said as John drew up a stool and reached for the pitcher of ale.

''Tis not the best kept secret in Europe,' John said. He had known this man for a long time and trusted him as much as he was able, which was not a great deal.

'King Philip is not a man to make up his mind quickly. But now that he is ready to strike, even the Duke of Medina-Sidonia cannot warn him away.'

John thought of the Duke's well-known qualms, the way he had first tried to turn down the 'honour' of the command, his worries about the lack of supplies, the poor weather. 'And the Queen? Is she ready to strike in return?'

The man shrugged. 'The English militias are woefully under-trained and lack arms, but the rumours of Spanish evils have spread quickly and they are ready to fight to the death if need be. If an army can be landed, that is.'

'But England has greater defences than any land army.'

The man looked surprised John knew such a thing. 'How many ships does King Philip command now?'

'It is hard to say precisely. Ten galleons from the Indian Guard, nine of the Portuguese navy, plus four galleasses and forty merchant ships. That is only of the first and second lines. Thirty-four pinnaces to serve as scouts. Perhaps one hundred and thirty in all.'

'Her Majesty has thirty-four galleons in her fleet, but Captain Hawkins has overseen their redesign most admirably,' the man said. John nodded. Everyone knew that Hawkins, as Treasurer of Marine Causes and an experienced mariner, had been most insistent over vociferous protests that the Queen's navy had to be modernised.

'They are longer in keel and narrower in beam, much sleeker now that the large fighting castles were removed. They're fast and slower to take on water. They can come about and fire on the old Spanish ships four times before they can even turn once.'

John absorbed this image as he sipped at the ale. 'A ship of six hundred tons will carry as good ordnance as one of twelve hundred.'

'Indeed. And Her Majesty's guns, though fewer than King Philip's, are newer. They have four-wheeled carriages, with longer barrels, and Hawkins's new ships have a new continuous gun deck which can hold near forty-three guns.'

John nodded grimly. The *San Lorenzo*, Spain's greatest galleon, held forty, but sixteen of them were small minions. Spain was indeed not prepared when it came to actual sea battle with England's modern navy. But Spain was counting on land war with Parma's superior forces, if they could be landed. 'England is ready for sea battle.'

'More than Spain could ever know or predict, I dare say.'

'Spain sails knowing God will send them a miracle.'

'So they will need it. Sailing with such an unwieldy, unprepared force can have no good end. Medina-Sidonia knows that.' The man gave him a long, dark look. 'To be on these ships is a dangerous proposition for any man.'

'I do know it well, too. But information obtained from inside the ships could be of much use later.'

'And once a path is decided upon, 'tis impossible to turn back. *I* know that well.' He finished his goblet of ale and rose to his feet. 'God's fortune to you, sir. I travel now to Portsmouth, one way or another, and will send your message to our mutual friend from there.'

John nodded and waited several minutes before following his contact from the ale house. He made his way back to his lodgings through streets turned empty and ghostly after the pageantry of the procession. The shutters were closed on the houses and everything seemed to hold its breath to see what would happen next.

John had been working towards this moment for so very long and, now that it was upon him, now that he was actually about to embark, he felt numb, distant from it all. He knew Sir Matthew would make sure his family's name was restored if he died on the voyage and he himself could bring new glory to the Huntleys if he survived. It was what he had worked for, but at the moment it all seemed strangely hollow.

He found the house where he had lodgings, near the river wharves, and made his way up the staircase at the back of the building. It was noisier there; the dock workers did not have the luxury of locking themselves away until the Armada had sailed. They had to prepare the ships for the long voyage, and quickly. The sounds of shouts, of creaking ropes and snapping sails, floated over the crooked rooftops.

He could hear it even in his rooms, the small, bare, rented space that was exactly the same sort of place where he had lived for years. He barely remembered what being in one place was like, having a home to belong to. He unbuckled his sword and draped the belt over a stool, unfastening his doublet as he poured out a measure of wine.

But he was not alone. He could feel the presence of someone else, hear the soft scratching of a pen across parchment. He followed the sound to his small sitting room and found Peter de Vargas at his desk, the man's pale head bent over a letter he was feverishly penning, as if time was running out. As it was for the men who were to sail at least.

John felt no alarm. Peter often borrowed his rooms, saying they were quieter than his family's lodgings, and Peter seemed to have much to accomplish, though John had not yet deciphered what that was. He was a strange man, was Peter. Half-English, but fervent in the Catholic cause. He had befriended John when they first met in Madrid, and was a source of much information from the inner circle of the King's court. John couldn't help but pity him, though; Peter was a pale, sickly young man, but afire with zeal for his cause and eager to bring others into its work when he could.

He glanced up at John and his pale blue eyes were red-rimmed, bright as if with fever. 'I did not see you at the cathedral,' he said.

'Nay, I could not find a place there, it was so crowded,' John answered. 'I watched from the street.'

'Glorious, was it not? The cheers as the Duke raised the sacred standard were most heartening. God will surely bring us a miracle.'

It would take God to do so, John thought wryly, considering that poor preparations of the Spanish king. 'Have you eaten?'

'It is a fasting day,' Peter answered. 'I took a little wine. I need to send these letters before we sail.'

'Who do you write to?' John asked. 'Your mother?'

'Among others. I want them to know the glory of this cause.' He glanced down at the letter he was working on. 'This one—I do not know if it will reach its goal. I pray it must, for if anyone has to know all…'

'It is this person?' John said. Peter had often spoken of some mysterious correspondent, someone whose rare letters he treasured, someone who must know everything. Thus far John had had little luck finding out who it was. He thought it might be someone in England, a contact of Peter's. He would soon find out who it was. Peter was a fool, dedicated to a cause that cared naught for him and would wreak destruction on half the world if it could. They had to be stopped and John would do whatever he had to in order to accomplish that.

If time did not run out for them all.

Chapter Four

Galway—September

Alys could not sleep, despite the great lateness of the hour. The icy wind, which had been gathering off the sea all day, had grown into a howling gale, beating against the stone walls of the castle as if demons demanded entrance. The rain that had pounded down for days had become freezing sleet, always pattering at her window.

Every time she managed to doze off for a little while, strange dreams pulled her back into wakefulness. Fire-breathing dragons chased her, or the castle was turned into an icy fortress with everyone inside frozen. The long days of not knowing what would happen next, of waiting for messengers on the long journey from Dublin.

They said the Armada had been driven from England, defeated by Queen Elizabeth's superior modern ships in battle at Gravelines, pushed back by great winds sent from God, but ships had been sighted wrecking in the storms off Ireland as they tried to flee along the coast and then towards home in Spain. They broke apart on the treacherous rocks, drowning hundreds, or the men straggled ashore to be robbed and killed.

Yet there were also tales, wilder tales, of armies storming ashore to burn Irish houses and take the plunder denied them in England. Or of Irish armies slaughtering any Spanish survivor who dared stagger on to land, mobs tearing them apart. The uncertainty was the worst and in the dark night nothing could distract her from her churning thoughts.

Alys finally pushed back the heavy tangle of blankets and slid down from her bed. The fire had died down to mere embers, leaving the chamber freezing cold. She quickly wrapped her fur-lined bed robe over her chemise and stirred the flames back to life before she went to peer out the window.

She could see little. During the day, her chamber looked down on to the front courtyard of the castle, where guests arrived and her father gathered his men when they had to ride out. Beyond the gates was a glimpse of the cliffs, the sea beyond. Tonight, the moon was hidden by the boiling dark clouds and the sky and the stormy sea melded into one. Only the churning white foam of the waves breaking on the rocks cast any light. It was a perilous night indeed. Any ship out there would be drowned.

Alys shivered and drew back from the cold wind howling past the fragile old glass. She had rarely been at sea, but she did remember the voyage that had brought her family to Ireland when she was a child. The coldness, the waves that tossed everything around, making her stomach cramp. The fear of the grey clouds suddenly whipping into a storm. How much worse it must be for men, weakened by battle and long weeks at sea, so far from their sunny homes.

She pushed her feet into her boots and slipped out of her chamber, unable to bear being alone any longer. Despite the late hour, the torches were still lit in their iron sconces along the corridor and the stairway, smoking and flickering. She couldn't see anyone, all the servants were surely long retired, but she could hear the echo of angry voices coming from the great hall below.

Messengers had been riding in and out of Dunboyton all day to meet with her father. She had seen little of them, for her father had sent her out of the hall to see to the wine and meat and bread being served, but the snatches she heard of their worried conversations was enough to worry her as well. What was left of the Armada was indeed sailing along the Irish coast, putting into ports where they could, but what would happen next, whether they would fight or surrender or how many there were, no one seemed to know.

The rumours that raced through the kitchens and the laundry were even wilder, and it took all her time to calm the servants and keep the household running. Invasion or not, they still needed bread baked, cheese strained and linen washed.

She tiptoed to the end of the corridor, where she could hear her father's weary voice, too low to make out any words, and the angry tone of his newest visitors. When they arrived after dinner, mud-splashed though they were, Alys saw they wore the livery of Sir William Fitzwilliam, Deputy of Ireland. Sir William had once savagely put down the Spanish and Papal troops who helped the Irish chieftains to rebel at Smerwick near ten years ago and vowed to do the same to any Armada survivors now, with the help of his brutal agent Richard Bingham.

Already stories flew that, farther south, soldiers and

scavengers scoured the coast, robbing corpses and stealing the very clothes off the weak survivors, killing them or leaving them to die of the cold.

Alys could hear drifts of their words now, caught in the cold draught of the corridor.

'…must be found wherever they land. The Irish people are easily led astray by foreign designs against the Queen's realm,' the deputy's man said, punctuated by the splash of wine. They would have to order more casks very soon. 'If the old chieftains join them…'

'We have not seen a hint of rebellion in years,' her father answered. 'The Spanish will never make it as far as Galway.'

'Ships have already been sighted from the fort. Sir William only has twelve hundred men in the field now. He has sent messages to all the Queen's governors along the coast to pass on his orders.'

'And what orders would those be?' her father asked wearily.

'That any Spaniard daring to come ashore shall be apprehended, questioned thoroughly, and executed forthwith by whatever means necessary.'

Alys, horrified, backed away from those cold, cruel voices, their terrible words. She spun around and hurried towards the winding stairs that led up to the walkway of the old tower. Men always kept watch on those parapets, which had a view of the sea and the roads all around, and tonight the guards were tripled. Torches lit up the night, flickering wildly in the wind and reflecting on the men's armour. The wind snatched at her cloak, but she held it close.

'Lady Alys!' one of the men cried. 'You shouldn't be out here in such cold.'

'I won't stay long,' she said. 'I just—I couldn't stay inside. I thought if I could just see…'

He gave an understanding nod. 'I know, my lady. Imagining can be worse than anything. My wife is sure we will be stabbed through in our beds with Spanish swords, she hasn't slept in days.'

Alys shivered. 'And shall we?'

He frowned fiercely. 'Not tonight, my lady. 'Tis quiet out there. Only a fool would brave the sea on a night like this.'

A fool—or a poor devil with no choice, whose wounded ship had been blown far off course. Alys did have fears, aye, just like this soldier's wife. Terrible things had happened in other lands conquered by the Spanish. But they were defeated now, beaten down and far from home. And how many of the men in those ships had been there of their own free will? Her fear warred with her pity.

She saw her father's spyglass abandoned on a parapet, and took it up to peer out at the night. She could see nothing but the dark sea, the moonlight struggling to break through. Then, for an instant, she thought she saw a pinprick of light bobbing far out to sea. She gasped and peered closer. Perhaps it was there, but then it vanished again.

Alys sighed. Now she was imaging things, just like everyone else at Dunboyton. She tucked the spyglass into the folds of her cloak and made her way back inside to try to sleep again.

The *Concepción* had become a floating hell, carrying its cargo of the damned farther from any hope at every moment.

John felt strangely dispassionate and numb as he studied the scene around him, as if he looked at it through a dream.

The *Concepción* had sustained a few blows at Gravelines, wounds that had been hastily patched, and her mainsail was shredded in the storm that blew them off course and pushed them far to the north of the Irish coast, out of sight of the other ships. But she had managed to limp along, praying that a clear course would open up and push them up and over the tip of the island and on a course for Scotland, where friendly Frenchmen might be found.

Yet the weather had only grown worse and worse, a howling gale that blew the vessel around haplessly, destroying what sails they had left and battering her decks with constant rain that leaked to the decks below. There were too many weak men and too few to raise the sails or steer. Salt was caked on the masts like frost.

Even if the skies did clear, the men were too ill to do much about it. They were like a ghost ship, tossed around by the towering waves.

John propped himself up by his elbow on his bunk to study the scene around him. The partitions that had been put up in Lisbon to separate the noble officers from the mere sailors had been torn down, leaving everyone in the same half-gloom, the same reeking mess. Everything was sodden, clothes, blankets, water seeping up from the floorboards and dripping on to their heads, but not a drop to drink except what rain could be caught. The ship's stores were long gone, except for a bit of crumbling, wormy biscuit. The smells of so many people packed into so small a space were overwhelming.

So many were starving, ill of ship's fever and scurvy, and could only lie in their bunks, moaning softly.

John wanted to shout with it all, but he feared he too lacked the energy to even say a word. There was little sleep to be had, with the constant pounding of the waves against the wounded hull, the whine of the pumps that couldn't keep up with the rising water, the groans of the men, the occasional sudden cries of ladies' names, ladies who would probably never be seen again.

John spent much time thinking over every minute that had happened since he left Lisbon, since he left England, really. All he had done to try to redeem his family's name, his own honour, all he had done thinking it would keep England safe. Surely he had given all he could, all his strength? What waited now? Perhaps the ease of death. But something told him he was not yet done with his earthly mission. More awaited him beyond these hellish decks.

He felt the press of his papers tucked beneath his shirt, carefully wrapped in oilskin to protect them. Would he ever have the chance to deliver them, to see the green fields of England he had fought so hard to protect? He could barely remember what Huntleyburg looked like. Perhaps he had lived a lie for too long now—it would be better if he died in it, too.

He heard a deep, rasping cough and looked to the next bunk where Peter de Vargas lay. Peter's greatest desire was to see England Catholic again; he spoke of it all the time. John found him innocent, if very foolish and fanatical, and willing to spill any secrets he had.

But now Peter burned with fever, as he had for days, and was too weakened to fight it away. At night, John heard him cry out to someone in his nightmares, his voice full of yearning. John gave him what water and food could be found, but he feared little could be done for the young man now.

Yet it seemed now Peter had summoned up a burst of strength and he sat up writing frantically with a stub of pencil. His golden hair, matted with salt, clung to his damp brow, and his eyes burned brightly.

'Peter, you should be resting,' John said. He climbed out of his own bunk, wincing as the salt sludge of the floor washed over his bare, bleeding feet. He was trying to save what was left of his boots, though he was not quite sure why now. He pulled them on. He wrapped the ragged edges of his blanket around Peter's thin shoulders.

'Nay, nay,' Peter muttered, still writing. 'I haven't much time. I must finish this. They must see…'

'See what?' John asked. He glanced at the slip of paper and could only glimpse a word or two, but mayhap it was of some import? Maybe Peter wrote to English relatives meant to help him, or secrets to send back to Spain. Even in the midst of floating hell, John's mind turned on what information could be useful to Walsingham and the Queen.

'The truth, of course. The truth of what I did. Love will come then. It must. It was promised.'

'Love?' John asked, puzzled. 'Who do you write to, Peter?'

'To England, of course. They are there. I think—yes, it must be…' His words faded into muttered incoherence, a mix of English and Spanish.

'Who in England? How shall you deliver it?' He studied the paper over Peter's shoulder again. The words were scribbled, smudged with salt water, with strange drawings in the margins. A code?

'It will find its way. It always does.' He looked up into

John's eyes, his face taut with longing and fear, his eyes burning bright. 'You must deliver it.'

John was shocked. Peter knew naught of his true work aboard the *Concepción*, no one could. But Peter was nodding confidently. 'Me, Peter? Why?'

'Because you are the strongest man left. You can make it ashore. You can carry this for me when we are all in the grave.'

'Where shall I deliver it?'

'They will know.'

'Who will know?'

'They know all.'

There was no time to say more. A peal of thunder, louder than any of the guns of battle, cracked overhead and there was a splintering crash. The mast that still stood had been split by lightning and a dagger-sharp spear of it drove into the deck below. The sea rushed in, a cold, killing wave that overwhelmed everything and swept wounded, weakly crying men out to sea.

'Take it!' Peter screamed, and stuffed his crumpled paper into John's hand.

John tucked it inside his doublet and shirt with the other papers he carried and grabbed Peter's arm just as the ship tilted on a wild roll. There was a massive creaking noise, as if something strained past the breaking point, and the ship split in two. More water rushed in, as cold as hundreds of needles driving into bare skin. John swam upward, dragging Peter with him.

The freezing water stole his breath and numbed his whole body. He could barely feel his legs as he forced himself to keep kicking, keep moving. A wild animal instinct to live drove him ever forward and he dug deep within himself to find a raw, powerful strength he didn't realise he possessed. A sharp splinter drove itself into his shoulder, but he pulled it out and kept moving.

He surfaced to find a world gone insane, filled with the howl of the wind, rain beating down on the churning waves. The great *Concepción* was breaking into pieces behind him and he could see men's heads bobbing in the sea all around.

John's shoulder crashed into something, sending sharp pain through his whole body, and he realised it was a wooden plank from the deck. He shoved Peter up on to it and clung to its splintered side as he kept kicking. He could see little in the driving silver sheets of rain, but he thought he glimpsed dots of light somewhere in the distance, a bobbing line like torches on shore. He feared it could be merely a mirage, the cold and hunger making him see such things, but he kicked towards it. There seemed no choice.

At last, after swimming until his legs felt they would fall off, his feet felt something beneath them, the shift of sand and rocks. The tide tried to push him back away from that tiny security, but he fought to regain it. With a great surge of a wave, they washed on to a rocky beach.

John collapsed on to his back, staring up into the boiling, stormy sky. He had never felt such pain in his life, even when he was stabbed through the thigh at Leiden or hit over the head with a chamber pot in a public-house brawl in Madrid, but mostly he felt—alive. The wind was cold on his face, as if giving him new breath, and even the pain sustained him because it meant he was still on earth.

'Peter,' he gasped. 'We're on land.' He turned his head and saw what he had feared all along—making land would not help poor, idealistic Peter now, for he was dead.

Dead, as John himself would surely be soon if he did not find a way out of the storm. He forced himself to stagger to his feet, even as stabbing, dagger-like pains shot through his body. He gritted his teeth, ignored it and kept moving forward. Always forward.

He came to a stand of boulders, which blocked the small spit of rocky land where he had washed up from a larger beachhead. He peered around the rocks to see a scene out of a poem. Towering cliffs, pale in the storm, rose to meet a castle at its crest, a strong, fortified crenelated building of dark grey stone, surrounded by tiny whitewashed cottages. That was where he had seen the light, a bobbing line of torches making their way down a steep set of stairs cut in the cliffs.

He opened his mouth to shout out, but some instinct held back his words. He could not know who these people were, friends or foes. They could not know who he was, either. If they were loyal Englishmen, they would consider him a Spanish enemy.

For a few moments, he watched as they moved closer and he glimpsed the gleam of torchlight on armoured breastplates. Soldiers, then.

He pushed back the waves of pain and managed to stagger up a sloping hill to a stand of boulders, half-hidden in reeds. He collapsed to his knees just as he heard the first screams, the first clash of blades.

'Nay...' he gasped, but the pain had dug its claws into him again. He collapsed and darkness closed in around him.

Chapter Five

Alys couldn't bear the shouting another minute.

She sat very still on the edge of her bed, trying to breathe, to turn her thoughts away from what she knew was happening outside, to pretend she was somewhere, anywhere else. When she was a child and her father often rode out to track down rebels and criminals, her mother would hold her all night and whisper tales of faraway Spain into her ear, tales of sunshine and strange music, to calm her and distract them both.

It wasn't working now.

It had come at dinner, when the household was eating their tense, silent meal in the great hall. Her father had tried to smile at her, to pretend naught was amiss. But she had seen the mud-splashed messengers hurrying in and out of the castle, had glimpsed rows of soldiers marching out from Galway City and the fort. Rumours had flown like sparks that Sir Richard Bingham, the lieutenant of Fitzwilliam who had so brutally put down the chieftains' rebellion, had been marching up the coast towards them, hunting for the shipwrecks. He had already taken and summarily executed dozens of shipwrecked Spanish sailors, and was marching now towards Galway.

Alys's father had sent her to her chamber, but she could still hear the panic of the castle outside. The servants were rushing around the corridors and stairs of Dunboyton, panic-stricken, and the great storm that had swept suddenly over the skies only added to the confusion and terror. The thunder pounded overhead and icy rain beat at her window.

Alys jumped down from her bed, unable to sit still any longer and let the not knowing sow fear in her mind. Facing a danger and fighting it was always better than endless waiting.

The corridor outside her chamber was empty, but she could still hear voices, fierce, low murmurs and high-pitched shrieks, coming from below. She followed the sound down the stairs to the great hall.

There she found a few of the servants gathered around the fire, whispering and talking together, their faces white with fear. A few soldiers who had already been out patrolling the ramparts were slumped on the benches in their wet clothes, gulping down hot spiced cider. Their unfinished supper still littered the tables, with her father's dogs fighting over a few bits of chicken and pork pies.

Alys caught a pageboy who was rushing past. 'Have you seen my father?'

He shook his head frantically, his eyes wide. 'Nay, Lady Alys. They say his lordship rode out hours ago.'

'Did they say where?'

'Nay, my lady.' The boy practically trembled with fear and excitement.

Alys knew he could tell her nothing. Likely no one could—or would. Not if Bingham was abroad. They said he enjoyed torturing his prisoners before he killed them, making them die slowly after he had robbed them of whatever they had. She hoped her father had not been summoned to his regiments.

She spun around and ran up the twisting stairs to the ramparts of the tower. She caught up her cloak from its hook and wrapped it over her woollen gown. The freezing rain beat at her hood and the howling, whipping wind caught at her skirts, but she barely noticed. She took up the spyglass and turned it on to the beach below.

What she saw made a cry escape her lips. Surely it was a nightmare. She was asleep in her bed, seeing phantoms conjured by all the fear around her.

She lowered the spyglass, closed her eyes, and shook her head.

But when she looked again, it was still there.

Out to sea, vanishing and reappearing in the surging waves, were two ships, breaking apart in the storm. Chunks of wood and furls of sail bobbed in the foaming waves. And on the beach was a straggling group of men, thin, barely clothed in rages, swaying on their feet, collapsing to the sand.

It seemed Bingham had already arrived, for soldiers in helmets and breastplates that gleamed in the glow of the lightning moved among the prisoners. As they passed them, the captives would collapse to the ground. As Alys watched, frozen and horror-stricken, a sword flashed out and one of the sailors fell to the rocky sand, his head rolling free. Weak screams were carried to her on the wind.

The Spanish *had* come to Galway, but certainly not as the maids had feared, as conquerors. They were now pitiful victims.

'Nay,' she cried out. This could not be happening, not here at her own home. She had heard the terrible tales of the rebellions, the murders and pillaging, but this was the first time she had seen such things and she found she could not bear it. Those men down there were obviously defeated and beaten, and they were her mother's fellow Spaniards.

She whirled around and ran as fast as she could back to the great hall. She had no clear thought now; she moved on pure instinct. No one seemed to pay her any attention as she ran out the door and across the bridge that led from the castle to the gardens and the cliff steps. It was meant to be guarded, but she saw no one there now. No doubt they had run to the beach for their share of the excitement and of any Spanish treasure that could wash ashore.

The steps cut into the cliffside, steps she had run up and down ever since she was a child, were slippery and perilous in the storm. Alys almost fell several times, but she pushed herself up and struggled onward. She didn't know where she was going, or what she would do once she got there, she only knew she had to try to stop some of that horror.

Once she reached the beach, the straggling group of half-drowned sailors was still far away, but she could see more. And she wished she could not. One of the starving sailors dropped to his knees, snatches of a prayer in Spanish carried to her on the wind. A soldier drove his sword through the man, then yanked a gold chain from his neck.

A surge of bitter sickness rose up at the back of Alys's throat, choking her. She clapped her hand over her mouth to hold it back. She didn't even like to see a cook kill a chicken for the pie pot. How could she bear such wanton cruelty?

She took a blind, lunging step forward and a hard hand caught her arm. She screamed at the cold jolt of surprise and spun around to find a soldier standing there. She could see little of his face beneath his helmet, just the hard set of his jaw.

'You should not be here, my lady,' he said. ''Tis not safe.'

'I see that.' She glanced back at the beach to see a clutch of people in cloaks and mantles, villagers, searching the beach for anything that might have washed ashore. 'Those men are no better than scarecrows now! Surely they are no threat. Perhaps they have information, or could be ransomed...'

'They are rabid Spanish dogs, my lady, and would have slaughtered us all if they could,' the man answered. 'This is war.'

Alys looked back to the beach and felt that bitter tang of sickness at the back of her throat again. 'This does not look like war.' It looked like wanton slaughter.

'Go back to the safety of the castle, my lady—*now*,' the soldier said, as implacable as stone.

'My father shall hear of this,' Alys said, though she feared he must already know. She marched away, leaving those horrors behind her, but she did not go back to the cliff steps. She made her way around through the sand dunes and the sodden reeds, hoping the rain would wash away her fury over what she had seen, her rage at her own helplessness.

Suddenly, above the whine of the wind, she heard a groan. She stopped, her senses on alert, half-fearful, half-hoping she was not alone. Yet it seemed it had been her imagination.

She started forward again. 'Please!' a hoarse voice called from the reeds. 'Please.'

She knew she had not imagined *that*. It was definitely

a person, someone in trouble. She ran to the reeds, which were higher than her waist, and searched through them.

'Please,' the voice came again, weaker this time, fading.

In the blinding curtain of rain, Alys tripped over him before she saw him. She stumbled over a booted foot and nearly tumbled to the marshy ground.

Cautiously, she leaned closer to study him. He was a tall man, probably once with powerfully broad shoulders and long, muscled legs. He wore what she could tell had once been very fine clothes, a velvet-and-leather doublet with gold embroidery on the high collar and expensive, well-wrought soft leather boots. But they were sodden and caked in mud and sea salt now, hanging loose off his thin figure.

Alys glanced up at his face. His hair, over-long and trailing like seaweed, and his beard were dark, his skin brown from the sun and weather of a long sea voyage. She could make out little of his features, but suddenly his eyes opened and focused directly on her. They were the brightest, clearest emerald green and they seemed to see deep into her very heart. She felt sure she knew those eyes.

'Please, mistress,' he said hoarsely, slowly, as if each letter was dragged painfully from a raw throat. 'I must go—I have messages...'

He had no hint of a Spanish accent, but then Alys's mother's words had not either. *Was* he Spanish, a noble soldier, or mayhap one of the English exiles they said sailed with the Armada, hoping to regain their lost estates? Either way, his life was in the gravest danger from that barbarity on the beach.

'Help me,' he said. 'I must deliver these.' He reached

for her hand. His fingers, roughened, torn and bloodied, barely touched her, but she felt a jolt of heat from his skin to hers, something that startled her and made her draw back. She saw a glint of gold on his hand, a ring on his smallest finger.

She glanced back frantically over her shoulder. She could see nothing from the reeds that closed around them, but she could hear the screams from the beach. She thought of her mother, of her dark Spanish eyes, her wistful smile, and Alys was completely torn.

Aye, this man could be the enemy and if she helped him she could find herself in much trouble. But as she looked into this man's eyes, practicality and danger gave way to human feeling. He was a person, a human being, and deserved a chance to tell his tale before he died, to deliver these messages that seemed so important to him. She thought of the men being killed so wantonly on the beach and she shuddered.

How could she ever face her mother in heaven if she did not help him?

She thought quickly and prayed she had enough strength to carry out such a wild plan. 'It is well now,' she said soothingly. 'I know where we can go. You can trust me. *Confía en mi, señor.*'

His eyes widened in surprise at her words in Spanish, and he nodded. *'Gracias.'*

'Can you stand at all? We must hurry.' The screams on the beach were growing louder and soon the looters would spread out in their search.

He nodded again, but Alys wasn't sure. He did look very pale, almost grey beneath his sun-brown. She slid her arm around his shoulders and helped him to sit. He was very lean, but she could feel the strength of his muscles beneath his sodden clothes. He must have been no idle nobleman. His jaw set in a grim line, and his skin went even paler, but he was able to push himself to his feet. He swayed there precariously and Alys braced her shoulder against his ribs to help hold him up.

She was not a tall woman and had inherited her mother's small-boned, delicate build, but carrying around baskets of laundry and digging in the kitchen garden had not been in vain. Between the two of them, he soon had his balance again.

'We must hurry,' she said. 'Follow me.'

They made their way through the sand dunes, crouching low to avoid being seen. The rain had slowed down and the clouds slid back and away from the moon, which was good and bad. She could see her way a bit clearer, but that meant so could the soldiers on the beach. She found the second set of stairs etched into the cliff, around the curve of the beach and more hidden. The steps went only up to the old abbey and were seldom used.

'Can you climb here?' she said. She looked up at him and saw that his face, starkly carved like an old Roman statue, was set in lines of determination. He nodded and closely followed her as she climbed the stairs. He swayed dangerously at one point, almost falling backward, and Alys caught his arm and pulled him up with her.

At last they reached their destination, the ruins of the ancient abbey. Alys had gone there often when she was a child, sneaking away from her nursemaids to pick flowers and just lie in the grass, staring up at the sky through the crumbling old stone arches. Sometimes her mother would take here there, too, for picnics and games.

It felt like another world to her from that of the crowded castle, a world of peace and beauty. But sometimes the sight of the abandoned cloisters seemed to make her mother sad. What had once been a grand and glorious place, with a soaring church and dozens of monks and priests, was abandoned and silent.

Alys had never seen it quite like this, with rain pounding down on the old stones, lightning casting an eerie glow through the empty window frames. The wind, howling around the collapsed vaults of the roof, sounded like the cries of the banished monks.

If they were there now, watching with ghostly eyes, Alys begged them for their help. She wanted to cry, to scream, but she knew she couldn't. She needed all her strength now.

She took a deep breath of the heavy, cold air and made herself focus carefully on what she was doing. The wounded man had walked so bravely up the stone steps and along the overgrown path to the abbey, though she could tell it pained him greatly. He held himself very stiffly, placing his steps carefully, and once or twice she heard a muffled moan. She gently touched his cheek and found it burning hot. He needed rest.

'Almost there now,' she said encouragingly, trying to smile.

'You should leave me here,' he answered. 'I am away from the soldiers, I can hide from them on my own.'

'You certainly cannot! You can't even walk on your own. I have taken too much trouble over you to abandon you now.' Alys thought of the terrible scene on the beach, the helpless, half-drowned men just cut down, and she shuddered. No one deserved such an end. Treating helpless prisoners thus cruelly made the English no better than the Spanish devils the maidservants had feared so much.

And this man did not seem to be a cruel demon, come to garrotte and brand English children. There was a kindness in his eyes, beneath the wariness.

She led him into what had once been the dairy for the abbey. It was one of the only buildings still mostly intact, with its roof and door. It was windowless and cool, the thick walls lined with shelves that still held buckets for milk and covered containers for butter and cheese. There was a hearth where cream would be stirred.

'Wait here,' she told him, propping him against the wall. A ghost of a smile flickered across his lips beneath his beard, as if her bossiness amused him. She hurried to find a pile of old canvas sacking, which she used to make an improvised pallet bed by the hearth. There was a bit of wood left in a basket by the fireplace, along with a flint and some twigs for kindling. It was a bit damp, but she managed to get an ember to catch.

She turned back to the man, whose tall body sagged against the wall. His eyes were closed, his skin very pale. Alys hurried to his side and slid her arm around him again. He was so very tall and she couldn't reach around his chest. Surely he would soon regain his health and be a fine figure of a man again.

'Come, sit down by the fire,' she said, trying to keep her voice calm, to hide her fear. 'It isn't much, but at least it's out of the rain. You can rest quietly.'

She helped him to lie down on the improvised mattress. He fell back to the sacking with a suppressed, painful sigh. He made no protest as she unfastened the buttons of his ruined doublet. The fine fabric was sodden and crusted with salt, but she saw that the buttons were silver and there were traces of metallic embroidery on the collar.

Who *was* he? She was greatly intrigued by the mystery of him and how he came to be on that ship. But her curiosity would have to wait.

As she peeled away the doublet to find a bloodstain on the torn shoulder of his fine linen shirt, a small packet of letters fell out. Alys reached for it, but despite his wounds he was faster. He snatched it away, holding it tightly in his long, elegant fingers. His gold ring glinted.

'Don't let these be lost,' he gasped. 'They must stay with me.'

'Of course,' Alys said gently, even as she burned with curiosity to know what those letters held. Her rescued sailor became ever more intriguing. 'Be easy, *señor*. They will go nowhere.'

He studied her closely with those otherworldly green eyes, until she felt her cheeks burn hot with a blush. At last, he nodded and laid back down again. When Alys was satisfied he rested calmly, she hurried back outside to find the cistern near the old refectory. She dipped him a pottery goblet of the clean water, and went back to kneel at his side. His eyes were still closed, but she could see the lines of pain etched around his mouth.

'Here, drink a bit of this,' she said. 'I need to look at your shoulder. I'll have to fetch some food and medicine for you from the castle and I should see what exactly I will need.'

He nodded and laid very still as she eased the salt-stiff shirt away from his shoulder. His chest was smoothly muscled, with pale brown hair lightening the sun-browned skin. But that perfect expanse of skin was marred with a deep gash at his shoulder, apparently from a dagger-like splinter.

Alys ripped a bit of canvas from the sacking and

dipped it into the clean water to dab at the wound. As she cleaned away the crusted blood, she saw that it was a long cut, but not terribly deep. She would need pincers to clear away the smaller splinters.

As she worked, she tried to focus only on her task, not on him, his breath as he moved against her, his eyes that watched her so closely. She had tended wounded men before, but somehow it had never felt quite like—this.

'Why are you doing this?' he asked. The sudden sound of his voice, so deep and dark, startled her and she glanced up at him. He still watched her and the glow of his green eyes made her somehow want to fall into them, to drown in their jewel-like colour and never leave him. 'I must be your enemy.'

Alys looked back to her work. 'If you are indeed an enemy, you must be honourably imprisoned and questioned, perhaps ransomed back to your family. You would surely fetch a fine price, to judge by your clothes and your fine manners.'

A wry smile touched his lips. 'You know the procedures to follow battle, then?'

'My father has been governor of Dunboyton Castle since I was a child and has fought to help put down many rebellions against the Queen. I have learned a thing or two.' She ripped another piece of canvas into a long strip for a bandage. 'And I know that what was happening there on the beach had naught to do with honourable battle. I am sure Queen Elizabeth would be appalled to have such barbarity done in her name.'

She could still feel him looking at her, that burning sensation she felt deep inside of herself. 'Is that all?'

Alys hesitated to say more. 'My—my mother was Spanish. She often told me about her home, her family and brothers. We are not monsters, even if we come from different countries. We are all people. If they...'

She couldn't say anything else, as tears choked her throat.

'I will help you to recover, if I can,' she said.

'Then send me to your father?'

Alys had not thought that far ahead. She could only think of getting food and medicine for him, of which herbs she would need. 'You can't stay in here for ever.' She tied off the end of the makeshift bandage and pushed herself to her feet. 'I will be back. I have to find you some food, some dry clothes and blankets. I won't be gone long.'

He reached out his hand, his fingers brushing hers and leaving a trail of tingling fire behind. 'May I at least know the name of my saviour?'

She looked down at him, and the firelight limned him in gold. Beneath the wild hair, the paleness of his illness, he was extraordinarily handsome. The most handsome man she had ever seen. Surely such allure made him doubly dangerous. 'I am Alys.'

'Alys,' he said and the word sounded like honeyed wine in his dark voice. 'I am—Juan.'

Alys tried to smile at him. 'I will be back, Juan. You rest now. You should be safe enough here.'

She hurried out of the small building, back out into the storm. Even the cold rain and howling wind could not frighten her. Only the emotions she had thought long buried inside of her, emotions this strange man was bringing out, could frighten her now.

He had been saved, snatched from the sea and the murderous soldiers, by an angel.

John laughed as he laid back against the rough canvas of his new bed. He would never have thought heaven would send *him* such a rescuer. He had done too many bad things in his life, had killed, cheated, stolen, to deserve it.

Yet, just when he thought death had come to claim him, he had opened his eyes and seen *her*. His angel. Alys.

She was so small, so frail-looking, with her long, rain-soaked dark hair and her pale, elfin face, yet she had the strength and determination of a warrior. So calm, so steady and unafraid. When he looked into her dark eyes, he forgot the pain, forgot the duty that had brought him to this place, forgot—everything. Because of her, he had a chance to finish his mission. He couldn't let his angel's sacrifice be in vain. He owed her so much.

John pushed away the waves of pain and crippling exhaustion that threatened to push him down and made himself sit up. Grimacing, he pulled off his ruined boots and stretched his freezing feet towards the fire. The warmth was something he barely remembered after months at sea and it was delicious. Almost as wondrous as Aly's touch on his hand.

He reached for the packet of papers. Their oilskin pouch had kept them relatively intact, their coded symbols and words still legible. He could recreate them before he delivered them to Walsingham. But Peter's letter had not fared quite as well. He could see it was in Spanish and could make out a few words. Perhaps it would be easier when it was light.

It had been so important to Peter that it be delivered, but to whom? Peter had often spoken of some friend, someone in England, who would know what to do when he found them. John would have to track them down now.

Another wave of crushing dizziness washed over him and he couldn't quite resist it this time. He hid the packet under the edge of the canvas bedding and laid back down. The ceiling above him was painted with a scene of angels peering down from the shelter of fluffy white clouds, an unexpected scene of beauty in such a strange place. John studied them as sleep overtook him, and he noticed that one of them had large brown eyes and a wary smile. Just like an angel named Alys…

Chapter Six

'What are you looking for, my lady?'

Alys spun around, startled by the sound of a maid-servant's voice in the doorway of the stillroom. She was filling her baskets with the herbs she needed, along with clean linen bandages and some wine, and was so absorbed in her own thoughts she heard little beyond the empty chamber.

'Some of the men are in need of healing poultices and tisanes after—after what happened last night,' she said. She remembered all too well the terrible scene on the beach and swallowed her fear to try and smile.

She knew she was not the only one affected by what had happened. The maid's eyes were red-rimmed, her apron askew. 'Oh, my lady, 'twas terrible! Will there be more of them, do you think? Will they reach the castle?'

Alys saw a flashing image in her mind, a scene of mayhem as soldiers stormed through the corridors of Dunboyton, tearing her life apart. *Nay*—she would never let such a thing happen. 'I'm sure Bingham's men have moved on to seek new prey. There will be little here for them and we will soon be as quiet as usual.'

'But the Spanish…'

'The Armada is destroyed!' Alys cried, thinking of those poor, starving wretches cut down on the beach. Of Juan, his beautiful eyes and his wounded body. 'They could not hurt even a seagull now. We must go about our tasks as always. Is my father's dinner ready?'

'I don't know, my lady.'

'Well, go see about it, please. Here is some mint for the lamb stew. Perhaps that will tempt his appetite a bit. I must go see to the garden.'

Alys took up her basket and hurried out of the still-room. She could tell that most of the servants were trying to go about their tasks as always, but there were still soldiers loitering in the gardens and the great room, and the air seemed heavy and oppressive. She went to fetch her parcel of clothes and linens, and made her way towards the garden, avoiding anyone's gaze.

She caught a glimpse of her father in the great hall and despite her worries the sight of him made her pause. He sat slumped in his chair near the fire, his head resting on his hand, and he looked so tired. So—old, suddenly. She left her baskets near the door, out of sight, and made her way to his side.

'Father?' she said and at first she feared he didn't hear her. He shook his head and slowly looked up at her. 'Father, are you unwell?'

'Nay, Alys my butterfly, I am well enough,' he answered, his voice tired and weak.

'Is your stomach aching again? I can mix you a tisane…' She had become used to mixing the certain combination of herbs that sometimes soothed him, as he had been plagued with illness ever since her mother died.

'It is no worse than usual.' He gave a deep sigh and

stared back into the fire. 'I have grown useless, Alys. I could not even do anything to stop that wanton slaughter last night.'

Alys's heart ached at his words. She knelt down beside his chair and pressed her hand to his trembling arm. 'Oh, Father. They say Bingham carried a royal order from Fitzwilliam, you could not go against that.'

'Royal order,' he snorted. 'Men like that follow no order but their own. Ransoms could have been made, perhaps, or valuable information obtained from those men. All for naught.'

Alys thought of Juan. Once he was recovered, what information could he give them? Perhaps if he could tell her father…

She shook her head. That had to be a secret for now, *her* secret, until Bingham's men were truly gone and she had found out what she could from Juan herself. 'Terrible things do happen in battle.'

'That was no battle, it was a slaughter of starving men who were defeated weeks ago. Thank the stars your mother was not here to see such wickedness. And I pray that you will never see such again, either. That you never see true battle.'

'That seems unlikely, Father. I am no warrior, am I?' She kissed his cheek and made herself give him a bright smile. 'I am sure Dunboyton will be as isolated as ever now that the ships have gone. I'll finish my tasks and dine with you this evening. There is lamb stew and a new apple pie.'

Her father patted her hand, but she could tell he was far away from her again, staring into the fire as if he could see images in the flames no one else glimpsed. She wondered if he saw her mother there, her Spanish mother.

Alys quickly fetched her baskets and hurried out of the castle. Juan had been alone for hours now and she worried what she would find at the abbey. Perhaps he had become feverish, or mayhap wandered away and was captured. She knew she should not be so worried for a man she did not know, a man who could bring much danger on to her, but still she hurried her steps towards him.

It was still cold and windy, but the rain had gone. She avoided the beach. They said the villagers had pillaged what they could from the sailors' bodies and from the cargo that had washed ashore from the ships, and the bodies were buried in the dunes. The English regiments had moved on along the coast, but she couldn't bear to see the place where she had witnessed such horrors. If she could help Juan, even though he was only one man…

Well, it was all she could do for some atonement, something for her mother.

As she came over the top of the cliffs, the ruins of the abbey came into view. The spires still reached towards the slate-grey skies, even though their walls were crumbling, one tiny spot of beauty left out of ruin. The empty windows and old walkways seemed as empty as always.

What would she find when she went to search for Juan?

The door to the old dairy was closed and no smoke curled from the chimney. It looked as abandoned as the rest of the cloisters.

Alys slowly pushed the door open. She held her breath, listening for any sign of life, but there was not even a rustle of noise. '*Holà…*' she called tentatively. Her words ended on a scream as her arm was suddenly grabbed and she was dragged into the room.

A hard, strong hand clamped over her mouth, cutting

off her words and her breath. Cold terror washed over her. She twisted frantically against her bonds, driving her elbow into her captor's ribs. She must have inadvertently hit a wound, for she was suddenly free and her captor stumbled back a step.

Alys whirled around, and saw it was Juan who had grabbed her. His face was grey, streaked with sweat, and his eyes were filled with a wild glow, like an animal cornered. Anger replaced her fear. Had she not done all she could to help him, despite everything? How dare he frighten her so!

'I am trying to help you, at great risk, and this is the thanks I get!' she cried. She scooped up some of the tumbled linen that had fallen from her basket when she dropped it and tossed it at his head. She knew she should still be scared; she had seen men in the aftershocks of battle before, they didn't always know where they were. And Juan was much larger and stronger than she was. But somehow, her fear was gone.

He caught the linen in one hand and the wild light in his eyes faded. A look of horror flashed across his face. 'Forgive me, *señorita*. I didn't realise it was you, I thought—it was most ungentlemanly. I...' His face went very white and he sagged against the wall.

Alys remembered his wounded shoulder, all he had been through, and she felt terrible for shouting at him, deserved or not. She rushed to his side and took his arm. He felt much too warm, as if his fever had not abated. 'Of course. I could have been one of Bingham's soldiers, though I dare say they would have made much more noise. Here, sit down, you are feverish still. I'll build up the fire.'

He went with her, though she sensed he went most reluctantly, trying to hold back, as if ashamed of his behaviour, his loss of control. 'Why have you not summoned the soldiers yourself?' he asked.

Alys shrugged, concentrating on stoking the fire. 'I do not like Bingham and his barbaric methods. He is a brute, who does not follow the proper procedures for battle. He just enjoys a bloodbath.' She sat back on her heels and watched as the flames caught and crackled, sending out their warmth into the cold, stone room. She nodded, as if she had decided on something. 'And my mother...'

'Ah, yes, you said she was Spanish,' he said. 'So was mine.'

She turned to look at him, wondering that there was someone else there like her, someone who might understand what it felt to be caught ever between two worlds. 'And your father?'

His jaw tightened. 'He was English.'

'Is that why you were with the Armada? For your mother?'

He was silent for a long moment, until she was sure he would not answer her. He looked like a rock, a cave made of stone she could not penetrate. 'I was there for many reasons. You would find my tale dull.'

Alys thought of his hidden packet of papers, that strange jumble of letters and symbols she had glimpsed for only an instant before he hid it again. She was sure the very last word to describe him would be *dull*. But she could tell he should not talk more today, the effort of holding his secrets had made him pale again and he shivered. She would have to discover more later.

Once the fire was blazing again, she gathered up her tumbled supplies and went to kneel beside him. He gave her a wary glance.

'I brought you some proper blankets and pillows, not much like a real bed, but better than that old canvas,' she said. 'Also, a clean shirt, and some bandages and healing herbs from my stillroom. Oh, and wine and bread, a bit of cheese and smoked fish. You look as if you haven't had a real meal in some time, so you must eat very slowly.'

He examined the supplies she laid out with a strange look on his face, almost a wonder, as if she had brought an array of gold and rubies. 'Where did you get all of this?'

'I told you, the herbs came from my stillroom and the food from the kitchen, of course. No one saw me gather it.' She measured out a mixture of feverfew and rosemary, carefully crushing them together and mixing them into some wine.

'You stole this? For me?'

Alys laughed. 'Certainly not. They are mine to take, since my father is governor of the castle. Except for the shirt. I did take that from him, but I will sew him a new one.'

'Then where am I, exactly?'

Alys glanced up from her herbs and saw a frown on his face. 'Dunboyton Castle in Galway. Did you not know?'

He shook his head. 'Our pilot died days ago and much of our navigational equipment was damaged. No one was well enough to steer, so we just—drifted. Until we followed another ship into a bay, trying to shelter from the gale.'

Alys tried to remember all the jumbled stories that had flown around when the ships were sighted. 'Aye, they did say there were two that went down, but there seems no sign of the other.'

'There were no survivors, then?'

Alys went back to her mixture, making a new one for the poultices. She did not want to tell him too much yet, not when he was still ill. 'I don't know. If there were, they weren't brought to the castle. Here, let me see to your shoulder. The bandages will need changing. Drink this.'

Juan drew back, glaring suspiciously at her array of herbs. 'What is that?'

'Merely feverfew, some yarrow, a bit of valerian, things of that sort,' she answered. 'It will help the fever and aid your blood in healing itself. I will make you a tea of chamomile later, to help you sleep. It is not poison, I promise. Why would I go to so much trouble to bring you here if I was just going to poison you?'

He laughed, and it sounded as if he had not done so in a long time. It was like drawing back a shutter and letting the light and warmth in again. 'A fine point, *señorita*.'

'You'll have to take off your shirt.'

To her amusement, his cheeks actually turned a bit red and he turned his back to strip off the torn, stained shirt. For a moment she could only stare, amazed, at the beauty of his sun-darkened skin lightly touched with the pink of those incongruous blushes. Her giggles faded when she saw the way he winced in pain at the movement and she hurried over to touch his arm.

'Here, sit down, Juan, let me look at your shoulder,' she said.

She could tell he was still wary, holding himself stiff under her touch, but he slowly sat down on the blankets she had arranged by the fire. He held his back very straight as she leaned closer to study the gash on his shoulder.

The wound was not as angrily red as it had been, but she saw she did need to remove the rest of the splinters and dress it with the poultice if it was not to poison his blood. She also realised he must have found the water cistern and bathed, for his gold-touched skin was clean and smooth to her touch, and he smelled of sweet rainwater with a hint of citrus.

He was really very, very handsome, with his sharply carved features, his strong jaw and blade-straight nose, and those sea-green eyes. His body, too, was tall and leanly muscled, like that of an ancient warrior.

Alys shook away the strange spell being close to him seemed to weave around her. She could not afford such distractions now. She quickly rinsed a rag in clean water and carefully dabbed at the dried blood that had seeped around his wound.

'What is this place?' he asked. 'Part of the castle?'

'Nay, it is the old abbey. It was abandoned long ago, in King Henry's time, and most of it is in ruins. It was dark when we came here, I am sure you couldn't see it well.'

'An abbey?'

'This was the old dairy and somehow it has survived with its roof intact. I think the shepherds use it sometimes, when they drive their flocks towards Galway City.'

'How do you know about it?'

Alys carefully dabbed her paste of herbs on the cleaned wound. His shoulder tensed under her touch and his skin felt like steel under silk. Distracting again. 'I came here with my mother when I was a child. The monks had large herb gardens and we would gather some of the remains, or we would sit on the old walls and she would tell me tales.'

'Tales of Spain?'

Alys thought of those sunny spring days, with the light flooding through the empty windows and the scent of mint on the air. 'Sometimes. She said it was always sunny and warm there, most unlike Ireland. Mostly fairy stories, or tales of old kings and warriors, though.'

'Will she find you here?'

Alys bit her lip as she wound the bandage tighter. 'Nay. She died many years ago.'

Juan reached up and gently touched her hand, making her skin turn warm at his touch. 'I am sorry.'

'It—it was a long time ago,' Alys stammered, confused at the feelings his touch awoke. 'Though I fear my father still mourns her greatly.' She slid her hand away to tie off the bandage. 'Some of the stories she did tell me were ghost tales. She loved those. I always wondered if the Spanish had such drama in their blood.'

'Ghost tales?'

'Of the monks who once lived here. On some nights, when the moon is bright, they go in procession, chanting through the old cloisters. Some of the maids say they have even seen lights up here, moving along the cliffs.'

'Have you ever seen them?'

Alys shook her head as she finished her nursing ministrations. 'Never. My mother said I was too practical to see the world beneath our own, that I was too concentrated on my everyday tasks.'

He smiled at her, and it was meltingly beautiful. 'And are you? Practical, Alys?'

Alys smiled back. She couldn't seem to stop herself. His smile looked like something she had been waiting to see all her life and she wanted to fall into it and be lost. 'I suppose I am, though I don't mind a pretty song or two when the *jongleurs* come to Dunboyton.' She offered him the clean shirt. 'Did the ghosts come to visit you last night?'

'Not yet, but I have no fear of them. I grew up in my father's house, which was also once an abbey, and there were ghosts aplenty there. Here cannot be much different.'

He tried to slip the shirt over his head, but he was still moving stiffly and the sleeve caught. Alys moved to help him and felt the soft brush of his hair, the warmth of his body against her. 'Have you been to many places since you left your father's house?'

He smiled up at her again, but now it was rueful. 'Many lands indeed. The Low Countries, France, Portugal…'

'I fear I have never left here. My father was sent here as governor when I was a child. Dunboyton is beautiful, but rather small, I fear, and my knowledge of the world must come from books and the stories of visitors.'

He looked into the fire as he tied the laces of the shirt, a wistful frown replacing his smile. 'I would have liked a real home, I think.'

'And I think I would have liked a bit of adventure.' Alys took up the wine and food from the basket and held out the loaf of bread. 'In exchange for my help, Señor Juan, I insist you tell me all about Lisbon and Paris. What they wear there, what they eat, their buildings and shops…'

Juan laughed. 'So tales are your price, my rescuer? One story for every bite of cheese?'

'If they are good stories, I may even bring you a pie or two. But you must still eat slowly and carefully. I don't want my efforts to come to nothing if you become ill again.'

'I am quite sure I will find my health quickly again, thanks to you.' He peered at her curiously as he sliced off a bit of cheese and slid it past his sensual lips. 'You are surely an angel.'

Alys turned away, flustered. 'I am sure my household would disagree with you. They say I am too bossy.' In fact, it would soon be time for her to oversee dinner. She poured out a measure of wine and mixed in a spoonful of valerian to help him rest. 'Here, you should drink this. I have to go now and see to my father's dinner, or I shall be missed. But I will be back later to see if you are well.'

'And to claim your first story?'

Alys laughed. 'And that. It had best be an amusing one.'

She gathered up her baskets and hurried out of the old dairy, making sure the door was firmly shut and no one watched her. It was quiet on the path along the cliffs that led back to Dunboyton, giving Alys too much time to think about Juan. About how shockingly handsome he was beneath the beard and sun-brown of his time at sea, like no one else she had ever seen in real life. He was like a hero or ancient warrior in a sonnet, all elegant, quiet strength. He spoke very well, too, his words polished and educated, his accent fine. She couldn't help but wonder more about his past. Where had he really come from? What had driven him on to those ships? He held many, many secrets, she was sure of that.

She knew she should be frightened of him. Certainly she should tell her father about him immediately. But something, some part of a fairy instinct her mother had claimed she lacked, told her that his secrets were not evil ones. He was a complicated man, yes, but not a wicked one.

At least she hoped he was not, that her trust in him was not misplaced. And he had called her his angel, in a sweet, wondering tone she had never heard before. She liked him thinking of her in that way. The memory of it made her laugh and then blush when she thought of how warm and smooth his bare skin was when she touched it. Aye, she was in danger of being overtaken by her emotions, for the first time in her life, and she could not let that happen. She had to be very careful, indeed, and find out for sure what Juan's true purpose was there. She prayed with all her might it was a good one. It looked as if her whole future depended on it.

When Alys was gone, the small room, which had felt so warm and welcoming while she was there, seemed to close around him. Yet he dared not go outside, not until he was strong enough to face any foe again.

John opened the door a crack and stared out into the night, and somehow its starlit beauty, its silence, made him recall too sharply the scenes of the past weeks. The bloody battles, the freezing, starving days on the ships, watching poor Peter—and so many other men—die. If not for Alys, he would be among them. He would be mouldering in a hastily dug grave on the beach and his quest to restore the Huntley name would be at a terrible end.

Aye, he owed her so very much. She declared she was not an angel, but he knew differently. When he had opened his eyes to see her face, to look into her dark eyes and hear her low, sweet, reassuring voice, it was like being raised into the bright light once more. He had a new chance at life, if he could make it safely to court, and he owed it all to her.

He thought of the way she took such care of his wounds, her cool, calm demeanour, her gentle smile.

She had saved a man, a stranger, and taken care of him with no sign of fear. Such remarkable courage and kindness, such as he had never seen before in either woman or man. Aye, of course she was an angel.

He thought of foolish Peter and the letters he had written so fervently, even in his final days. John wondered if it was a woman Peter wrote to, a woman who had stolen his heart, who shared the cause that made a martyr of him. It would explain his worshipful expression, his adamant insistence that he would see the person he wrote to once more.

Aye—perhaps a woman had once helped Peter, as Alys had helped him. The thought gave him pause. He knew he could not lose his heart so fervently, or at all. His work was still incomplete. But he did want Alys to know how she had helped him. How she had changed him.

He reached for a small block of wood from the stack of fuel for the fireplace, and studied its angles and shape carefully. He had once spent long hours waiting for battle, or aboard ship, in carving, he was sure he could remember how to do it now. This piece of wood would work, and it would definitely help pass the time as he recovered his full strength and plotted his return to court.

It would also remind him of Alys in the long, quiet hours until then.

Chapter Seven

Alys made her way along the path to the abbey the next morning, carrying a large hamper of fresh supplies. No one had noticed her slipping out of the castle not long after first light. Bingham's men had all marched off to find more shipwrecked sailors further down the coast and all seemed quiet again. But Dunboyton was not yet quite back to normal. Everyone was still too unsettled, too excited by the violent interruption to their daily routines. The maids still cried into their aprons, the pages still carried around kitchen knives 'just in case' and everyone jumped at the merest loud noise.

The maids would no doubt be relieved not to have their lady watching them as they whispered together over their kettles and dusting cloths instead of working. And she had not seen her father all night or morning, he was shut up in his library with his steward and the captain of his guards. There was no one to see her pack up wine and food, gather up bandages and herbs from the stillroom. At least she truly hoped no one had.

Alys glanced over her shoulder and saw nothing but the sweep of the empty meadows down to the cliffs and the sea beyond. The great gale that wrecked the ships had blown away, but there was still a chill to the wind and there were no fishing boats putting out to sea. Most of the villagers, along with Dunboyton's household, stayed behind their locked doors for the time being.

She hoisted her basket higher in her arms and turned towards the path to the abbey. Once again, like old friends, the spires against the grey sky greeted her. A warm sense of anticipation rose up in her at the sight. She looked forward to seeing Juan, to checking that her nursing skills were working, to see if she could coax more stories from him. He owed her a few more tales; after all, that was their bargain.

And, if she was honest, it was not just the prospect of nursing that made her steps grow quicker as she reached the edge of the crumbling cloister wall. She looked forward to seeing *him* again, to hearing the secret smile in his voice as he talked to her, the way his green eyes glowed.

Life at Dunboyton was not a bad existence, but Alys admitted it *was* a quiet one. The same people, the same tasks, every day. Juan was like no one else she had ever met. He was a complete puzzle, one she wanted to fit together so very much. She wanted to know more about his Spanish mother, whether she had told him tales of her homeland as Alys's had to her. The feeling of belonging to two different worlds was one they shared. Alys could not see things as everyone else did, as English and Spanish and thus different, for she knew they were not. Did Juan feel the same?

And, if she was being doubly honest with herself, she had to admit that she was deeply attracted to her shipwrecked sailor. The thought of giggling over something so frivolous in the midst of such a terrible time made her chide herself, laugh at herself for her silliness. Who would have thought dull, practical Alys could sigh so over a pair of lovely green eyes.

She hurried through the open, sky-lit sanctuary and found the dairy. She was almost afraid he would have gone, but then she saw the silvery smoke snaking from the chimney. She knocked carefully at the door, and called out, ''Tis Lady Alys.' As much as she wanted to see him, she wanted no repeat of yesterday's rough greeting when she surprised him.

The door cracked open and he stood before her. He smiled, making his eyes crinkle most invitingly, and held out his hand. She could tell with a glance that he looked better, his skin not so pale and his figure standing straighter, taller. 'Lady Alys. I was afraid you might not come today. I have been watching for you.'

He had been watching for her? Did he...*want* to see her, as she wanted to see him? She felt her cheeks turn warm at the thought and she set quickly about her tasks to hide her confusion. 'I had to make sure breakfast was prepared for the household. They are so disordered, nothing seems to be getting done at all. I am sorry, you must be hungry.'

'You did promise me a pie,' he said teasingly. 'I have been trying to come up with a story fine enough to deserve it.'

Alys brushed by him to the fireplace and he followed her. She was achingly aware of the heat of him, his tall strength right behind her. Pretending nothing was amiss, she knelt beside the hearth and started to unpack her basket. Beside her was his makeshift bed, a nest of tumbled blankets and pillows, and she tried not to imagine what he looked like lying there, at his ease beside the fire as the flames turned his bare skin to pure gold…

Silly girl, she chided herself. Her hands shook as she measured out her packets of herbs.

'I am very comfortable here,' he said. 'In fact, I do not think I have ever been in such a comfortable place. The silence and peace all to myself is most wondrous.'

'I am sure being packed into a ship for months at a time cannot provide much silence at all,' she answered, handing him a serving of bread and cheese and pouring out some wine. She wondered where he had been before that ship, what kinds of lodgings he had known in Paris and Antwerp and Lisbon. Surely he was only being polite now; a makeshift pallet on a stone floor could not compare to fine Parisian chambers. Though he *had* made it cosy for himself. Besides the bed, there was a small milking stool he had found somewhere and the canvas sacking formed into draperies to soften the cold walls. There was also a small block of wood on the stool along with a fruit knife, it looked as if he was carving something.

'What are you working on there?' she asked.

He gave her a sheepish smile and swept the wooden object and its shavings under the edge of a blanket. ''Tis nothing. A bit of nonsense to pass the time. My carving skills are grown rusty, I fear.'

'So you are an artist as well as a sailor?' As well as a spy, mayhap? Her curiosity about him grew every time she saw him, discovered yet another half-hidden facet of this gorgeous man.

He laughed and his eyes crinkled again. It made him look so much younger, so much freer and happier. Alys found she longed to make him smile again, would do anything to see that facet of Juan once more. 'I am neither artist nor sailor.'

'Are you not? Then what are you?'

His laughter faded in an instant, faster than that storm blowing up from the sea. His changeableness was startling, almost frightening. He looked down to tear open the loaf of bread. 'I am nothing at all, I suppose. A wanderer. A seeker.'

A seeker. Alys knew how that felt, even though she could seek only in books. To see, to know—it was tempting indeed. Perhaps that was what had drawn him to the ships, the need for adventure. She poured out more wine, including some for herself. 'I suppose I could call myself a seeker, as well, though I cannot look for what I desire in the world as you can. I can only read of it. I envy you.'

He sat down beside her, their backs to the fire. Once again, he studied her closely with those brilliant eyes that seemed to mesmerise and capture, as if he sought out her secrets just as she sought his. He was much too easy to talk to, she knew she would have to carefully guard her words when he looked at her like that. 'What do you seek in your books?'

Alys hesitated a moment before she spoke. 'I'm not sure. I suppose I want to know what the world is really like beyond Dunboyton and the only way to find that is in books, and the tales my mother used to tell me. I want to see London, the churches and shops and palaces, but I would also like to know what the sea looks like beyond our bay. I'd like to see Spain, taste real oranges there, feel the sun on my face. And Paris—' She broke off with a little laugh. 'It must seem silly to you, who have actually seen all those things.'

He gave her a gentle smile. 'The world outside this

place does hold many beauties,' he said. 'But it can also be a cruel and ugly place, and it is lonely to see it by oneself.' He reached out to softly touch a strand of loose dark hair that had fallen from its pins. Alys held her breath at his nearness, the warmth of his hand so close to her cheek. 'I can see why your family would want to protect you, to keep that—that sweetness in your eyes.'

Alys swallowed hard and leaned away from his touch. She feared if she stayed there, looking into those eyes of his, she would lean *into* him instead and kiss him. She ached to know what his lips might feel like on her own and that was one thing she should never try. She turned away to unroll a pile of bandages and then roll them again. 'Even Dunboyton can be filled with cruelty, as we saw all too clearly only days ago. If I knew more of the world—of how to shield myself—' She broke off, overcome by the memory of those poor men on the beach. By how easily Juan could have been one of them.

He laid his hand against her arm, lightly, as if he feared she would break away. She did not. 'Of course. It was most hideous. I didn't mean to imply you were some sort of swooning maiden in a tower. You are obviously very brave, as well as kind. See how you help a stranger, at peril to yourself.'

Ah, but Juan was not just *any* stranger. Alys came to see that, fear that, more and more as she knew him. 'You said you grew up in an English abbey.'

He looked surprised at the sudden change in topic, but he recovered quickly and smiled. She thought she glimpsed something in his eyes behind that smile, a flash of wariness. 'So I did. My father's estate. His grandfather bought it from King Henry.'

'But you did not stay there.'

'Nay, I left to study at Cambridge and then went to the Netherlands in a company of soldiers with my godfather.'

He fought for the *English* in the Netherlands? Alys wondered if her suspicions were right and he was a spy. But for whom? 'And from there you went to Spain? To find your mother's family, mayhap?'

He looked down, hiding those eyes from her as he crumbled the remains of the bread. 'I have never known anything about my Spanish family. My understanding is that I have no living Spanish kin.'

It sounded unbearably sad, a tiny child left without his mother, without even a sense of where she came from or what kind of person she was. At least Alys had known and loved her mother, known something of Spain. 'I am sorry. I am glad I did know my mother and stories about her family. I could imagine what it was like, even here in Ireland, though I will never see it for myself.' She laughed. 'I will probably never even see London, let alone Madrid! You are lucky in your travels.'

He flashed her a smile, but it looked sad. 'I have never felt so fortunate. Always being in a different place is a very lonely life indeed.'

'But an endlessly fascinating one, I am sure.'

'I did say I would tell you some tales of my travels.' He stared up at the painted ceiling for a moment. 'Amsterdam, for instance. It is a city built on water, as Venice is, but the two are very different despite their canals. Venice is old, full of crumbling stones and ancient bridges, of mysterious eyes peering from behind shuttered windows. Amsterdam is clean and orderly, with barges going about their marketing business and tall, painted houses along every walkway. And Portugal…'

'Is it as sunny as everyone says?'

'It might be, but it's hard to know, since the houses are built so close together. Their roofs almost touch on the streets overhead, blocking the light, until one comes to the river. Then, all the lanes open up on to wide wharfs and ships bound for every port wait at anchor to set sail for the New World, or mayhap for India.'

'India.' Alys sighed, thinking of silks and spices, and warm sunshine. She did have dreams of the royal court at London, which sometimes seemed as distant as India could be, but she thought there were more worlds to be seen than anyone could ever dream of. Amsterdam, Venice, Paris…

'How many adventures you must have had,' she said sadly.

He knelt down beside her next to the fire, watching her closely. He seemed to hide nothing from her now, his eyes clear, speaking of a sadness she could barely fathom.

'Lady Alys,' he said softly. 'There were many reasons I was on that ship, but I am bound by my honour not to speak of them. I only want you to know that you and your father's household have naught to fear from me. I will do nothing to harm you and never would have.'

Alys studied him very closely for a long, tensely silent moment. For that time, they seemed bound close together with shimmering, invisible cords that could not break. Their breath, their very heartbeats, seemed as one. 'I—I think I always did know that. We do live in such a world of secrets, and as I said I know little of the lands beyond Dunboyton. But I do know that the Queen's throne is not a steady one and she needs help from the shadows.'

He suddenly leaned back, away from her, and she glimpsed the surprise and suspicion on his face. Had she found out something, then? Guessed correctly about his work?

She quickly turned away. He still needed his bandages changed and she mixed up her herbal poultice with trembling hands. 'How will you find your way to where you are going? After you have recovered your strength, of course.'

'I will find some way, Lady Alys, never fear. And I will not burden you with my presence here long at all, I promise. I think I am strong enough to move now, thanks to you.'

She glanced back at him and saw that even sitting there talking to her, holding tight to his secrets, had tired him. His skin was pale again, his eyes dark-shadowed. 'I vow you are not! You need more rest and good food. Here, sit here and let me look at your bandages, then you must have some of this spiced wine. It does strengthen the blood.' Alys busied herself with those familiar tasks, the herbs and the bandages, to try to force away one desolate thought—Dunboyton would be even lonelier, even more dull, when he was gone.

He sat down on the stool near the fire and went very still as she eased back the laces of his borrowed shirt and unwound the old dressings. He was warm now, but from the fire and not fever, and his skin was so deliciously golden she longed to touch it, to feel the silken heat of him under her fingers. If she closed her eyes, she could picture exactly what it would be like to do, to breathe in the scent of him, and lean closer and closer until...

Nay! She had to focus on her tasks, not on things that were impossible.

'Tell me of your days here,' he said quietly.

Alys smiled. His wound was healing well, no streaks

of reddened infection at all. She smoothed on the new poultice, trying not to linger. 'They are dull indeed, especially compared to what you must have known in your travels. Sometimes, when my father has visitors, I must play hostess to them in the great hall, but that is not often. I go to market in the village, I oversee the laundry and the kitchens, I work in my stillroom…'

'Where you learned your great knowledge of healing herbs?'

'My mother taught me. The stillroom is my little sanctuary.'

'Your sanctuary from what?'

Alys shook her head. 'I should have not said that. Dunboyton is not so terrible as all that. But sometimes I have to escape the quarrels of the maidservants. They do find an extraordinary number of things to disagree about. Or escape from doing the same things every day. The stillroom is always quiet and it smells lovely…'

'So that is where you get it.'

She looked up at him, confused, and found him smiling down at her. 'Get…what?'

'You smell so lovely, Lady Alys. Like a meadow in the summertime.' He caught up her loosened strand of hair and lifted it to his nose to smell it. It was as if he inhaled all of her, all she was and knew.

She felt her cheeks turn warm and pulled away. Her hair slid between his fingers. ''Tis lavender and rosewater.'

'Is that what you are using to heal me, too?' he said, gesturing to the herbs in her basket.

Alys was most glad of the change of subject. 'I doubt rosewater would help you, though a rosehip syrup couldn't hurt. This is feverfew and yarrow, to bring down your fever. And I will give you some valerian for your wine for tonight, to help you sleep and purify your blood.'

He was silent for a moment, studying the dried and powdered herbs as she pointed to them. 'So when do you read, if you are so busy gathering your herbs and physicking everyone? When you walk here to the abbey?'

'Sometimes. The abbey is a bit like the stillroom—an escape. It isn't often we get new books here and I like to savour them with no one to interrupt me.'

'And what do you read? Poetry? History?'

Alys bit her lip, afraid he would think her rather—unfeminine. 'Whatever I can find. I read my prayer books, of course, and histories of England. I do love poetry, tales of adventure and romance. When we receive French volumes, they are the best, but that's a rare treat. And I like reading of courtly life. I want to…'

His head tilted as he studied her. 'Want to what?'

'Well, imagine what life is like there, I suppose, at the Queen's court. What it would be like to meet her, serve her, see people from foreign lands. The fashions, the music. My father often shows me drawings of London and I would like to see it for myself.'

'Will he send you to court as a Maid of Honour, perhaps?'

Alys thought of all the letters that had come to her father, all the messages refusing to summon him to court because of his Spanish wife. She feared a palace life could never be hers. 'Perhaps one day.'

'I am surprised you are not yet married.'

His voice sounded tight when he said the words and she glanced up to see a flash of something like jealousy cross his face. Or perhaps that was her wishful imagining. 'I have not thought about it. I think I would rather go to court for a time before I must go from managing Dunboyton to another household just like it. I am not so very old as that yet.' Though it was true many girls younger than she were wed here in Ireland, she had met no one she would even consider as husband.

She feared no man would measure up to Juan now, either. It was a great pity.

He laughed. 'You are not so old at all, Lady Alys. And I do understand your wishes.'

She thought of all the places he had been, all his adventures. She could not picture him quiet by his own hearth. 'I am sure you do, or surely you would not have gone on such dangerous travels.' Or put himself so near death. She shivered at the thought of how close he had come.

'Royal courts are glittering places indeed,' he said. 'But a lady such as you should never stay there long. There can be many dangers there.'

Alys laughed. 'I told you, Juan—I am no delicate angel. I am sure that, given time and instruction, I could find my way.'

'I am sure you could do anything you set your mind to, Lady Alys. But I must disagree with one thing. You are most assuredly an angel.'

He reached for her hand, raising it to his lips for a gentle kiss as courtly as any she could imagine receiving in a palace. His lips were soft against her skin, and lingered in a sweet caress. Alys leaned closer, drawn to him as she would be to a fire on a cold night, as if his touch was necessary to her very breath. He looked up at her, his eyes so very, very green…

And suddenly something dropped down from the thatched roof above them, something long and horribly shimmering. It landed on Juan's shoulder and fell to the ground, rearing up to bare sharp, needle-like fangs.

'A snake!' Alys cried. How was that possible? She had never even seen a snake at Dunboyton and here was one right at her feet, about to strike. She felt paralysed, staring down at it, as if time had slowed to a terrible crawl.

But it never struck. Juan tossed a dagger at it, quick as flash of lightning and with unerring aim. The blade sank deep in the viper's neck and it fell to the dirt floor with a hiss.

Juan sucked in a deep breath. 'You did not warn me I shared my accommodations.'

Alys swallowed hard, trying to find her voice. 'I—I have never seen such a thing here before. They say St Patrick drove all snakes away from here.'

'He obviously missed some.'

Alys choked on a laugh, even as she shivered with a sudden fear. Was the snake a terrible sign? A warning?

What evils would befall her, and Dunboyton, if she did not heed it?

Alys ran up the path towards the gates of Dunboyton, as fast as if even more snakes chased at the hem of her skirts. She was so distracted when she returned to the castle that she didn't notice the servants and her father's soldiers hurrying past, didn't notice the usual clamour and bustle that always surrounded mealtimes. She didn't notice the wind that cut through her cloak as it swept around the courtyard.

All she could see in her mind was Juan, the tenderness of his touch as he reached for her hair, the sweetness of his kiss on her hand. The fierce, quick strength when he killed the snake. The glow of his beautiful eyes.

At the foot of the stone steps that led to the inner door, she did notice something out of place—a fine grey horse that did not belong to the Dunboyton stable. It stood at attention, the centre of a circle of gaping grooms, its silver-and-green velvet trappings shimmering. It was too fine for anyone Alys knew nearby. Could it be that Bingham or even Fitzwilliam had returned, searching for Juan?

Pushing down her fear, she ran into the house and, after she hid her baskets and cloak in the stillroom, went to find her father in the great hall. She had been worried about him of late, worried about how tired he seemed, but now he was talking with great animation, even a smile, to the man who sat next to him beside the fireplace.

She didn't know the man, but she could tell at a glance he must be someone of some consequence. He was tall and lean, with the erect bearing of a soldier, his thick iron-grey hair brushed back from austere, hawk-like features. He wore travelling clothes of the finest grey wool and velvet, a cloak of green velvet that matched the horse's trappings spread before the fire to dry.

'Oh, Alys, there you are,' her father called. 'A guest has just arrived this afternoon.'

Alys made her way forward as their visitor rose and gave her a bow. Standing, he was even taller, more imposing, even while dressed so simply and sombrely. He seemed to notice everything around him in one quick glance with his grey eyes and Alys was suddenly aware of how windblown and flustered she must look. She pushed the loose lock of hair back into its pins and smoothed her red-wool skirts.

'I am sorry I wasn't here to greet you, sir,' she said. 'I had some tasks in the outbuildings and did not know anyone was expected.'

''Tis of no matter, my lady,' he answered, his tone perfectly civil and soft. 'I did not expect to stop here on my journey. I have spent a most pleasant hour with Sir William, hearing all about this most intriguing place.'

'Alys, my dear, this is Sir Matthew Morgan, an agent from the Queen's court. We knew each other long ago, when I was at Cambridge, and it's an unexpected pleasure to see him again. Sir Matthew, this is my daughter, Lady Alys.'

The Queen's agent? Would they send someone like this to track down fleeing Spanish sailors? Alys could think of no other reason he would be there and knew she had to warn Juan. But for now, faced with those sombre grey eyes that seemed to see too much, she had to stay calm and polite. To give nothing away.

'I am most pleased to meet you, Sir Matthew. My father often speaks so fondly of his days at Cambridge, and to see a new face at Dunboyton is always most welcome, though I fear you will find us much less than "intriguing". Our days are usually quite dull.' She gestured to one of the servants to bring more wine, and sat down on the cushioned stool next to her father. Their guest resumed his seat across from them, smiling pleasantly. But Alys could not quite shake away that lingering fear.

'Not dull in recent days, I fear,' Sir Matthew said.

'Unfortunately not,' her father answered. 'I much prefer my quiet routine. But Bingham has taken his men off along the coast now, he won't come back here any time soon. We saw only two ships break up in the bay below our cliffs and he dragged away the few survivors.'

'Is it Bingham you seek, then, Sir Matthew?' Alys asked, pouring out the fresh wine.

'I would like to speak with him, of course,' Sir Matthew said. 'He has much to answer for to the Queen. My task now is to make some sense of what has happened here for an account to Her Majesty. She wishes to be sure any valuable survivors are questioned by her own men and kept here in honourable imprisonment until they can be ransomed back to Spain. They say there were many men of the most noble families in Spain and Portugal aboard these ships. England cannot face such an invasion again, but neither can she be seen to be unmerciful.'

Alys bit her lip, thinking of how she had found Juan, ill and injured, freezing in the reeds. And he was the fortunate one. She couldn't let him be found now.

'I am afraid we can be of little help to you here, Matthew,' her father said. 'Bingham did not linger here long and, as far as I know, he took only one valuable prisoner, a nobleman named Perez. Many were killed and my men could not stop it, I am ashamed to say.'

Sir Matthew took a slow sip of the wine, his austere face completely unreadable. 'One of the ships that went down near here was called the *Concepción*, I believe. A valuable galleon of the Biscay Squadron.'

'Aye, they did say that was one. The other is yet unknown,' her father said.

'I would like to question your household, with your permission,' Sir Matthew said. 'Many times people witness something of great import and do not even realise it. I must be as thorough as I can in my report, not an easy task after time has gone past.'

'Of course,' her father answered, though his expression looked rather reluctant. He had been governor of Dunboyton for many years and Alys knew how protective he was of all his household.

'I shall not be more than a day or two, William, and will go gently,' Sir Matthew said.

'You must stay with us, then,' Alys said. 'I will have the maids air the chamber here above the great hall—I fear it is seldom used. There is a sitting room, too, which you can use for your enquiries.'

'I am most grateful for the hospitality, Lady Alys,' Sir Matthew said. 'I have been sleeping in the saddle for too many days now.'

'Then, over dinner, you must tell me all about the Queen's court,' Alys said with a smile. Perhaps she could lure a titbit of information from him, if she was careful. Something that might tell her what he really sought at Dunboyton. 'I am so eager to hear all about it all! It must be so magical.'

Her father chuckled. 'Alys is quite obsessed with the latest fashions and dances.'

Sir Matthew smiled indulgently. 'I fear I am not a dancing man myself, but I will tell you all I can remember from the royal banquets. I have the feeling, though, that ruffs and sleeves are not quite all that interests you, Lady Alys.'

Alys tried to cover her surprise with a quick smile of her own. 'If you know anything of new embroidery patterns at all…'

He laughed and held out his goblet for more wine. 'Now there, I would be of no help at all.'

'Well, your company is welcome none the less, Sir Matthew,' Alys said and rose to her feet as slowly as she could. She couldn't go running away now. 'If you will excuse me, I shall see to your chamber.'

As she made her way out of the great hall, she heard her father say, 'My poor daughter. It is a lonely life here at Dunboyton. I have been trying to secure a place for her at court for some time.'

'She would grace it with her presence, she is quite pretty,' Sir Matthew answered. 'And with all your services to the Queen, especially of late, there should be no difficulty. Any who have aided in the defeat of the Armada will be rewarded. Perhaps I could be of some help?'

Alys hurried away before she could hear her father's answer. A bribe of sorts, to find information from her father? Alys did not quite trust Sir Matthew, despite his polite smiles. She had to make her way back to Juan soon and warn him the Queen's men were here. He deserved the chance to go to them himself and tell them his tale, if her suspicions of his spying activity were correct.

And if she was wrong about him, about everything— she was in too much trouble for even a position at the Queen's court to fix.

Chapter Eight

'There. What do you think?' Alys asked, balancing carefully on the stool as she tied the painted cloth to the wall of the old dairy. The bright colours of the scene seemed to make the dim, dank little room a bit more vivid, a bit less dreary. 'I don't think anyone could recover their health in such darkness, with nothing pretty to look at.'

Juan laughed. 'I have recovered my health completely, thanks to my ministering angel. And you have made a cosy little home here in such little time. I've never lived anywhere so comfortable.'

Alys studied the room, which she had tidied and feathered with new cushions, blankets and the cloth. It *was* rather cosy, she thought, and not a bad place to recover a measure of health, but she doubted it was the best place he had ever lived, not after being in so many fine cities. 'I don't think that can be true—have you not visited palaces and such?'

'Oh, nay, I assure you—it is by far the best.' He took her hand to help her down from the stool and his touch was warm on her skin. She hated to let him go. They sat down together on the newly cushioned stools, near the teetering stacks of books she had loaned him to pass the time. 'Palaces, though certainly grand in their state rooms, are small, cramped and damp in their accommodations. They are old places, by and large, and cold even in summer. Not to mention crowded and smelly. Here I have this space all to myself and may read and think all day. I can't remember ever having such luxuries.'

'I think I should still like to see a palace, even if they're cold and cramped!' Alys said. 'Dunboyton is very old and often dank, and always crowded, but we have no marble pillars and fine carpets to look at, such as the Queen must possess. There must be amusements there we don't have, as well.'

'There are amusements, true,' Juan said. 'Banquets and dancing almost every night, and in the summer there are often river pageants and picnics, hunts, ceremonies to welcome foreign ambassadors, always music and fine food.'

Alys sighed happily to envision it, a crowd of velvet-clad courtiers dancing under gilded ceilings. 'It would be lovely to see new people sometimes, not always the same faces all the time.'

'You must have gatherings here? Dancing and music?'

'We do dance here, especially at Christmas,' she said. 'But I am sure it can't be nearly as elegant as the courtly dances.'

'Well, shall we compare them?' Juan said. He rose to his feet and offered her his hand as he gave a bow.

Alys laughed at the contrast between his elaborate bow, low over his outstretched leg, and his rough borrowed clothes, their simple surroundings. 'Compare?'

'Aye. You must imagine you are in the Queen's own

hall. There is the dais where sits her velvet-and-gilt throne, an embroidered canopy of state over it. And there are the carved panels of the wall, the cabinet piled high with glittering gold-and-silver plate. The musicians are in their gallery above our heads, playing a royal galliard on their lutes and drums. All the courtiers are taking their places. Now, my lady, will you honour me with this dance?'

Alys dipped into a low curtsy. 'I shall, kind sir.'

He took her hand in his and led her to the empty centre of their little room. His touch was warm on her fingers, slightly rough from his work on the ships, and for a moment she imagined they *were* in a palace. That she was surrounded by velvet and satin gowns, tapestries sparkling with gold thread, the scent of rich, flowery perfumes. That she herself wore bright silk and flashing jewels.

'Now, imagine the music like this,' Juan said, and hummed a few bars. 'One, *two*, one, *two*, three, three. Right, left, right, left and jump, landing with one leg ahead of the other. Like so.'

He showed her the patterns slowly at first, then quicker as she followed, his movements as lithe as a mountain lynx. Alys saw it was not so very different from their Dunboyton dances, and she copied him, landing with a little twirl. She hoped against hope he thought she was almost as graceful as those court ladies.

'Very good,' he said with a laugh. 'Are you sure you have not done courtly dances before?'

'You must be a fine teacher,' she answered with a teasing smile.

'We shall see when you dance before the Queen,' he

said, holding her hand up as she made another little twirl. 'Now, let go of my hand and face me, like this.'

She came to a stop close to him, mere inches from his shoulder. She didn't dare to look up at him, into those magical eyes. The warmth of his nearness made her breath catch. 'Now—now what?'

'I put my hand on your waist, like this,' he answered hoarsely as his hand landed lightly on her waist. 'You touch my shoulder and we turn.'

They spun around each other, slowly at first, their steps twining around each other, perfectly matched, as if they had always danced just like that. Alys held on to his strong shoulder, letting him guide her, trusting him.

But then she got ahead of him and his leg tangled in her skirt. She felt herself tip off balance, toppling towards the floor. She caught at his shoulders, her stomach lurching, and he swung her up high in the air.

Alys laughed, her head floating giddily. 'Is this part of the dance?'

'It is now! Our own new step.' He twirled her around and around, as if she was a mere feather, and indeed she felt like one. Like she floated free high above the world.

She laughed helplessly until her sides ached and tears prickled at her eyes. She couldn't remember ever laughing so much, or ever being with anyone who made her feel as Juan did—free and light, as if she could be herself for a moment. Their strange, rough little refuge seemed changed entirely to a fairyland.

'Oh, stop, stop!' she cried, her feelings overwhelming her.

He lowered her slowly to her feet, but it still felt as if the room spun around them. She clung to him, gasping with laughter. She hadn't felt so free since she was a child!

'I think we could start a new fashion in dancing,' he said, his voice thick with his own laughter.

For an instant, Alys imagined what it might be like to be at court with him. Walking on his arm past those crowds of richly clad people, knowing he was hers and she his. Shyly, she glanced up at him and she was shocked to see he had dropped his careful mask. She glimpsed a stark, naked longing in his eyes, a haunted pain.

Then it was gone, banished behind laughter. He stepped away and bowed again.

Alys fell back a step and rubbed at her arms, suddenly cold again.

'Thank you for the dance, my lady,' he said. 'I think you are quite ready to impress the Queen.'

'I do doubt it,' she murmured. She turned away from him, flustered. 'It—it is cold in here, is it not? I shall bring more blankets when I come back.'

'I am perfectly comfortable here, Lady Alys,' he said. 'You have made it like a true home.'

She glanced around and found that everything did look different than it had only days before, a new place of colour and interest. He made it so; he made the world look different, made her imagine different things, a different life. If only it could be so.

'I must go now, or I'll be missed,' she said. 'But I will return later.'

He reached for her hand, holding it lightly balanced on his palm as he raised it to his lips. His kiss was warm, soft and light as a cloud and it made her tremble. 'Thank you, my fair rescuer,' he whispered.

Alys couldn't answer. She spun around and hurried

out of the room, catching up her shawl to wrap it tightly around her shoulders. The wind outside was chilly, but she welcomed its cold brush against her face. It helped steady her, helped wash away the clouds of dreams that had dared to come into her mind. Dreams of court life, of romance, of dances and kisses. With Juan.

'Don't be so silly,' she told herself as she hurried along the cliffs towards home. Those moments with Juan were only that, dreams, and soon enough they would be gone. But she knew, deep inside, that she herself would never be quite the same again.

Chapter Nine

Alys tiptoed out of the castle, holding a basket of fresh supplies on her hip. It was growing late, the servants were at their own supper in the kitchens, her father was in his chamber and she had not seen their mysterious guest since their own dinner. It seemed a good time to go to Juan, with the risen moon lighting her path.

She felt a fizzing excitement as she made her way towards the abbey and it made her want to laugh and cry all at the same time. Looking forward to seeing him made her feel *alive*, in a way she never had before. She dreaded what it would be like when he left again, as he surely would very soon. Dunboyton would be quiet once more, her days filled with her household routines.

Yet she would have memories of him to go over in years to come. That would be enough. It *had* to be enough.

Alys paused at the top of the cliff steps to shift her basket. It had grown heavier with the climb. The moon shimmered with a silvery glow on the old stones of the abbey, turning their ruin into something jewel-like and magical. It seemed like a night when fairies might appear, when anything could happen.

For an instant, she thought she heard something, a rustle or a footstep.

She whirled around, her heart pounding. Was it the ghosts of the monks, gathering for their prayers under the moon? Or mayhap a far more corporeal danger. There was no guarantee that all Bingham's men had left the area.

And then there had been the snake. Surely it had not just come out of nowhere, as a sign or a warning. Her old nursemaid would have said it was a demon.

Yet she saw nothing now. She was alone, except for the brush of the wind through the trees.

'Don't be so silly,' she told herself sternly and turned to make her way towards the dairy.

As always when she came to Juan, for a moment she feared he would be gone already, that she would find the old building deserted. She knocked quickly. ''Tis me— Alys,' she called softly.

The door swung open and Juan stood there. He looked almost as if he had been sleeping, his dark hair tousled, his shirt lacings loosened to reveal a vee of golden skin. A smile broke over his sensual lips, wide and delighted, bright as the sun of a summer day, and it made her smile, too. 'I feared I wouldn't see you tonight,' he said as he took the basket from her.

'Our evening meal took longer than usual,' she answered. 'My father has had guests for a couple of days now.'

'Guests?' He knelt down to stir the fire, making the flames leap higher. The light gilded his skin, making him seem like a golden god.

To distract herself, Alys started unpacking the food and wine from the basket, laying it out on a blanket as a makeshift table. 'Not to worry, it wasn't Bingham's soldiers returning. I brought you some of the beef and chicken pies that were left, and some of the cook's fine honey cakes. She doesn't make them very often.'

'Then I am most grateful to your guests. I confess I have a terrible sweet tooth.' He popped one of the small cakes into his mouth and grinned, making Alys laugh.

'Have you been too bored today?' Alys asked, pouring herself some wine.

'Not at all. I read some of the fine books you brought and watched the birds among the ruins. I don't think I have ever felt so very peaceful in a long time. Maybe never. There truly is a magic in this place.'

Alys remembered when she would come to the abbey with her mother, climbing over the stones, lying in the meadows with the sun on her face. The way it had sheltered her after she lost her mother. 'It brings me great peace, as well. My nursemaid used to tell me there were fairies living here.'

'That reminds me, fair Alys—you do owe me a story still. Remember our bargain?'

Alys laughed. 'I can't think of any good tales now.'

'Certainly you can. What of those fairies? Come, entertain me while I eat. I have been alone all day, after all.' He gave her an exaggerated sad look that made her laugh again.

'There is a tale I loved as a child,' she said. 'It rather reminds me of you.'

'Of me?' he said with a laugh.

'Aye. There are many fairies who live near us and they watch what we do even as we have no awareness of them.

Some of them wish evil on humans; some are only mischievous. And some do love us, in their own way, even though their fairy love can destroy us as easily as the illness-causing evil fairies.'

'Am I an evil fairy, then?'

Alys studied him carefully, his easy smile, his beautiful eyes. 'Nay. You are the sort who draw unwary mortals closer and closer, until they long for the fairy realm and forget their own homes. Just as the tale my old nurse told me, about a fairy king who sought to wed a human princess. She was betrothed to another prince, but when she saw the fairy king, he mesmerised her with his eyes, and drew her to him, until she vanished to her family and fiancé.'

'He had magical eyes?'

'Aye. A beautiful emerald-green, like your own, if I remember the story right.'

Juan gave a sad sigh. 'But alas, I have found no princess to love me.'

Alys laughed. 'You just have not looked close enough, I would wager. I am sure princesses from Antwerp to Lisbon have looked into your eyes and been lost. Mayhap your mother was not Spanish after all, but fey folk…' Emerald-green eyes. Alys smiled as she thought of their rare beauty and felt the deepest sympathy for the lost human princess. They were mesmerising indeed. Just like…

Like the green eyes of the boy who had once saved her and soothed her tears away.

Startled by her own memory, she looked up at Juan and saw there the boy. The green-eyed boy with the floppy dark hair and sweet smile. He had come back to her now, when she had thought never to see him again.

Flustered, she looked away. 'I should look at your

shoulder and make sure it is healing properly before I go,' she said. 'Does it give you any pain?'

He rolled his shoulder with seeming ease. 'Not at all. You have worked miracles. A healing angel.'

Alys felt her cheeks turn warm with a pleased blush. 'Nay, not I, it's just the herbs. My mother used to say any wound could heal, if kept clean and dosed with the right herbs. The earth knows what is needed.'

'Then she was a most wise woman. I'm fortunate she had such a daughter.'

Alys smiled and tentatively eased back his shirt. The linen was warm from his body and when she was so close to him it was hard to remain sensible. She forced herself to concentrate only on his wound, not on the way he smelled, the smooth, hot satin of his skin.

She turned back the bandage and saw that the poultice was doing its work. She reached for the new mixture of herbs from the basket and wound a fresh bandage around his shoulder. The familiar work distracted her from old memories.

'Do you remember anything at all of your own mother?' she asked.

'Very little. She died when I was very young. I think I recall the way her perfume smelled, of summer roses, and her smile, which was sad and sweet. After she was gone, I fear our house was not a home at all. The buildings began crumbling, a wreck just like my father turned into.'

Alys felt a pang of sadness for him as a little boy, left alone to face a cold world. 'I am sorry. Dunboyton might be dull and chilly, but it is never cruel. The home my mother tried to make is still here.'

'Is it *your* home, Alys?'

She thought about that carefully. 'Not the castle, no. But my memories, the people I love—that makes it home, I suppose.'

'Will you miss it when you marry and leave?' he said tightly.

Alys peeked up at him and found he watched her carefully, his bright eyes narrowed. 'Of course. But thanks to my mother, I will know how to make a new home. What of you, Juan? Will you find a fine lady to marry and make a new home?'

He gave a bark of laughter. 'Nay, I would not know how to do that. I have never known a home.'

'But would you like to?'

He was quiet for a long moment. 'I think I might. A home—it does sound like a fine thing.'

There was a note of sadness in his voice that made Alys's heart ache all over again. She rested her hands on his shoulders and leaned against him, longing to bring him comfort. To bring that to herself.

Suddenly, the air between them seemed to change, growing charged as the sky was just before a lightning strike. She could hardly breathe, especially when he reached for her and drew her closer. She had never been so close to a man. How dizzying it was! All her senses tilted and whirled, and all she knew in that moment was him. The way he felt under her touch, so alive and strong and warm.

'Alys…' he said hoarsely.

'I—I am here,' she whispered.

As if in a hazy dream, far away, yet more immediate and real than anything she had ever known before, his head tilted down towards her and he kissed her.

The brush of his lips was so soft at first, like warm velvet, pressing softly once, twice, as if he expected her to run. But Alys could not have moved away from him. As she moved up to meet him, his kiss deepened. It became hotter, more urgent—the most urgent, hungry thing she had ever known.

Something deep inside her heart responded to that urgency, a rough excitement that grew and grew until she thought she would burst from it. She moaned, parting her lips to the shocking feel of his tongue seeking entrance, sliding over hers. There was only *him*, not the world outside, only him and that one perfect moment.

But the outside world insisted on breaking into her dream. A sound like a branch falling against the roof shocked her, making her fall back from him. She jumped to her feet, her whole body shaking. She longed to jump back into his arms, yet she knew she could not. If she did, she might never free herself again.

'Alys, I am so very sorry…' he said, his sea-green eyes grown dark.

'Nay. Please don't say you are sorry for what happened,' she gasped. 'I could not bear it. I just—I must go now.'

She whirled around and ran out of the dairy, hearing him call after her. She couldn't stop, though. She hurried out of the abbey's ruins as if the ghosts were indeed running after her. She didn't feel the cold wind, even though she had left her shawl behind, and she could hear nothing at all but the wild beat of her heart in her ears.

She paused at the kitchen-garden wall to try to catch her breath. If her father was awake, she knew she could not let him see her in such a state. But as she studied the castle, she saw that no windows were alight, except the one in the guest chamber of the tower. The one where Sir Matthew stayed. She felt as if someone watched from behind those blank windows, someone who sought all her secrets.

Chapter Ten

He was not alone in his hiding place. John could sense it. And whoever lurked outside, it was not Alys. She would have dashed inside, her basket in her arms, and lit up the darkness with her smile.

John's extensive training during his work with Walsingham had sharpened his sixth sense to an exceptional degree. He always knew when he was being followed, being watched. It had served him well in the palace corridors of Madrid and Paris, and the back alleys of Lisbon. Last night, when he was alone after Alys left, he felt the sharp prickle of that sense. He had tried to shrug it away, to attribute it to the darkness of the sky and Alys's tales of ghostly monks and fairies. Now he saw how foolish shrugging it away had been.

John held the hilt of the only weapon he now had, the eating knife, lightly on his palm and stepped silently to the half-open door.

He could feel whoever it was moving closer, like the slow slide of a length of silk over his skin, barely a whisper.

Then he heard it. The merest crackle of a fallen leaf

on the old, cracked flagstones. It could have merely been blown by the wind, but he knew it wasn't. He heard another sound, the brush of wool against the wall, and he lunged out the door, his dagger raised. His other hand shot out towards a shadow looming in the darkness and caught a fistful of that woollen cloak.

The figure inside the cloak was too tall, too muscular to be petite Alys. He shoved the man against the wall, into the ray of light coming out of the door, and pressed his knife to a throat, just at the vulnerable spot beneath the chin. Before he could drive the blade home, the cloak's hood fell back and he saw the man's face.

It was as familiar to him as his own in its sharp, hawk-like angles, in the wry smile that curved the lips. 'I see I taught you well enough, John,' Sir Matthew Morgan said, his smile growing.

John drew back the blade. Shock and happiness shot through him at the sight of his godfather. It had been too long since he had seen anything familiar, had felt close to home again. Whatever home was. 'Sir Matthew! What are you doing here?'

'Whatever do you think I would be doing in the wilds of Ireland? Looking for you, of course.'

Looking for him? He had always known Matthew was good at his job, but perhaps now he had some second sight. Or perhaps the Queen's astrologer, John Dee, had led him. 'How did you find me?'

Matthew shrugged. 'Perhaps we would be more comfortable talking inside?'

John nodded and led the way back into his little sanctuary. Matthew took it in with a flicker of a glance. 'You have found a fine nest. I suppose the pretty Lady Alys made it so, since I remember the squalor of your Cambridge lodgings. You never had a talent for housekeeping.'

At the mention of Alys, John turned wary, his senses heightened in that prickling, warning way again. He closed the door softly behind them and leaned against it with his arms crossed. No one could be permitted to harm Alys, even his godfather, even if she was, technically speaking, a traitor to the crown. She had been moved by humanity alone to save his life and he would die to keep her from being punished for it. 'Is that how you found me? Through her?'

'In a way, though I must say she was remarkably careful for a lady with no experience as an intelligencer. She made sure she was followed by no servants or soldiers from the castle and gave no clue even to her father. Perhaps Walsingham could recruit her?'

John shook his head in anger. His gentle Alys, subjected to the things he had seen and done in Walsingham's service? He regretted nothing; it had been done to protect the Queen and the peace of England. But Alys could never know those horrors. 'Don't you dare approach her, Sir Matthew. She may be careful, but she is also an innocent.'

Matthew glanced at John, his brow raised in an expression of curiosity. 'Indeed? 'Tis a pity. We could use her. We have few men here in this part of the world. Even spies can't stomach it.'

'You must have a few, though, to have found me so quickly.'

Matthew turned to the fire, his back to John as he held his hands closer to the flames. 'We have been carefully tracking all the Armada ships that escaped from Gravelines. We heard the *Concepción* had been blown this way in the storm and I set off as soon as I heard. The Queen's pinnaces are much faster and safer than your clumsy Spanish galleons. I prayed you had survived.'

'And so I did. But how did you know I was here? Bingham's soldiers were killing anyone they could find on sight.'

'Surely you must know I have my own men with Bingham? They have sharp eyes and knew the right questions to ask, even in the midst of such chaos. They had not seen you. And I took shelter at Dunboyton. Sir William Drury is an old friend of mine and a smart man. I hoped he could help in some way.'

'So you found Alys there.'

'*Alys*, is it? Aye, so I did. Sir William had no knowledge of you, nor of any Englishman seeking shelter, and I could tell he was not lying. His daughter, on the other hand…'

'You did not question her, did you?' John asked sharply, that cold fear returning.

Matthew frowned. 'Certainly not. As I said, for a civilian and a sheltered lady she was not a bad liar. She hid her fears well enough and was quite gracious. But she was not quite good enough. I could tell she was hiding something and when I saw her slip out of the castle with a rather large basket, I was sure of it. I followed her, simple as that.'

'How did you know she was coming to me?'

'I did not, of course. It could have been anyone she was helping, but I had a sense.' A smile flickered on his face. 'I do know the effect you have on fair ladies, John. It has served you well with the French *mademoiselles* and Spanish *doñas*, I trust.'

John shook his head. Aye, he had done things in the

past he was not proud of, flirted with ladies of every age and station, coaxed secrets from them. But Alys—she was different. Different from every other lady he had ever known, with her sweetness and her laughter, even with her sensible help when he was injured. Aye, Alys was different. 'I did not seduce her into helping me, Sir Matthew. She has a good, kind heart and it was wounded seeing Bingham's brutality.'

For an instant, Matthew looked surprised. 'I am sure she was.' That unguarded expression was gone as fast as it was there, hidden behind that small smile. 'I knew Sir William when we were young and I remember Elena Lorca, who became Elena Drury. She was a gentle beauty as well and Sir William thought her love worthy of exile from court. Her daughter looks much like her.'

'Are you saying you think I am considering staying here?' John asked. He had not thought of such a thing before, but now that it had occurred to him it seemed— alluring. A home, a hearth of his own, with a lady like Alys by his side. No more wandering, no more lies.

It was alluring indeed, but he knew it could never be. His past made him unworthy of someone like Alys and his duty was to his work still. He shook away the brief image of a life of his own and faced his godfather again with a scowl.

Matthew shrugged. 'The life of an intelligencer is a difficult one, even as necessary as it is, and most men do not last in it as many years as I have. It can grow most wearisome.'

John nodded. Wearisome indeed. He had craved adventure, sought it, and it had come to him in spades. Yet he had not done what he wanted the most—to retrieve the honour of his family name from the depths his father had dragged it to, to restore Huntleyburg. He still had much work to do and sweet Alys could be no part of it.

'I have been injured, true,' John said. 'But I am regaining my health. I still have services I can perform for the Queen. And Alys—she deserves better than I could give her. She deserves a husband with a calm disposition and a fine estate.'

Matthew studied him for a long, tense moment and finally nodded. 'As you say, there is still much you can do for Queen Elizabeth, for England. You have already done far more than even I could have imagined. As for Lady Alys…'

'She must not be harmed!'

'Never. She shall be rewarded in some way for her bravery in saving your life, I shall see to that. Perhaps a rich marriage? Some titled gentleman from the court?' Matthew smiled at John's involuntary scoffing sound. 'You do not like that idea, I see, John. Well, we shall think of something for her later. For now, we must be gone. We sail on the dawn tide.'

'So soon?' John asked, startled.

'We must return to the Queen as soon as possible. We have much to tell her of what has happened here and the danger from Spain has not passed. They say some of the ships have regrouped at Ostend and may yet connect with Parma's army. And there are rumours that some of the English Catholic exiles have already secretly reached England's shores. I do not want Sir William or any of the men here to know such things. Also, most importantly, the spy who was in contact with Peter de Vargas is still at the Queen's court and we do not know who it is. They must be found and you are the only one who can do it.'

'But I must thank Alys for all she has done. She…'

She had done *everything*. She had summoned him back to life, both his body and soul, when he had been on the edge of surrendering it. She was a flash of light and joy in darkness. How could he give that up now, now that he had seen what could be? Yet he knew he had to. For her sake. Especially if Peter's spy was still at court. Matthew was right—the danger was not past. It was never past.

Matthew came to John and laid his hands gently on his shoulders, looking into his eyes most solemnly. 'I know how it is. I know the longings in a lonely heart. But you have chosen a different path in life, a dark and rocky one, and you must see it to its close. Lady Alys is gentle and beautiful, as her mother was. Do you not want to spare her such dangers?'

'Of course I do.' John was sure of that. He did care about Alys too much, owed her too much, to expose her to the dangers of his own life. 'Very well.'

Matthew nodded. 'I do know how it feels. I had to make such choices myself, in my youth, and I watched the lady I loved have a better life for it. Lady Alys will be well, I promise you.'

Lady Alys would be well. John nodded, but he could not answer. His throat was tight with all the feelings his heart dared not admit.

'Now, we must be going,' Matthew said briskly. He re-tied his cloak and turned for the door.

John quickly gathered up his few possessions. He knew well that this was for the best, that it was necessary, but still he felt he had to say farewell to Alys in some way, to let her know she would never be forgotten by him. As he piled his shirts into a bundle, he saw the block of wood he had been carving to pass the hours, an almost completed angel with delicate wings and a soft

smile. He had thought of Alys as he carved it, for he
would always think of her as his angel.

As Matthew put out the fire, John carefully placed
the angel where Alys would find her. He hoped she saw
the message of it. The dying light of the flames caught
on the ring he always wore, the ring carved with arms
of his mother's families, and impulsively he tugged it
off his finger and left it caught on the tip of the angel's
wing. The ring had helped keep him safe on his travels;
now he hoped it would do the same for Alys.

As he closed the door behind him, John paused for one
glance back. He had never been sorry to leave a place
before. Temporary lodgings in Antwerp or Paris or Lisbon never felt like home and he was always glad to see
the last of them, to go on to the next adventure. But this
place, this makeshift dairy chamber…

He knew he would always remember it. The sweetness he had known for those few moments with Alys, the
forgetfulness he found in her kiss, the laughter, he had
never known such things before. He hoped with all he
had that somehow she would know the great gift she had
given him, that she would remember *him* for the man he
wished he could be, not the wandering deceiver he was.

But Matthew was right. Alys was too good for the
life he led, the man he had to be. She had been a gift to
him, one he had to let go of now for her own happiness.

He followed Matthew to the cliff steps. He glimpsed a
ship below, a small, sleek pinnace riding the waves, waiting to shoot out of the bay and into the sea beyond. He
glanced back at the castle and saw a few lights at the windows, pinpricks in the pre-dawn gloom. And beyond…

In the sky beyond there was a strange, pinkish glow.
A suspicious light.

Matthew looked back as if to see that John still followed and his expression shifted as he, too, glimpsed the glow in the sky. His mouth hardened.

'Not everyone here, it seems, is as loyal as William Drury and his daughter,' Matthew said.

John remembered Bingham, the killing in the name of the Queen. He remembered other towns in the Low Countries and Portugal, burned for harbouring fugitives, for keeping secrets. 'What have you done here?'

'What you yourself have done many times, John. What we all must do to keep Queen Elizabeth safe. That village was disloyal. Now, we must go or we shall miss the tide.'

John turned to run back to the castle, to shout the warnings, but Matthew seized his arm in a hard grasp. 'Remember your vows, your work, John. If you do not leave with me now, it shall go worse for everyone here. If it is thought Lady Alys helped a suspected Spanish spy, what will happen to her? Come now. The Queen is waiting.'

John stared at his godfather for a long moment and in those cold grey eyes he saw his own soul, his own past. His own future. It was a bleak one, but it was the one he had chosen. He had to protect Alys now by leaving her behind. He nodded and followed Matthew to the ship, not looking back again.

Chapter Eleven

Alys awoke to complete chaos.

At first she thought it was merely part of her dreams, which had been tumultuous for many nights, filled with stormy seas and falling skies. Shouts and the pounding of racing feet only seemed to be a part of that. She groaned and rolled over, pulling the blankets over her head and waiting for it to be quiet again.

But the noise only grew louder, maids sobbing in the corridor, men's loud voices from the courtyard below her window, bells ringing from the chapel. Suddenly, Alys realised it was not a dream at all. Peace had not yet returned to Dunboyton.

She thought of Juan, hidden at the abbey, and she sat straight up in bed. Had he been discovered? Was he being dragged to Bingham even now? Cold fear raced through her.

She jumped to the floor and wrapped her bed robe around her shoulders as she ran to the window. It was still night, but surely near dawn, for the darkness was touched at the horizon with a faint glow. The courtyard below was crowded with her father's men, many of them just fastening their jerkins and pulling on cloaks as if they had been hastily summoned from their beds. She couldn't see any organisation to their racings and shouts, though.

She had to find Juan.

She hastily pulled on her gown, a simple woollen house dress she could lace herself, with no sleeves. She stuffed her feet into her boots and hurried into the corridor. She saw servants running towards the stairs and some coming up them, but could make no sense to it.

She glimpsed Molly from the laundry and grabbed the girl's arm as she dashed past. 'Molly! What is happening?'

The girl turned her freckled, tearstained face towards Alys. 'Oh, my lady! They say the village has been set afire. We're being attacked!'

Alys stared at her in shock. 'The village? Have Bingham's men returned?'

'I don't know, my lady. Maybe it's the Spanish! They've come to kill us in our beds after all!'

Alys thought again of Juan and hoped he stayed where he was in the dairy. 'Where is my father? Or his guest, Sir Matthew Morgan?'

'I haven't seen Sir Matthew. Sir William is in the courtyard.' Her sobs broke out again and she covered her face with her apron.

Alys gave her a little shake. She almost wanted to start crying in confusion herself, but there was not time to be wasted thus. She had to keep her wits about her if she was to find out what was happening. 'Go gather some supplies to take into the village, then. No matter what, there are people who will need food and blankets come morning. I will find my father.'

As Alys hurried to the stairs, she remembered the

strange feeling Sir Matthew had given her, as if he watched everything around him too carefully, especially her. Could he be a spy of some sort, his visit to Dunboyton a cover for something? She made her way up the stairs to his chamber and knocked on the door. There was no reply, no sound at all, and when she peeked inside she found it was empty. All his possessions were gone.

Panicked now in truth, she ran out to the courtyard and found her father just as he was swinging into his saddle. He wore chainmail beneath his cloak and his face was taut and grey in the torchlight.

'Father!' she called out. She dashed past the other horsemen and foot soldiers, grasping his stirrup. 'What is happening?'

He gave her a grim smile. 'I fear the village has been set alight, but no one seems to know why. There are rumours they were hiding Spanish spies.'

Juan. Had he been found? 'Is it Bingham again? What has he found exactly?'

'I don't know yet, but I am riding out now to find out. You must stay here, bar the doors until I return.'

'Sir Matthew has gone.'

Her father nodded grimly. 'Aye, I thought as much. He has his work to do, just as we do. I must go now, Alys. Do as I say!'

Her father spurred his horse onward and Alys watched as his men followed him out of the castle. The gates to the courtyard swung shut behind them. She knew she had to hurry.

She didn't even go back to the castle to grab a cloak, she just ran to the kitchen-garden wall and climbed it to make her way to the steps up to the abbey. The dawn was coming now, lighting the familiar path. She tried to focus on one step after another, not thinking about what might lie in wait at the abbey. Could it be in flames, too?

Much to her relief, when she came over the top of the hill and glimpsed the old stones of the abbey, she saw all was quiet there. Perhaps too quiet? There was no smoke from the chimney of the dairy, no sign of any life at all.

'Juan? Are you here?' she called as she pushed open the door. But she knew even as she said the words that he was gone. There was only the chill staleness of abandonment about the room again.

It was almost as if he had never been there at all.

Alys tiptoed to the middle of the chamber and turned in a circle to take it all in. The fire was gone, leaving only ashes in the grate, the blankets of his makeshift bed folded and piled in a corner. There were no clothes. Had it truly been a dream? Had *he* been a dream?

Alys closed her eyes, and in her imagination she remembered their kiss. The fire and sweetness of it, the way it made her feel as if she could fly free into the sunshine. She thought of his sea-green eyes, the way they crinkled at the corners when he smiled at her. The deep, rich sound of his laughter.

Nay. It had not been a dream. But perhaps it had been her imagining, those feelings, that smile. It had not meant to him what it had to her. How could it?

She opened her eyes and saw that the room was not entirely abandoned. She glimpsed something perched atop the old milking stool. As she moved closer, she saw it was the small block of wood he had been carving. It was not blank now, though, but formed into the delicate shape of an angel. Her pointed wings were etched with elegant feathers, her hands clasped before the folds of her robe, her expression one of sweet smiling. Her long hair tumbled over her shoulders, a whisper of a halo around her head.

Alys lifted it up and examined it closely, as if it could tell her the secrets of Juan, where he had gone, who he truly was. She remembered how he had called her his angel, his merciful rescuer, but she feared she was no angel. She was too frightened, too angry at his sudden departure from her life to find any such heavenly serenity.

And this carved angel was mute. Alys tucked her into the hidden pocket of her skirt and, as she did so, something fell from the tip of its carved wing and fell with a clink to the floor. A beam of moonlight gleamed on it.

Alys stooped to pick it up. It was the gold ring she had seen so often on Juan's finger. Now, up close, she saw the band was worn with use. There was something etched on its face, but she could not make it out in the shadows.

'Where is he?' she whispered as she turned the ring over on her palm. Who was he, really? Such desperate longings rose up in her to know, yet she feared she never would now. He was gone and whatever he was to her was gone with him.

She slid the ring on to her finger, and ran to the door as if she could look hard enough to find him again. Yet she knew she would not see him, no matter how far she ran or how hard she looked. He was gone, vanished from her life as quickly as he had appeared. That glimpse of excitement and adventure she had with him, the fire of his kiss, the feeling of not being alone at last—it was gone.

She had known such a moment would soon come. He could not stay hidden here at the abbey for ever. Yet losing him so quickly hurt far more than she would have expected. It was like an arrow through her chest, almost a physical pain.

She made her way back to the castle in a daze, only habit guiding her footsteps. On the steps to the beach, she found a group of people running up and noticed their faces and garments were streaked with smoke.

She caught the arm of one of them as they hurried past. 'Are you from the village?' she asked, her daze cleared completely. 'What has happened?'

'They burned some of the houses,' the man said angrily. His wife held on to his other hand, sobbing.

'Who did this?' Alys asked.

'Some of the Lord Constable's men, they say. They claimed we were harbouring spies, but we never! This fight is none of ours and look what has happened to us.'

'My father, Sir William Drury, is he there now?' Alys said, her fear and anger growing within her, as sharp as the pain from losing Juan. Surely Sir Matthew Morgan had something to do with this, with his sudden appearance and just as sudden departure. And Juan—was Juan with him? Had he given him the information that destroyed the village, whatever it was?

She prayed it was not so.

'Aye, they're putting out the flames now,' the man said. He spat at the ground before he turned away to follow the others. 'It matters not what side we're on, we'll pay the price for this war in the end.'

Alys continued on towards the castle, that anger growing inside her so she could barely see anything else. If Juan had done this and she had helped him—nay, she could not think that, or it would drive her mad. She had to forget him now, forget him as if she had never known him at all, no matter what had happened. He did not deserve her tenderness if this was his doing, and if it was not—then she could not go on dreaming of him for ever. Aye, she had to forget him, one way or another.

Yet she knew even as she made that vow that it would be the hardest one to keep.

Chapter Twelve

Several weeks later

'Most exciting news, Alys!'

Alys glanced up from her sewing and smiled to see her father's enthusiasm as he came into the great hall, waving a letter in the air. He had been in such low spirits since the horror of the Armada, staying in his library all hours, only emerging to eat dinner, grey-faced and silent. Messengers passed back and forth, but she knew not what letters they bore.

In truth, she had not been in good spirits herself. The village houses were being rebuilt and life at Dunboyton was slowly returning to its old routines. There were tasks to do, meals to be cooked and gardens to be tended. Yet something so deep and fundamental seemed to have changed. The days did not have their old smooth rhythms and distrust and fear seemed to hang in the air like smoke from the village fires.

Alys touched the ring she wore on its chain beneath her gown, then abruptly dropped her hand. She had to push away all thoughts of Juan, as she always did when his face appeared in her mind. She put down her sewing and turned to her father. 'Good news is welcome indeed, Father. What has happened?'

'What I have been waiting for so long.' He sat down in the chair across from hers and gently touched her hand. 'You are summoned to court as Maid of Honour to Queen Elizabeth.'

Alys stared at her father in shock. She shook her head. Surely she had not heard his words right? 'What? Now? But I thought…'

'As did I. Yet it seems I am not without friends in London after all.'

Alys frowned in suspicion. 'Did Sir Matthew…?'

Her father sat back in his chair with a huff. 'I know you think he had something to do with the village that night, Alys.'

'He must have! He vanished soon after.' And he took Juan with him. The uncertainty, the not knowing who they really were and what really happened, nagged at her.

'Sir Matthew has his own work. But we have known each other for many years. It does seem he has helped me now.'

Alys did not want such a man's favours. But then again—what if Juan was at court? 'I should not leave you now, Father. Not with everything that has happened of late.'

'That is exactly why you must go, Alys! Now more than ever. There is nothing here for you.'

'There is you.'

'And I am old. My dearest daughter, to see you settled and happy is all I long for now. There are prospects at court, many paths you could take, and there are none here.' His face, so set in worried lines, softened as he smiled at her. 'And you could help me much, when you have the Queen's ear.'

Alys hurried over to hug him close, her heart torn. For one thing, she did worry about her father, worried he would have no one to watch over him. For another—he was right. She could help him at court, make friends for them, perhaps find him another post in a warmer place where his health could improve. How could she *not* do that for him?

And that feeling of adventure she had pushed down so firmly since Juan left, it was calling her again, the faint song of a siren. London, court, the Queen. Anything could happen there.

'Oh, Father, I would do anything to help you, you know that. And it does sound exciting, I admit. But what do I know of court life? I have nothing to wear, for a start.'

'Perhaps you can use some of your mother's old things to make some travelling clothes? She had some fine velvets and furs, I remember. You can order a whole new wardrobe from London merchants once you are there.'

'When must I leave?'

'As soon as may be. The Queen says many of her ladies have left court of late and she requires your attendance at the Christmas celebrations.'

Christmas—only weeks away now. She would have to travel fast. She glanced around the great hall, the room she had known all her life, and felt the cold prickling touch of those doubts. Yet still, there was the prospect of what she might find at court. What she might learn. 'I should start to pack, then.'

Her father patted her hand with a wide smile. 'I knew

you would not fail me, my Alys. You will enjoy court life, I promise you that.'

Alys was not quite so certain of that. She would have to learn so much so fast, dances and deportment, and she would have to find friends. It was daunting, but also intriguing. And there, amid the bustle and splendour of court, maybe she could start to forget.

She hugged her father again and made her way out of the great hall to instruct the maids on the dinner preparations before she hurried up to the attic chambers where her mother's old trunks were stored. She sorted through them, finding old satin gowns trimmed with laces and furs, pearl-edged sleeves and brocade robes. They were of old styles, to be sure, but she could use them to make new underskirts and bodices, remake the trims for new girdles and the lace for ruffs in the wider fashion.

As she held up a length of forest-green velvet to her shoulders, it reminded her of the colour of Juan's eyes. Before she could push it away, she remembered his kiss, the soft feel of his lips on her hers, the sweet excitement of it.

Perhaps he was at court? He had hinted he had secret work for the Queen. Mayhap it had taken him back to her royal side. But if she *did* see him…

'God's teeth,' she cried and tossed down the velvet. She hoped he was not at court. She had finally ceased to dream of him at night and court was to be a new beginning for her. He had left her, with the village aflame behind him. Surely, if he was indeed an English spy, he was gone on another mission, cozening other ladies. And if he was a Spanish spy—surely then he had vanished for ever.

Either way, it would do her no good to see him again.

Her father has asked for her help at court and that was what she had to concentrate on now.

It was a new life for her. She would not waste it on old, fantastical dreams that could never have come true.

Chapter Thirteen

Greenwich Palace

The court was a buzzing hive today, John thought as he left the boat and climbed the water steps to the walls of Greenwich Palace. He could hear it even outside, even in the winter-bare gardens. The high-pitched music of constant voices, punctuated with laughter and the strum of lutes. It was a tune that played constantly at court, from a group of troubadour courtiers who never rested, and he had become accustomed to it in the last few weeks. It had become mere background buzz to his own thoughts.

But now, after a few days in London, John found the noise and excitement had grown to near deafening levels. It was the Christmas season and the Queen had vowed it would be the most merry, the most lavish one ever in her reign. God had driven the Spanish from England's shores, Queen Elizabeth was victorious and the world would see it all for the festive season.

As John strolled down the corridor, he saw it all, heard it all, just as he was trained to take in everything around him, but it felt like a scene in one of the Southwark playhouses. A masque put on to impress, but little to do with him.

It was obvious the Queen was in residence at Greenwich, for the winding corridors were lined with the richest tapestries, scenes of summer winemaking and dancing glittering with metallic threads. The flagstone floors were covered with red-and-blue Turkey carpets meant to warm the old rooms and muffle the velvet shoes of the courtiers. Portraits of the Queen's ancestors stared down from their gilt frames and lapdogs ran past barking.

The Queen's ladies gathered together near the windows of the gallery, a flock of exotic birds in their jewel-trimmed velvets and satins, feathers and tinsel ornaments shimmering in their fashionably high-piled curls. They paid no attention to the view of the winter-grey river and pale sunlight outside the tall windows, for they were too busy creating wreaths and swags for the Yule decorations. They looped red-and-gold ribbons through the boughs of evergreen branches and holly, and laughingly created kissing balls of mistletoe.

But they were not too busy to notice the gentlemen strolling past, who gave them elaborate bows and flirtatious smiles. They were just as brightly arrayed as the ladies, for the styles of the season were for slashed satin doublets and striped stockings, tall plumes in their velvet caps.

John eschewed such styles for simple black and purple velvet doublets and embroidered short cloaks, plain caps, but he did not go unnoticed either. One of the ladies, a pretty, peachy blonde, waved her be-ringed fingers at him as he passed and giggled. John gave her a bow, and a flirtatious smile automatically touched his lips. He, too, had long ago learned to play his part in the masque. The part of a gallant, courtly favour-seeker, not seeing beyond the plumed edge of his cap. It was a part he knew he played well and no one ever questioned his activities at court. What he did behind the gaudy painted sets.

And perhaps, before the Armada, before Ireland, he would have taken advantage of the small rewards of that role. Coin for a game of primero; a fine horse won in a race. Beautiful ladies-in-waiting, eager for admiration, well-versed in their own games.

But now—now when he looked at those ladies, heard their practised laughter, all he could see was Alys. Her open smile, her endless night-dark eyes, her sweetness. He tasted her kiss every night in his imaginings, as he tried in vain to find sleep. He knew nothing now could compare to it.

He turned away from the lady's giggles and walked away along the length of the gallery. Alys followed him even now, as truly as if she held his arm and smiled up at him. He hoped she gave him a kind thought now and then, but he doubted it.

'Sir John!' he heard a lady call out.

He turned to see Lady Ellen Braithwaite, one of the Queen's most sought-after Maids of Honour. She was a great beauty, tall and slim with waving red-gold hair and a ready laugh. But John always sensed something behind her laughter, from one actor to another. There were rumours her brother was in financial straits and her role at court, her search for a fine husband, was most vital to her family. Perhaps it was that that gave a desperate edge to her smile.

Such tales at court were too common and John certainly sympathised greatly with those who fought single-handedly to rescue their family honour in such perilous times. He had been fighting for that himself for years.

Yet still there was something about Lady Ellen he could not trust, a hard edge to her charm. She stood with her usual circle of admirers, a fantastical figure in red-and-gold brocade, rubies dotted in her hair. As he bowed to her, she waved him over with her feathered fan.

'You have been gone from court for many days, Sir John,' she said.

'I had business to attend to in London that could not wait,' he answered.

She gave him a shrewd glance over the edge of those feathers. ''Tis fortunate you missed none of the Queen's Yule revels, then. It all promises to be most splendid.'

'So I see,' John said, gesturing to the feverish preparations going on around them.

'So many new people have arrived at court of late, I am quite giddy trying to remember them all! Have you met Lord Merton and Sir Walter Terrence? They have just arrived from their estates in Kent, and before that they were in Paris. Their tales are quite wondrous. Did you not visit Paris in your own travels, Sir John?'

John bowed to Lord Merton and Sir Walter, both of them dressed in the height of fashion, both of them hard-eyed as they bowed back. 'Once or twice, my lady. Paris has its beauties, but nothing like those to be found right here before us in England. Or in this very corridor, I would vow.' He bowed low again over Lady Ellen's hand as she giggled, but surreptitiously he studied her new companions again. They did not look familiar to him, under those names or any other, and that planted a small seed of suspicion in his mind. He knew that many things went on abroad that had to be known to Walsingham and, if they had gained passports, now they had to be of some import.

Sir Walter looked rather young, wide-eyed, with angelic blond curls and a quick smile. Lord Merton was older, bearded, harder, but still clad in the elaborate satins and furs court demanded. They smiled and he could read nothing behind those polite gestures. Perhaps a bit of jealousy on Sir Walter's part, as Lady Ellen seemed to favour a newcomer over him.

Aye, they had been abroad, but he himself had been gone for a long time and they all had secrets. The world of the Armada, the too-brief shelter of Ireland, had been like a different world entirely. He still had not adjusted entirely to court life, and his instincts needed honing.

'We must exchange tales of Paris soon, gentlemen,' he said. 'I am eager to hear of some friends I left there.'

'Indeed,' Lord Merton answered. 'It is a fascinating time to be abroad. Perhaps now Europe will take England seriously at last, as she deserves.'

'I would so love to see Paris.' Lady Ellen sighed. 'Or Venice! Or anywhere but here. Until the dancing begins, it is dull. Will you walk with us now, Sir John?'

'I fear I have an appointment I must keep and thus must tear myself away,' Johns said, kissing her hand again.

'Then perhaps we shall have a dance together at the banquet tonight,' she said lightly. 'I would like to hear more of London. Greenwich is not so far from the city, but it feels so, does it not?'

'It only feels far when I am separated from the joys of court,' he said. 'A dance tonight, then.'

He walked away from Lady Ellen and her little group, greeting other friends he saw in the gallery as he tried to figure out what it was that bothered him about her new friends. It was most odd.

He found his godfather in a small office along a winding corridor in one of the palace's towers. Sir Matthew sat at a desk behind a towering pile of documents, while two black-robed secretaries wrote feverishly in the corners.

It was a stark room, furnished only with the desks and benches, but with a warm fire blazing in the hearth and rich draperies at the window to keep the river draughts away. Sir Matthew matched his chamber, clad in sombre dark grey in contrast to the brilliant court, a simple cap on his head, but with fine fur at his throat and wrists. He glanced up and before his smile of greeting crossed his face John could see the lines of strain.

'John,' Sir Matthew said, his smile widening. 'You have returned from London. Any news?'

John sat down in the chair across from his godfather's desk and stripped off his gloves, sighing at the welcome warmth of the fire. But even the heat could not burn away the frustration inside of him for every dead end he had encountered in the city in his search for Peter de Vargas's English contact.

He had gone to London following a lead, only to find a shopkeeper who had recently—and suddenly—died and no new clues. 'Not as yet. The man was dead, most of his household vanished. Have your secretaries had luck breaking the code?'

'They have broken it, but we can tell little from the messages. They seem a muddled mix of love poems and exhortations to remain faithful to the true church.'

'Perhaps it is a double code,' one of the secretaries said. 'We are still working on it. It will break before us, as all do.'

'Or perhaps it was the mere rantings of a poor man whose mind had snapped,' Sir Matthew said. 'You said Master Peter was not well.'

'Those ships were a floating hell,' John answered quietly. 'The hunger and the stink. It would drive anyone mad. Yet Peter was always so—so afire about this person he wrote to, about the importance of their connection. He knew what he was about when it came to that.'

'Hmm.' Sir Matthew frowned. 'And we do know there was a spy here at the heart of the court, who must have been his contact. They did not have enough information, but they did pass on ship movements we would rather were not known. Someone as fanatical about Spain and the Catholic cause as Master Peter could still cause much trouble if they are not found.'

'Or just as fanatical about some rich Spanish reward,' John said, thinking of Westmoreland and Paget, and their conviction that if they helped King Philip he would return their estates.

'Either way, we are agreed this could make them even more dangerous now, if they feel they are denied their rightful reward,' Sir Matthew said. 'I have seen such things over and over. The vipers strike when they are trod upon.'

John remembered the snake that had fallen from the ceiling of the dairy, Alys trembling in his arms. What would happen to people like her, innocents, if such serpents were allowed to escape? 'Perhaps they have left court now.'

Sir Matthew shook his head. 'Nay, they are still lurking here. I can feel it and my sense of danger has never yet failed me in my work. It is how I have stayed alive this long. Mayhap they have gone to ground, but we shall root them out before they cause more harm. Now, have you messages for me?'

John handed over the letters from London. As Sir Matthew sorted through them, he asked, 'How fares Walsingham?'

'Most ill, I fear,' Sir Matthew muttered. 'He has taken to his bed with the stones again. I think we won't see him this Yule season.'

If Walsingham died, it would leave England in a perilous position indeed, one spies such as Peter's friend could take advantage of. 'There do seem to be many new people at court now.'

'It is a time of victory. Many will be seeking rewards they have not earned. Though a few have been given what is long overdue.' Sir Matthew looked up, a strange smile on his face. 'I have heard from my old friend Sir William Drury.'

John was surprised to hear that name so suddenly, but he managed to smile back politely, blandly. Managed to not demand to know how Alys fared. 'Indeed?'

That smile widened. 'I know you have much reason to be grateful to that name, as I am. It seems his daughter will soon be at court to serve the Queen. Perhaps even in time for the Christmas revelries.'

Alys would soon be there? John pushed down the excitement that rose in him at the thought that he might see her again. It felt like a marvellous thing, but he knew well it was not. 'She does indeed deserve reward. She saved my life.'

Sir Matthew sat back in his chair, his hands folded neatly. 'A most courageous and kind lady. I think we did agree back in Ireland that I should help her if I could. Not as pretty as most court ladies, mayhap…'

John felt a rush of anger. 'She is far lovelier than any woman I have yet seen here.'

'Ah.' Sir Matthew's smile faded in a look of concern. 'It is most natural that you should be grateful to her, to admire her. But our work here is most vital and there can be no distractions. We must root out this spy forthwith.'

John took a deep breath, forcing all emotion away until he felt his heart grow chilly again. Alys here at court— would she be a target for the spy, if they knew how she had saved him in Ireland? 'I will not be distracted, Sir Matthew. You have trained me well enough.'

'Aye. You are a professional, John, I am most assured of that. In your work for us abroad you always kept a cool head in the most dangerous of circumstances. But a pretty face can often wreak havoc on the coldest heads.' Sir Matthew shook his head ruefully. 'I do remember well when I met Lady Alys's mother…'

'Lady Elena? Aye, you did speak of her in Ireland.'

'Yes, Elena. A truly gentle, angelic lady, with such dark eyes, like the night itself. Lady Alys rather reminded me of her.'

There was a wistfulness to his voice that made John realise what he should have long ago—Sir Matthew had been in love with Alys's mother. 'Sir Matthew…'

'Go now, you must prepare for tonight's banquet. Muddy boots and a dusty cloak will never do for Her Majesty,' Sir Matthew said, turning abruptly back to his papers. He waved John away, signalling the end to their interview. 'Keep close watch on everyone tonight. We must find Master Peter's spy soon.'

John nodded, and bowed as he left the room, his thoughts turning over and over. Sir Matthew had given up his love to help keep England safe and now he expected John to do the same. And he *would* do it, he had vowed his life to it. But now there was something even more precious he would have to keep safe in the midst of the viper pit of court—Alys Drury.

Chapter Fourteen

Alys sat bundled in her new fur-lined cloak at the back of the barge as they slid along the half-frozen, sluggish Thames. The wind was icy and biting, but she pushed her hood back to watch the scenery as it glided past. The weather made her think she might never have left Ireland at all, it was so grey and windy, spitting with sleet and snow, but the buildings were decidedly different. Red brick faced with pale stone made up the newer homes of the Queen's courtiers, half-hidden up steps from the river and behind gates. There were older mansions, more like palaces with their towers and narrow windows, and in the distance she could glimpse smoke from the chimneys of villages and towns.

The people were different, too, ladies and gentlemen in passing boats, swathed in velvets and furs, laughing, listening to the strains of lute music as they travelled. On the walkways and waiting at the docks she saw clergymen in stark black and white, merchants' wives in warm woollens, beggar children skittering around in their rags and pale faces, fine ladies carrying lapdogs. People of all sorts and stations, all mingling as they hurried about their days, and so many of them, too. It was very different from Dunboyton.

Yet she had savoured the journey, even when it was stormy or the people strange, for it took her away from thoughts of John for a while. He always waited when she closed her eyes at night, keeping her from sleep with memories of him. If she was honest with herself, she had to admit that his tales of courtly life, his small dance lesson, had been a comfort to her. It felt as if she knew court life a tiny bit now and would not be entirely taken by surprise.

She shivered now as she wondered what waited at court.

The barge slowed as the oarsmen eased around a turn in the river and Alys caught her first glimpse of Greenwich Palace itself.

She remembered tales her mother would read her when she was a child, of enchanted princesses caught in ancient castles, held by spells in its old halls. Surely this was the sort of palace those tales spoke of. It was not like stout, squat Irish castles, meant to defend sieges and house regiments, but vast and low, elegant in its pale grey stone, with fanciful towers at each corner and windows shining in the pale sunlight. The pitched roof was as dark grey as the winter sky, the curls of smoke from the dozens of chimneys drifting into the clouds. It seemed all made of grey, but the walls were faced in red brick and white stone carved into curlicues and flowers, more warm and welcoming.

There was no moat or fortifications, as Irish castles would have, for the stretch of the river past Greenwich's walls was serene and silent. Instead, a sea of windows glinted like diamonds. Alys couldn't help but imagine the many eyes that watched from behind those panes, waiting.

The barge pulled up to a dock, rocking in the water as the rowers leaped out to tie it fast to its moorings. One of them held out his hand to help her to the dock. For an instant, she swayed dizzily. It had been so long since she stood long on solid land, her legs seemed to have forgotten how to balance! First the long, stormy voyage across the Irish Sea, and then the river voyage to London, which she only glimpsed from its outskirts. But she was there now, at her destination at last.

She glanced back down the river, half-wondering if she could flee back the way she had come. Yet she knew she could not. She was summoned to court and could never shame her father by such behaviour—or herself. She was a Drury. The thought gave her courage and she straightened her shoulders and marched up the steep wooden steps to the bottom of the walls of Greenwich's gardens.

And then—she knew not quite what to do. It was silent there, she could hear nothing beyond the gate and only faint footsteps of the guards on the walls above. She knocked hard on the gate and waited. It became harder to hold on to her bravado with every moment that passed, until a guard peered outside.

'I am Lady Alys Drury, the new Maid of Honour to the Queen,' she said. 'I am to meet the Mistress of the Maids here.'

'Of course, my lady,' the guard said as he swung open the gate and ushered her into a covered corridor at the end of another narrow staircase. 'If you will wait here.'

Then there was more waiting. Alys shivered in her cloak, listening to the whine of the wind on the wooden roof above her head. She wondered if she should have come in more state, instead of just with three guards and Molly as maid, but no more could be spared. And even an entourage of hundreds couldn't lessen the flutter in her stomach now.

At last she heard the click of fine shoes against the wooden floor and whirled around to see a lady hurrying down the stairs. It wasn't a maidservant, or a guard like the one who had left Alys like a package at the gate. This was an older lady, wrapped in solemn dignity along with her dark green velvet gown trimmed with yellow silk. Her grey-streaked dark hair was pinned beneath a lace-edged cap and her blue eyes, though faded, seemed to take in everything around her.

Her gaze swept over Alys, quiet and quick, taking in her face, hair and attire in one sweep. Her lips pursed and Alys felt every grubby inch from the very long journey. She remembered her father's warnings, the importance of her work here, and she quickly smoothed the creased folds of her red-wool skirt and pasted on a smile. Her mother had been the daughter of ancient nobility, albeit Spanish nobility. She would not disgrace her now.

'Lady Alys Drury?' the woman said and her voice, while brisk, was not unkind. 'I am Mrs Jones, Her Majesty's Mistress of the Maids. We have been expecting you these last few days.'

Alys dipped into a polite curtsy. 'I am sorry, Mistress Jones, the journey proved longer than expected. I am most honoured to be here.'

A small smile curved Mrs Jones's lips. 'And so you should be. Dozens of families write every month seeking places for their daughters. There has not been a vacancy among the Queen's ladies for some time and I can recall no ladies from Ireland who have served here.'

Alys tilted up her chin. 'My father's family estate is actually in Devon. He has long been posted as governor to the Queen at Dunboyton.'

'Is it? Then I hope you shall know something of our ways here. We will keep you very busy, Lady Alys, with the Christmas festivities upon us and Her Grace still celebrating her great victory. The Queen has ordered every lavish trimming for the holiday and there will be little time for you to learn courtly ways.'

'I have always much enjoyed Christmas, Mistress Jones, and my parents celebrated every year with banquets and dancing,' Alys said. 'I am most eager to serve Her Grace.'

'That is good, as I am to take you to the Queen now so she can inspect you. One of the other maids will then show to your lodgings.'

'Now?' Alys gasped and struggled to grasp the shreds of her pride again. She was to meet Queen Elizabeth *now*, in her travel-stained gown and cloak?

Mistress Jones sniffed. 'As I said, Lady Alys. This is a very busy time. Her Grace has few spare moments.'

'O-of course,' Alys stammered. 'Whatever the Queen wishes.'

Mistress Jones nodded and turned to hurry up the stairs without another word. Alys scrambled to follow, surreptitiously trying to smooth her hair beneath its knitted caul and flat cap, to brush the dust from her skirt.

At first they followed narrow, bare, winding corridors, nothing like what she would imagine to find in a palace. Until they turned a corner and she found herself facing a wide gallery, bright with tall windows looking down to the river and filled with every colour, every shimmering bit of gold and silver imaginable.

Alys could scarcely take in the luxury around her, the fine tapestries on the wood-panelled walls, the gilt ornaments displayed on tall chests, the crowds of satin- and fur-clad courtiers who paused in their laughing chatter to stare at her curiously. It was all so very different from Dunboyton's rough simplicity, its everyday bustle and noise. Alys longed to sink into the floor, to hide under those plush carpets under her feet, but she knew she could not. She held her head high and smiled, looking neither to right or left, and glided onward.

For an instant, she remembered another, very different place—a tiny, bare, cold abbey dairy that had felt like the grandest palace for all too short a time. She remembered laughing with Juan next to their fire, talking to him about her innermost feelings and secrets as she could never have talked to anyone else. Remembered his kiss, the touch of his hand.

She pushed those memories away. That place did not exist now and to keep longing for it was of no use. She was at the royal court now. She had a duty to help her father, and that was all that mattered.

It *had* to be all that mattered. Remembering Juan would only drive her mad.

'The maids' chamber is just over there, along that corridor,' Mistress Jones said, gesturing to the left. 'Your maidservant will be waiting there for you with your baggage.'

Her words pulled Alys fully back into the present, into the crowded palace, and the laughter and noise was loud in her ears again, a discordant song. She glanced back towards where her lodgings would be and saw two young ladies in white-and-silver silk gowns emerging from the doorway. Their heads, dressed with piled-up curls and decorated with pearls and ivory combs, bent together as they giggled.

They vanished as Mistress Jones led Alys down yet another twisting hallway, up and down stairs. Alys was sure she would soon enough forget Juan and their dairy sanctuary. She would be too occupied with being lost.

They went up one more short staircase and emerged into another crowded chamber. 'These are the royal apartments,' Mistress Jones said. 'When the Queen sends you with a message for someone, they will probably be here in the Privy Chamber.'

Alys stared out at the long, narrow room, filled with yet more lavishly dressed people playing cards, sewing, chatting, so careless and idle. She could sense the taut air of anticipation, the desperation that hovered just beneath the expensive perfumes. Everyone here needed something; everyone waited, hoped, feared the Queen's favour.

Just like Alys's father.

'How will I ever know who is who?' she said. The brilliant colours, blue, red, green, yellow, black, all the large, starched lace ruffles and plumed caps, all the curled hair and rouged cheeks, made everyone look alike. It was all a blur.

Mistress Jones laughed. 'You will learn soon enough. We all do. Come along now.'

Alys hurried to follow her from the crowds of the Privy Chamber, through a smaller room filled with fine musical instruments: a set of lovely inlaid virginals, a harp, a lute on its stand. A narrow doorway led into a room obviously meant for dining. Carved tables and cushioned chairs were lined up against the panelled walls, carved with cornucopia of fruit in the fine-grained woods. Buffets were laden with shining gold-and-silver plate, ewers, salt cellars, covered goblets, too many to count.

For a moment, Alys was distracted from feeling nervous by the beauty of it all. All the chilly fears returned in an icy rush, like the winter river outside, when Mistress Jones said, 'Hurry along!' They moved into the mysterious hush of the Presence Chamber, where a red-velvet throne waited empty beneath a green-and-gold cloth of state.

Beyond that had to be the royal bedchamber itself.

As they stepped through the door, Alys was surprised to see the Queen's bedchamber was not large and there were only a few small windows to let in the grey, wintry sunlight. A fire blazed merrily in the large stone grate, crackling and snapping as it tried valiantly to warm the small space.

The whole room was dominated by a grand bed set high on a dais, which Alys was sure must be larger than her whole chamber at Dunboyton. It was a carved edifice of pale wood, carved vines and flowers twisting up its posts, thick as tree trunks. It was piled high with satin cushions and velvet quilts, edged with fur. The green-and-gold hangings were looped back with thick gold cords.

A dressing table in the corner glittered with bottles and pots of jewel-like Venetian glass and a gilded box spilled out creamy pearls and a rope of rubies.

A few stools and cushions were scattered by the fireplace, occupied by a cluster of ladies and their prancing lapdogs, tumbling over their flower-petal silk skirts. They all looked up eagerly as the door opened, as if longing for any distraction, even a travel-rumpled maid from Ireland.

Alys glimpsed a lady writing at a table by the window and realised it must be the Queen herself. Alys only knew her from portraits and from her parents' tales of their days at court before they were sent to Ireland. The reality was not entirely what she had expected.

Alys quickly swallowed her surprise and put back on her careful smile. She knew the Queen was no longer young, of course. Queen Elizabeth was now fifty-five. Yet she was *Queen*, ageless. This Queen was still as slender as a girl, upright and willowy, dressed in a loose gown of white silk trimmed with glossy sable fur, pearls looped around her neck. Her hair was still a bright red but was obviously false, curled very tightly and pinned with more pearls.

The quill went still in her bejewelled fingers and she glanced over her shoulder. She wore a thick mask of white make-up with spots of bright pink slashed across her high, sharp cheekbones. It gave her a ghostly, otherworldly air. But her eyes were dark, burning and alive.

Alys gasped on a breath, afraid she wouldn't be able to speak. It would be like trying to converse with the statue of a Greek god come to life.

'Is that Lady Alys Drury?' the Queen called. Her voice, too, was still young, soft as velvet but filled with a steel, unmistakable authority.

'Yes, Your Majesty,' Mistress Jones said, curtsying deeply.

Alys hurried to follow. She had been preparing for this moment for so long. She couldn't make a mess of it now. 'Your Majesty. My father sends his most reverent greetings to you. We are very honoured to serve you.'

'I do remember your father. He was a handsome man, though I dare say the climate of Ireland has done him little good.' The Queen rose from her chair, moving a bit slowly, stiffly. She held out her hand, long, elegant, white fingers decorated with rubies and emeralds, the heavy, dark stone of her coronation ring. The tips were stained with ink.

Alys quickly kissed the offered hand and the Queen drew her impatiently to her feet. Queen Elizabeth smelled of a jasmine scent, richer than any Alys could distil in her stillroom, along with the sugared fruit suckets everyone said she liked, and the violet-like tinge of her powder and rouge.

'We are in need of new company for the Christmas season, Lady Alys. Hopefully you are eager to celebrate with us.'

Celebrating had been the furthest thing from Alys's mind for many months. The fear of the approaching Armada and its aftermath, her sweet moments with Juan and then their sudden vanishing, had held her under a cloud. But now, with the Queen's burning dark gaze on her, she would have agreed to anything at all.

'Of course, Your Majesty,' she said.

'Very good. We do have much to celebrate this year, with England's deliverance from Spain.' Queen Elizabeth sat back down at her desk. She glanced at her whispering ladies clustered by the fireplace. 'Tell me, Lady Alys, do you wish to marry? Have you come to court to seek a husband?'

Alys swallowed hard. A vision of Juan again flashed through her mind, his green eyes smiling at her, the touch of his hand. Perhaps, if life had been different, if they two had been different, she might have married him and rejoiced for it. But he was almost certainly a betrayer, who had let the village be burned and left her without a word. He did not deserve her tenderness. And she would give it to no one else now.

The ladies went very quiet, as if they held their breath to hear her answer.

'Nay, Your Majesty,' she said firmly. 'I have no thoughts of marriage.'

'I am glad to hear it.' The Queen reached for her pen. 'The married state has its uses and is necessary for some, of course. But I do not like to lose my ladies to its clutches. I must have their utmost loyalty.'

Alys curtsied again. She had heard tales, even at Dunboyton, of some of the Queen's ladies and courtiers who had landed in the Tower for marrying without her permission. It was surely a good thing Alys had other thoughts now, thoughts of making a finer future for herself and her father. She would need no husband for that, not yet.

'I wish only to serve Your Majesty,' she answered truthfully. She never again wanted to feel that terrible, empty, hollow ache that had plagued her when Juan left.

'So you shall, starting this very night,' Queen Elizabeth said. She sorted through her papers, no longer looking at Alys. Being released from the hold of those dark eyes was like surfacing from the ocean, able to gasp a breath again. 'We are having a banquet to welcome some new members of the French embassy.'

A banquet already? Where she would be faced with not only the court, but French ambassadors? 'I—of course, Your Majesty,' Alys whispered, her mind whirling. What would she wear? What could she say? She had never felt quite so alone before, not even on the ramparts of Dunboyton.

'Very good. Lady Ellen Braithwaite will see you to

your quarters and tell you what is expected. I need Mistress Jones's assistance right now.'

At a brusque wave of Queen Elizabeth's jewelled hand, a lady broke away from the group by the fireplace. She was very pretty indeed, tall and slim in her white gown, with red-gold hair twisted up into a gold caul. She smiled, warm and welcoming, and made a small curtsy. 'Lady Alys? If you will follow me.'

Alys only had time to curtsy once more and thank the Queen for her favour, but Elizabeth paid her no heed. The pretty Lady Ellen took Alys's arm and led her away with a merry, confiding smile that did not quite reach her eyes. Lady Ellen was so beautiful, so elegant, she made Alys feel quite small. Still, any chance to make a friend should be seized, she told herself. She needed as much help as she could find at court.

'How do you do, Lady Alys,' she said, and her voice was as low and sweet as it should be, full of hidden laughter. 'I am Lady Ellen Braithwaite. I can't tell you how excited we all are to see you here!'

'Excited to see *me*, Lady Ellen? But surely I am quite unknown to anyone here.'

'Oh, not at all! You cannot know yet just how long and tedious our days are here at court. Once the victory celebrations were over in the autumn, and poor Lord Leicester died, it has been quite dreary here. And there have been no new ladies for months. It's always the same people all the time.'

Alys laughed. She did know how such monotony felt, but she couldn't imagine ever growing bored of the colourful court. 'I am not sure I can help make things more interesting for you. I know so little of court life.'

'But you are someone new! You will have new stories to tell us, new gossip to share.' Ellen led her towards the noise of the Privy Chamber and stopped to wave and giggle at two elaborately dressed gentlemen in the doorway. They bowed and smiled back, following her with admiring eyes. 'And aren't you from Ireland? You must have fascinating tales of such a wild place.'

Alys thought of Dunboyton, the walls and corridors she had known all her life. Mayhap for a while it had been exciting—*too* exciting, with shipwrecks and fires and rescued sailors who pitilessly stole hearts. But not most of the time. 'It is very different from here.'

A small frown fluttered over Ellen's pretty face. 'Were not some of the Armada ships wrecked there? That must have been quite a tale.'

Something held Alys back from answering entirely. Surely at least the memory of Juan was hers and hers alone? Not something she ever had to speak about again. And she did not want to remember the wrecks, the poor men killed. 'My father kept me quite sheltered at our home.'

'You could see nothing of any of the ships? We heard such dramatic tales of it all. The ladies were quite aghast.'

Alys shook her head. 'As I said, my father is most protective.'

Ellen sighed and laughed, her frown vanished as if it had never been there. 'Aren't they all? Brothers, too, though my brother is quite sweet, really. I am sure they sent me here because they thought it would keep me out of trouble. Little do they know...'

Alys was rather intrigued by this hint of domestic drama. 'Do you have many suitors at your home that they want to keep you from?'

'Suitors? Nay, nothing of the sort, I fear. I have yet to

meet a man who would suit me. Knights in poems are so much more fascinating, don't you think?'

'Sometimes,' Alys answered slowly. Men who seemed like knights in poems, though handsome and mysterious, were surely trouble.

'What of you? Were you betrothed to some wild Irish chieftain?'

Alys laughed. 'I don't think I've ever even seen a wild Irish chieftain. All my father has talked about for as long as I can remember is returning to England, making me an English lady. But I'm afraid I will disappoint him, since I know so little of courtly ways.'

'That is not so hard,' Ellen said lightly. She led them deftly through the crowds, giving one or two other gentlemen a smile, but not stopping. 'A Maid of Honour's duties are few, really. We walk with the Queen in the gardens, even now when the winter wind blows, go with her to church, stand around looking pretty as she greets diplomats. We sew and read with her, as you saw in her chamber. Most important, we run away and duck when she loses her temper and throws things.'

Alys was so startled by the image of the Queen hurling things about that she laughed. 'Throws things?'

'Aye. Shoes or scent bottles, usually. But her anger fades fast enough and mostly she just ignores us.'

'Then what do we maids do with the rest of our time?'

'Come to see who is waiting in the Privy Chamber, mostly. There is usually a card game going on, or someone to gossip with for a bit.' She waved her hand around the crowded room, as if to emphasise the fact that there was never the lack of company.

The chamber seemed even more full than before, the air hot and close with the scent of so many people, so many different perfumes. Everyone had turned towards them as they heard the doors to the inner chambers open, their expressions full of hope and fear, only to have that hope fade quickly when they saw it was only some of the Queen's ladies. The chatter rose again, like a wave.

'Lady Ellen!' a man in a peacock-blue doublet slashed with purple and green called out, pushing his way through the crowd. He was tall and rather handsome in an English country type of way, blond and red-cheeked, and his smile to Ellen seemed to say they were good friends. 'We have been talking about the new style of sleeve and cannot decide if they suit us or not. You must come help us decide.'

Ellen laughed brightly and stroked one of the bright streaks of green. 'I *am* quite the expert on sleeves, I confess. Show me what you think, Lord Merton.'

Alys tried to follow their conversation, which quickly moved from sleeves to shoes, but the long journey suddenly seemed to catch up with her. A wave of dizziness flooded over her mind, leaving it dim and fuzzy. For a moment, she leaned against the panelled wall and suddenly Ellen was lost to view in the sea of jewelled satins and lacy ruffs. The laughter around her buzzed in her ears like the flocks of seagulls over the beach at Galway.

Everything grew hazy before her eyes and she squeezed them shut. She couldn't faint now and disgrace herself, on her very first day at court!

She forced her eyes to open again and studied the crowd pressed around her. They were such a blur of bright colours, she could not see anyone clearly. Suddenly, just above their heads, she glimpsed someone taller. Someone with glossy dark hair, a pearl earring and a quick, flashing, *familiar* smile.

It was him. Juan.

'Nay,' Alys whispered. She closed her eyes again and shook her head. She was just tired, just seeing dream-like things. She needed to rest. That was all.

And yet—yet for that instant he had looked so real.

It was not him, she told herself. Juan was gone from her life. Yes, she had once wondered fleetingly if he was at court, but surely she would never see him again. Except in her dreams at night.

She had to be sure. She pushed herself away from the wall and clasped her hands at her waist to stop them from trembling. She had to appear calm; she had to *be* calm. She was just beginning her life at court and whether or not that was Juan she had glimpsed, she could not afford to let it make a difference.

Yet that glimpse, that one beautiful image of his face in the sea of courtiers…

'Lady Alys!' Ellen called, pushing back to her side. 'There you are. Do come meet my friends, Lord Merton and Sir Walter Terrence. Lady Alys is the one we have been waiting for, from Ireland.'

Alys forced herself to focus on the two men at Ellen's sides. One was the man in the slashed doublet, another an older gentleman in blue satin. He raised a glass to his eyes to examine her. 'Ireland!' he exclaimed. 'You must tell us everything. It sounds so dramatic.'

'Better than a Southwark playhouse,' the other man said.

Alys laughed, trying to be polite even as she longed to break free, to run through the crowd looking for Juan. 'I did tell Lady Ellen, I saw nothing dramatic at all. My life in Ireland is quite dull. I am glad to be here at court.'

'But you must tell us something!' the other man cried.

'I am longing to know about the Irish rebel chieftains. Do they really wear wolf skins and tie bones in their beards?'

'You are so silly, Walter, I am sure they dress much as we do,' Ellen said. 'Except for these sleeves. You were quite right to be wary of them.'

'Lady Ellen, I vow you are too cruel! I think they suit me well.'

Ellen laughed, but her laughter suddenly faded as she looked over her friend's shoulder. Her eyes widened, the light in them growing softer. 'Oh, but here is our other newcomer to court,' she said, waving her fan at someone Alys couldn't yet see. 'Do join us, my lord. You ran away so quickly before.'

Alys put on her courtly smile, prepared to meet another of Ellen's peacock friends—and her smile froze before it could form.

It had not been an illusion, a fleeting trick of her tired mind. It *was* him, Juan. Right there before her, when she had been so sure she would never see him again, *could* never see him again. She shivered and fell back a step, suddenly feeling so very cold.

He did not quite look like her Juan, bearded and ragged from the sea. He was just as tall, but his shoulders were broader and he wore no beard to hide the elegant angles of his sculpted face, his high cheekbones and sharp jawline, his sensual lips. He wore courtly clothes of purple velvet trimmed with silver, a high, narrow ruff at his throat. But his eyes—those brilliant summer-green eyes she had once so cherished—widened when his glance fell on her.

For an instant, his polished smile, his elegant façade that covered him like a velvet cloak, fell away and there she glimpsed her Juan in the flash of his smile.

But a veil quickly dropped over his face, and his smile

turned cool, small. His eyes narrowed. He was all care-less boredom.

Why was he even there? Alys wondered wildly. Why was he lounging here at court, looking so bored? Was it part of some plan, some betrayal? And if so—of whom? She had never felt so confused, so uncertain.

'Lady Ellen,' he said with a bow, making Ellen giggle. 'You shine like the sun on this dismal room.'

Shine like the sun? The Juan Alys had known would never have said such silly words, not in such a silly way. She remembered how he had called her an angel, had kissed her hand. That had been the truest, sweetest moment she ever knew. Where had that man gone?

Lady Ellen did not seem to find it silly. She giggled again and blushed, and laid her hand on his purple-velvet sleeve. Alys noticed that some of the other ladies nearby watched the couple most closely, their expressions sour as Juan kissed Ellen's hand. So he was popular with the la-dies at court, was he? Alys gave a sniff and looked away.

'This is the newest Maid of Honour here at court, Sir John,' Ellen said. 'Lady Alys Drury, of—of somewhere in Ireland.'

'Of Dunboyton,' Alys said. 'A most interesting place.'

'Not compared to Paris or Venice, I would vow,' John said in a bored voice, looking away to flick a lace-edged handkerchief at a speck of dust on his sleeve. 'I have heard it is naught but bogs and rebels.'

Ellen giggled nervously. 'But Alys promises to tell us all about its beauties. If you can cease to be rude, she might tell you as well. Lady Alys, this rogue is Sir John Huntley. He has just returned from London.'

'It must have been something important to take you away from court at Christmas, Sir John,' Alys said.

His gaze met hers and again she saw the flicker of the man she had known. Something knowing, full of laughter, behind the boredom. 'Important indeed. But I'm glad I made it back to Greenwich just in time.'

'Lady Ellen,' a page in the Queen's green-and-white livery called. 'Lady Ellen Braithwaite! The Queen requires you for an errand.'

'Oh, God's teeth, but what now?' Ellen said impatiently, with scowl and a toss of her head. 'Lady Alys, I am sorry. I shall return anon and show you to our lodgings.'

'I can see Lady Alys to her chamber,' Juan—John—said, still in that bored drawl.

Alys looked up at him, startled. Behind the cover of her heavy skirts, he gave her hand a quick, warning squeeze. Alys swallowed hard and tried to keep smiling, even as she couldn't breathe at the thought of being alone with him.

Ellen laughed. 'I dare say you do know where the maids' chamber is, Sir John! Aye, do see Lady Alys there. I shall meet you both when I have finished whatever errand this is. Lord Merton, will you walk with me?'

'Lady Alys?' John said, holding out his arm.

Alys still felt that cold uncertainty, that fear that she didn't know which way to leap now. But she noticed many people watching them, waiting. Ellen had already vanished. She could not make a scene and cause gossip already. She reached out and gently laid her fingers on his sleeve. Even with such a light touch, she could feel his warmth, his strength, beneath the fine fabric and it brought back every moment they had spent together in Ireland. His touch, the feel of him, the safety she thought she had found in his arms.

He led her out of the crowded chamber, past the knots of laughing, pushing, eager people and into the corridor. At the end of the hall, rather than lead her up the stairs towards where Mistress Jones had said the maids lodged, John pushed open a door and drew her into a tiny, dark closet before she could even gasp.

After the brightness and noise of the courtly chambers, for an instant Alys couldn't see anything but shifting shadows. Yet John was there, so close to her, watching her. She could feel it with every fibre of her being. His skin smelled the same, of clean water and crisp, citrus linen, and he felt the same, too. Large, strong, enough to keep her safe from anything.

But there was nothing to keep her safe from him.

She wanted to flee, but something held her where she was, pressed against him in that dark silence. That old, shimmering, invisible bond that had seemed to bring them together in Ireland was still strong, even after everything. After all they had shared, how could she feel so frightened now?

Yet all was changed. He was, and yet was not, her Juan. He looked like him, felt like him, but that man had never really existed at all. Now here was this courtly stranger, with Juan's eyes.

She stepped back from him until she found her back to the wall. The room was so small she could not go far. Her eyes had adjusted to the darkness and only now did she allow herself to look at him fully. To study his face, his eyes.

That bored, careless man of the Privy Chamber was gone and now John watched her solemnly, closely. 'Hello, Alys,' he said softly. 'You must be surprised to see me, I would wager.'

Alys stared up at him in the shadows of their hiding place. How different he looked here at court and it was not just the clean-shaven jaw or the fine clothes. He seemed harder, colder, like a man turned into a perfectly sculpted marble statue. A very handsome statue, but she could see nothing of laughter or emotion in his eyes.

She, however, feared she would drown in the emotions that had seized her at seeing him again. The last time she saw him they had kissed and it had felt as if the world opened up to her at last, only to slam closed once more. She only realised now how very angry and hurt she had truly been when John left Dunboyton without a word.

She twisted her fists in her skirt to stop her hands from trembling.

'Of course it is a surprise,' she said. 'How could I have known you came here? I didn't know where you went at all.'

'I am most sorry I had to leave in such haste,' he said quietly. 'I owe you so very much, Alys. If not for my duty…'

His duty? 'Duty?' The word snapped out sharper than she intended. 'I, too, have a duty, and I was foolish enough to neglect it. When the village burned the night you left—I saw how I never should have trusted you, not for a moment.'

He took a small step back. 'The village?'

'Aye. They said that the villagers had harboured spies, though when none were found they set the blaze anyway. Luckily none were killed.' As she spoke, she remembered the feelings of that terrible night, the panic and fear so thick at the castle she could hardly breathe. And then John was gone. 'It must have happened as you were leaving.'

'Alys, you must believe me—I never would have done such a deed.'

'But you *are* a spy, are you not?' Alys cried. And who could trust a man with such a career, a profession built on lies.

He said nothing, but the long, taut silence was its own answer. She spun around and reached for the door. He was too quick for her. He grabbed her hand, holding her with him.

'Let me go,' she whispered. His grasp just tightened and they were so very close together in the shadows. The warmth of him, the vitality and *life* of him that drew her to him in their strange abbey sanctuary, was still there. It wrapped all around her like velvet-soft bonds, bonds that had not even snapped in the months since she last saw him.

'Alys, please,' he said, his voice deep and rough, as if he, too, held back his emotions. 'Truly, I never meant to hurt you in any way. I—I have missed you.'

He had missed her? For an instant, Alys felt glad of it, a raising of her heart, but then it all crashed down again. Had she not just vowed not to trust? 'Surely there has been too much to occupy you here at court for such sentiment. Ladies to woo, dances, cards, tournaments. You must be much in demand with the Queen and her ladies.'

'Alys, that is not like you,' he said. 'In Ireland, your sweetness saved me. Your kindness…'

'Like an angel?' she said, thinking of the little carving in her trunk. 'But so many things are different now. *I* am different and so are you.'

His free hand gently touched the edging of her bodice, where the thin gold chain was looped around her neck.

Before she could know what he was doing, he drew his hidden ring free. 'Not so very different, though.'

Alys jerked away from his touch and the chain fell free. 'You are a stranger to me.'

'I am not different, Alys. When I was with you, I was more myself than I have been in a very long time. You gave me that.'

He raised her hand, the hand he still held, and pressed his mouth to the hollow of her palm. His kiss was warm, soft, and it made her legs tremble. How traitorous her body was, longing for his kiss again!

She snatched her hand back and buried it in her skirts. 'I must go now. And so should you. Surely we both have much work to do.'

'Alys, please, meet with me again. Let me tell you…'

Tell her—what? More lies? She could not let her heart be vulnerable again. She shook her head frantically and tore herself away from his too-alluring touch. She pulled the door to their hiding place open and dashed out. She wasn't sure which direction she should go, she only knew she had to get away.

She had thought a new life at court could not become any more complicated. But she had been terribly wrong. Only once she was alone in the maids' empty chamber did she realise the ring she had worn against her heart for so many weeks was gone.

Chapter Fifteen

Alys climbed up on her trunk to peer out the narrow window at the end of the long, narrow maids' chamber. The dormitory looked on to one of Greenwich's three large courtyard gardens, slumbering in the winter chill. The flowerbeds, carefully laid out diamond shapes between the gravel walkways, were brown and brittle now, the towering trees skeletal bare, all the marble fountains quiet. But she could see that in summer it would be spectacular, bursting with colour amid a riot of roses, lilies, violets, scented herbs and skeins of glossy green ivy twining over the trellises. Perfect for her stillroom.

Right now, the only colour was from the courtiers strolling the pathways, their velvet cloaks and the ladies' trains as bright as any birds. She found herself searching for a hint of purple doublet among them, but there was none to be seen.

Alys sighed as she watched the gardens. Her storm of tears had tired her, but it had also released something in her, some tight knot of uncertainty and fear she had carried ever since John left her in Ireland. That was unravelled and gone now, leaving her feeling lighter, but hollow as well. Drained of all emotion. She had no idea of what would happen next, but she did know she had to get ready for the Queen's banquet.

Alys turned away from the window to study the chamber more closely. The space shared by the Maids of Honour was a long, narrow rectangle of a room, lined with narrow beds on each side. They were small but pretty, with carved posts, spread with green-and-white woollen quilts and hung with thick curtain to keep out the draughts. A clothes chest and washstand stood by each bed and at the far end was even a precious looking glass. It was peaceful when empty, but was surely all chaos and clamour when all the maids were dressing there. Very different from her own chamber at Dunboyton.

Alys knew Molly was meant to be her maid here, but since she had no idea where the girl was she knew she had to find her banquet gown herself. She opened the travelling chest and took out the layers of new satin and silk clothes, smoothing them carefully as she tried to decide what to wear. After seeing all the court finery, she feared even these fresh, unworn bodices, sleeves, and stockings would be sadly out of fashion.

What would John think when he saw her in them? Would he think her a different lady altogether from the simple girl in Ireland, as she feared he was so different now?

'Don't think of such things now!' she told herself sternly. She tossed down the white bodice she held, embroidered with silver, and spun around, as if she could leave him behind.

Luckily, the door flew open and Ellen appeared, a timely distraction.

'Oh, good!' Ellen exclaimed as she dashed between

rows. 'My bed is next to yours. We can whisper at night.' She perched on the edge of her bed, which was indeed the one beside Alys's, and swung her embroidered shoes from under the hem of her skirts. 'Tell me, Alys—did you mean it when you told the Queen you do not seek a husband?'

Alys's head was spinning with her new friend's sudden appearance and this sudden change of topic. She laughed and looked down at her clothes. She feared she would never cease to be confused at court. 'I have met no man I could stand to be married to, not thus far anyway.'

'I feel just the same,' Ellen said fervently. 'Men are always such nuisances. There are far more important things in life, don't you think? Oh, Alys, you should wear those silver sleeves tonight! The ribbons are ever so cunning. Did you find them in Ireland?'

As Ellen leaned closer to examine Alys's clothes, Alys glimpsed something tucked into the depths of her trunk— the pale wood of her carved angel. She smiled up, always so serene, so knowing. Alys had not been able to leave her behind, even as much as the creator of her angel hurt her.

She tucked the angel deeper beneath the folded garments, where she could not be seen, and turned to Ellen with a determined smile. 'Nay, I found them in London, as soon as I arrived...'

All the maids giggled and whispered as they moved in procession from their bedchamber along the long river gallery. Their voices were muffled by the tapestries that lined one wall and the glass of the windows that looked down on the Thames, giving them an otherworldly quality. Their white-and-silver skirts shimmered in the gathering night shadows and rustled and flared. Even Alys was distracted by the angelic beauty of the scene and could hardly believe she was a part of it all. She was one of the white-clad creatures and soon she would be dancing before the Queen.

She wished her father could see her, and her mother, too. How proud they would be! And how she wished things could be as simple as that pride, as happiness at being at court. If John was not there...

If he was not there, he would still haunt her. Alys had to admit that. She just wished she knew exactly where she would see him again. She did not want to be surprised, to act so foolish, again.

'Isn't it splendid, Alys?' Ellen whispered. 'The first day of Christmas! Who shall you dance with?'

Alys smiled at her. 'I don't know anyone to dance with at all.'

'All the gentlemen shall be falling over themselves to claim your first galliard,' Ellen said. She gave Alys a sideways glance, a sly smile. 'Sir John Huntley was rather eager to show you to your chamber.'

Alys frowned. 'That was all he did, I promise. He is a man of few words, is he not? I could get nothing interesting from him.'

'Few words, maybe, but he is one of the most fascinating men at court. All the ladies are quite in love with him. Those eyes, you see...'

Alys felt a small, insidious prick of something that felt too much like jealousy. She pushed it away. 'Are *you* in love with him, Ellen?'

Ellen laughed. 'I? Certainly not. I need a man who adores me, you know, and Sir John treats all ladies the same, with unfailing courtesy and terrible boredom. I think Lord Merton would be a better bargain.'

'Despite his terrible sleeves?'

'His fine estates would more than make up for that. Perhaps *you* might care to know him better?'

'I told the Queen I did not mean to marry.'

'None of us mean to marry while at court. Such a nuisance a trip to the Tower would be! But eventually...' The doors at the end of the gallery opened and the ladies in front of them surged forward on a wave of laughter. Alys and Ellen had no choice but to be swept along.

The gallery suddenly opened on to the vast Great Hall and for an instant Alys was sure all of England must be waiting there in glittering array.

She thought of her father's stories of the English court, of its dazzle and splendour. They were tales she had never quite believed when she was a child; to her the world was the grey, stony chill of Dunboyton, the never-ending crash of the cold sea. Now she saw he had not exaggerated.

It looked like something out of a tale of gods and goddesses, not a room of human proportions at all. The Queen's Great Hall was a hundred feet long and thirty feet wide, the walls and floor painted to look like marble, the high, timbered ceiling held aloft with gilded beams and painted with Tudor roses and silver ER monograms. Silken banners and bright tapestries warmed the space and gave it brilliant colour, along with the shimmer of the gold-and-silver plate displayed everywhere.

And the people were as sparkling as the room. Violet velvet, cloth of silver, rose-red satin, bumble bee–yellow silk... It all shone with pearls and gold embroidery, on the men as well as the women, and the stark white of delicate lace in the ruffs. Alys felt quite a country mouse in her gown of white silk trimmed with silver ribbons and her small ruff, but all the maids had to wear white and she could hide among them.

'We sit over here, Alys,' Ellen said, leading her to a long table at the far-left side of the room, where some of the maids were already seated. At the head of the room was the Queen's dais, with its great velvet chair and cloth of estate, but it was still empty.

Alys slid on to the bench next to Ellen and studied the setting around her, wondering where John would sit. The tables were all spread with spotless white-damask cloths, embroidered with roses and crowns; the benches were lined with soft gold-velvet cushions, even at the lowest seats. In the centre of the table was a dazzling silver-gilt salt cellar, etched with more roses and curling ERs, and each place held its own small loaf of fine white manchet bread, wrapped in embroidered linen, and a silver wine goblet. As more courtiers filed in and were seated, pages appeared bearing an endless procession of dishes—venison, capons, partridges in ginger sauce, eels in oranges— and pouring out rich red spiced wine. Even as they waited for the Queen, the feasting began.

A blast of trumpets heralded the royal entrance. The doors opened and Queen Elizabeth swept in, as glorious as a phoenix in a gown of scarlet-and-gold brocade, a golden crown studded with rubies atop her high-piled red hair, sleeves of cloth-of-gold that swept almost to the floor. She held the arms of two of her handsome young courtiers and everyone leaped up to bow and curtsy as she processed past.

She seated herself on her dais and waved a page forward with his ewer of wine. 'Please, my good people, dance—dance! This holiday is made for enjoyment, is it not? I would see everyone dance.'

Alys thought of her dance lesson at Dunboyton with John, the way she had felt as if she could spin free in his arms for ever, and a wave of sadness washed over her. She looked down into her goblet, staring into the dark red wine as if she could find a way there to vanish into the past again—or to banish it from her mind for ever.

'Would you care to dance, my lady?' she heard him say and for an instant she wondered if her wish had worked.

She glanced up, startled, to find John standing before her. But she had not gone back into the past. The Juan of those magical moments, with his rough borrowed shirt and beard, that sparkle in his beautiful eyes, was gone and before her stood a gentleman of the Queen's court, splendid in purple velvet and gold satin, an amethyst sparkling in his ear. His expression was most solemn as he watched her.

'I—I am not sure I know how to dance here,' she said.

'I do remember you were a splendid dancer indeed,' he answered. 'And I am sure the Queen would wish to see you dance.'

Alys glanced around the room and saw that all the other maids were joining the dance, as the Queen clapped her hands and encouraged them. The crowd had closed behind her and she had no place to run.

'Very well,' she said. 'I shall dance with you, if I must.'

A small smile quirked at his lips. 'I am favoured indeed with such enthusiasm.'

He held out his hand and Alys slowly slid her fingers into his grasp. He did feel the same still, warm and strong, his fingers slightly callused. The ring she had once worn flashed again on his little finger. He led her into their place in the line of the dance and she held her head high, making herself smile as everyone else did.

The music started, a lively tune, quicker than she would have imagined from their lesson. He squeezed her hand, as if to reassure her, and they stepped off with the others—right, left, right, left, jump, twirl.

She had to laugh as the little leaping cadence came off just right, as if by some magic. For a moment, she even forgot where she really was, who *he* really was, and just enjoyed the quick, light movements. She let herself be guided by his touch and they moved in perfect unison, jumping, twirling, spinning between the intertwined lines of dancers. He laughed with her and for a moment they truly were just Alys and Juan again, in their own little world.

But such an instant could not last. All too soon, the music ended with a flourish and she whirled to a stop. The other courtiers closed in around her again and she heard the Queen crying out, 'Splendid indeed! Now another, I insist. Something Venetian, I beg you, musicians.'

'Shall we dance again?' John asked quietly.

Alys looked up into his eyes, that bright green that had held her so spellbound, and she shook her head. If she danced with him again, she feared she would never free herself from the past at all. 'I must go,' she said, and hastily curtsied.

She hurried out of the crowded hall, not sure where she was going. She only knew she had to be alone, had to forget. Yet she feared she never really could, not now. Not when she had danced with him again.

Chapter Sixteen

It was a cold, blustery day, but Alys soon realised that no amount of chilliness could distract Queen Elizabeth from her exercise—or from making her ladies accompany her. The Queen strode quickly along the garden paths, her ermine-lined black-velvet cloak billowing around her. Despite her age, she moved with a quick, lithe grace that left her younger ladies scrambling to catch up.

Alys found herself at the end of the train of ladies, which gave her space to examine the gardens. They were vast, an interconnecting avenue of courtyards laid out in careful beds and pathways, with vistas leading to fountains and classical statues, all left bare in the winter, but surely lush and full of colour in the summer. The river, hidden beyond the walls, could be heard in a constant, soft rushing noise.

Alys hadn't realised how closed away she was feeling in the crowded palace. At Dunboyton, she walked outdoors every day, wandering the cliffs and fields whenever she chose to go. The cold breeze on her face now felt delicious.

'Hurry along now, ladies!' the Queen called out. 'No lagging behind. It is a wonderful, brisk day for a walk.'

Most of the ladies looked as if they would heartily disagree, their faces pale and pinched under the hoods and caps. The Queen's secretaries, too, looked as if they would rather be anywhere else, as they dashed after her waving documents to be signed. Queen Elizabeth waved them away and kept striding forward.

Other courtiers loitered around the winding pathways, obviously waiting to catch the Queen's attention. They leaped up eagerly as she approached. She sometimes paused to nod at them, but she didn't stop.

Their train turned a corner into a circular labyrinth of pathways and Alys suddenly longed to turn back when she saw who was among the group waiting there. It was John, even more handsome than ever. Unlike the others, who shivered miserably, he looked as if he did not feel the cold at all in his dark blue velvet doublet, a black short cloak lined with sable tossed carelessly over one shoulder. His face was in shadows under the gold braided edge of his black cap, hiding his expression.

On his finger gleamed the gold ring Alys had worn for so long, now back with its true owner.

Alys lifted her chin and studied the men who stood with him. To her unpleasant surprise, beside John was Sir Matthew Morgan, just as sombrely dressed as he had been at Dunboyton, and behind him was a cluster of young, eager courtiers. They were a strange group, a mix of solemn older men in their greys and blacks, and court peacocks in plumes and pearls.

Alys hastily composed herself as they bowed to the ladies, but she feared that the instant of surprise at seeing Sir Matthew again had shown on her face. She was determined they would see nothing more of her confusion. She was learning to be a courtier now.

She pasted a bright smile on her face and marched forward to greet them. 'Sir Matthew. Such a surprise to see you here. It has been much too long.'

He gave her a bow, a small, expressionless smile on his face. 'Lady Alys. How lovely you look today. The fresh air certainly agrees with you.'

'I do miss the exercise I am accustomed to at home,' she answered. She was aware that John watched her closely; she could feel the warmth of his gaze, like a living touch, on her skin. But she would not look at him, not now.

'I'm glad to have the opportunity to thank you properly for your help at Dunboyton, Lady Alys. It was very good to see your father again and in such fine health.'

Alys remembered that Sir Matthew had once known her father, and her mother, when they were young. It made his betrayal at Dunboyton all the worse. 'I fear the climate at Dunboyton does him little good at his age. And he so seldom gets to see his old friends.'

Sir Matthew gave another of his bland little smiles that said nothing. 'I'm sure he will be able to return to England very soon.' He turned to John. 'Perhaps you have met my godson, Sir John Huntley?'

His *godson*? No wonder he had come to snatch John away from Dunboyton. But how did these two men work together now? 'Of course. Hello, Sir John.'

'Lady Alys. I'm glad to see you're adjusting to court life so well.'

'It is endlessly interesting,' she answered.

'It looks as if Her Majesty has got far ahead of you, Lady Alys,' Sir Matthew commented.

Alys glanced back to see that the Queen had indeed strode around to the next courtyard, her cloak a black, shadowy blur. Her ladies from that distance looked like a flock of bright birds, fluttering and twittering. Only Ellen hung back from them, studying Alys. Alys waved to her and she smiled and waved back.

'I should catch up to them,' Alys said. 'I cannot be neglecting my duties so soon after arriving here.'

'Let me walk with you, Lady Alys,' John said.

Walking with John, so far from the others, was the last thing Alys wanted. She was able to guard her tongue now, but she feared what would happen if he was too near. Yet she had no choice, no ready excuse to avoid his gallant offer. 'Thank you, Sir John.'

He offered her his arm and she slid her fingertips lightly over his velvet sleeves. The hard, taut muscles beneath tensed at her touch. They strolled away from his friends, towards the Queen, and Alys tried to concentrate on the crowd in the distance. Not on the man who stood so close to her.

'How are you faring thus far in the Queen's service?' he asked, his tone carefully bored. 'You seemed to be enjoying last night's banquet.'

'Well enough, I think. My duties are certainly not too onerous, merely a bit of Christmas feasting and walks, and I have done nothing yet to draw the royal wrath as some ladies have.' She shuddered as she thought of the footstool Queen Elizabeth had chucked at one maid's head that morning when she pinched her with a necklace clasp. Luckily, the stool had missed its mark.

John laughed. 'I don't see how you could ever draw anyone's wrath, Alys.'

'Because I am so adept at courtly ways?'

'Because of your kind nature. Queen Elizabeth is fortunate to have you in her train.'

'Surely everyone would say I am the fortunate one. To be here at court and everything.'

'We are all fortunate to have such a queen.' He paused and glanced down at Alys, his face still shadowed, but she could see the small frown on his lips. 'I do fear for you at times, Alys.'

Alys felt a flash of anger at his presumption. 'Fear for me? The Queen's palace is surely well guarded.'

'But are you? I said your heart is kind and I know you don't want to think ill of anyone—except for me.'

'Is it not deserved? I do think well of people, until they give me reason not to.'

'That is well earned, Alys, I admit. But I must warn you to take much care. So many people at court are not what they seem.'

Alys opened her mouth to argue, to protest that he had no place to warn her about anything, but something in his serious demeanour held her back. He seemed so very sincere. But perhaps that was just another instance of people not being what they seemed. 'Is there anyone in particular I must beware of?'

'Not yet. Soon I do hope to know much more. But for now—be most careful in where you go and who you speak to privily. Promise me you will do that.'

'I will do that. I hope I am always cautious.' Except when it came to John. She had not been cautious at all then. She hoped she had learned her lesson.

There was no time for him to say anything more, for they had nearly reached the hurrying crowd that trailed behind the Queen. Ellen was still waiting for her there.

'I will leave you here,' John said. 'Just remember what I have told you.'

Alys nodded, feeling even more confused than ever. She hurried to join Ellen and glanced back only once at John. He was already far away from her, re-joining his godfather.

'I did not know you were acquainted with Sir Matthew Morgan, Alys,' Ellen said.

'He knows my father,' Alys answered carefully, remembering the warning not to give away too much information to anyone. 'But they have not seen each other in a long time.'

'He is much too quiet. I cannot trust him,' Ellen said with a sigh. 'It is too bad, for he is rather handsome.' She linked her arm with Alys's and led her back towards the Queen. 'Now, what do you suppose is going to happen at tonight's banquet? A Lord of Misrule will be chosen! So exciting. I wonder who it will be…'

That evening's banquet took place not in the Great Hall, but in a smaller chamber which made it feel like a much more intimate party, almost like a holiday gathering Alys had known at her father's home, where everyone was crowded in close and conversation and laughter were easy to hear. Yet it was no less grand than any banquet at court could ever be, with the walls hung with bright painted cloths depicting scenes of a royal journey complete with silken tents and brilliantly caparisoned horse. The gold-and-silver threads woven through them made them seem to dance in the candlelight. A fire roared in the marble grate, casting a glow over the gilded beams of the low ceilings and the fine silver plate lining the round table.

Some of the Queen's musicians played a lively tune as the courtiers processed to the tables, nearly drowned out by the laughter. The scent of spiced wine, roasted meats and floral perfumes made Alys feel dizzy.

'Alys, over here!' she heard Ellen call and she followed her to the maids' table near the Queen's seat at the far end of the room. Pages were pouring wine into the goblets as everyone found their places and Alys sipped at hers as she studied the crowd. Lord Merton and Sir Walter Terrence were nearby and waved at Ellen, who laughed back at them. Alys found she was beginning to recognise some of the other faces in the glittering sea of jewels and furs, to remember their names, just as Mistress Jones had said she would.

Yet the face she looked for most closely, John's, was nowhere to be seen. Alys sighed, with relief or disappointment she was not sure, and settled back on her bench. She sipped at the wine, so much finer and sweeter than any they had at Dunboyton, and listened to Ellen and the other ladies as they chattered about the fashions around them, who was said to be in love with whom now and what might happen with the Lord of Misrule. It was a pleasant distraction from worrying about John.

'Look at Lady Withersley,' Ellen whispered. 'No style at all. She would be better leaving such low-cut bodices to her daughter.'

Alys looked to where Ellen pointed, to a tall, very thin lady seated across the room, dressed in an eye-catching gown of peacock-green velvet striped with gold and a stiff gold lace ruff. 'You would never see a gown like that at Dunboyton! The ladies would freeze to death.'

'When I am a grand old married lady I shall wear partlets up to my chin and sit around loudly telling my granddaughters how we had modesty in *my* day. Just as my grandmother always did,' Ellen said with a laugh. 'I will enjoy being old and not grasp after the past like Lady Withersley.'

'Or like the Queen,' one of the bolder maids said, but only in a whisper.

'The Queen thinks we cannot see that her skin grows lined beneath all that white paste, but strangely it only makes the furrows deeper,' Ellen said thoughtfully. ''Tis better to admit the truth.'

'And has your family found you a betrothal, Ellen?' another maid asked.

Ellen popped a sugared almond into her mouth and glanced away. 'My brother must find a wife first.'

'A wealthy wife?'

Ellen frowned and Alys had the impression she did not wish to continue this conversation at all. 'Better to wife wealthily whenever possible. Don't you agree, Alys?'

Before Alys could think of what to answer, a fanfare of sackbuts and flutes broke over the noisy crowd and everyone's birdlike chatter fell silent. Queen Elizabeth herself appeared in the doorway on the arm of one of her courtiers, an awe-inspiring sight in a gown of green-and-white satin, trimmed with pearls and ermine. Her curled bright red hair was piled high and crowned with a sable-trimmed gold cap. She glided forward like a ship in full sail.

Several men followed in her train and Alys felt a shock of surprise when she glimpsed John among them. He, too, wore green, a fine velvet doublet the same colour as his eyes, and a short cloak of white brocade lined in sable tossed over one shoulder. He smiled, but his smile was like a mask, the same one he had worn almost every moment Alys had seen him at court. Only when he stood with her alone in the darkened closet had that mask slipped, had she dared hope the man she had once known was still there somewhere.

But even if he was, even if her Juan lurked in his soul somewhere, what good would it do? He could not come out, not here, and she could not look for him now.

She turned quickly away, smiling her own smile, which she feared was already becoming too practised. Gossip flowed around her as freely as the wine, the laughter growing louder.

The Queen stood at her dais, holding up her hand, and the room fell silent once again. 'My good friends!' she said, her voice hoarse, as if the cold walk had done her little good that day. But she smiled, creases forming in her white make-up. 'I do thank you for joining me tonight on our Christmas revels. We do have much to celebrate, yet also much sadness to banish with the lighting of our Yule logs.' She closed her eyes for a moment and Alys wondered if she thought of her Lord Leicester, so recently deceased. Everyone said her grief for him had been sharp. But then she opened them and smiled once again. 'But first, every Yule must have its Lord of Misrule!' She clapped her hands and the doors opened again to admit a flock of liveried footmen bearing a large platter high above their heads. The crowd could just barely glimpse the cake there, an edifice of white marzipan and gold leaf.

Behind them marched two rows of gentlemen, who had obviously slipped away from the banquet to make a grand entrance, clad in their finest courtly satins and feathers. Lord Merton was there, with his friend Sir Walter, both of them in bright green and cloth of silver. Lord

Merton waved and bowed to the both sides, grinning as if it was his own princely procession.

Alys watched him with a small frown. She could not like the man and she was not sure why. He was Ellen's friend and always most mannerly, but such a peacocky show-off. She burned to look at John, but knew she could not and reached for her goblet of wine to take a deep gulp. Ellen gave her a concerned glance.

'In my father's time,' Queen Elizabeth said, 'a Lord of Misrule was chosen for the Christmas season by finding a bean hidden in a special cake. The odds seem perilously against such a thing, don't they? But my cooks swear to me it is in there and these gentlemen have bravely volunteered to find it. So, my dear gallants, choose your piece and go to!'

Slices of the cake, a rich amber colour filled with jewel-like bits of candied fruit and iced in thick white marzipan, were handed out. Amid much chewing, and shouted encouragement from the onlookers, the cake was consumed in great gulps, as if the men were starving.

Alys watched John as he reached for the cake, laughing at a joke someone else told, and in that moment the careful courtly gentleman vanished and the Juan she knew in Ireland peered forward from behind the mask. It was gone too quickly, but she almost cried at the glimpse.

'I have found it!' Lord Merton cried. He held aloft something on his palm, too tiny to be seen.

Queen Elizabeth clapped her hands. 'Excellent, Lord Merton! I declare you to be King of the Bean, Lord of Misrule.' He knelt before her, and she borrowed one of her courtier's swords to give him an elaborate mock dubbing that made everyone laugh even louder. 'What shall your first act be?'

Lord Merton leaped to his feet. 'A dance, of course! I declare everyone must perform a galliard to begin our Christmas revels. Lady Ellen, will you partner me?'

'I shall indeed,' Ellen answered and took his arm to vanish into the crowd, leaving Alys standing alone.

Yet she was not alone for long.

'Would you care to dance with me, Lady Alys?' she heard John say and she spun around to find him standing behind her. He smiled, but it was tight, wary, not reaching his eyes.

She remembered all too well what had happened the last time she danced with him, the longing that had swept over her. 'I—I do not care to dance tonight,' she said and hurried away before she could change her mind and give in to the temptation to touch him again.

She felt him watching her even after the crowd closed between them.

'You were late at the revels, John,' Sir Matthew said as John came into his office. He didn't look up from the document he was writing. Even in the middle of the night, by meagre candlelight, he did not cease to work.

'No one can leave before the Queen does,' John answered as he took the chair across from the desk. He sat down and stretched his long legs before him, feeling the weariness in his mind and his muscles. Courtly evenings were long ones and dull. He thought of the fireside of the small room at Dunboyton, laughing there with Alys, and he found himself wishing such evenings could be his more.

But he knew they could not. That had been a dream; this was the life he had to live.

'Aye, she will outlive us all,' Matthew said with a sigh.

'Your work for her wearies you before your time, Matthew.'

'What choice do we have? England is safe from Spain now, but five years from now? The Queen's enemies will always regroup.' Matthew sat back and carefully laid aside his pen. 'Have you discovered anything at the royal revels?'

John quickly told him of conversations overheard, strange glances exchanged, alliances that seemed to be shifting. The everyday matters of court.

'Very good,' Matthew responded. 'I fear I have a different errand for you at the moment, though. I have received information about a lodging house in London, where our old friend Señor Peter may have stayed when he was last in England. It is near the Deptford docks, many foreigners seem to feel comfortable lodging there, and a young man matching his description was there for many weeks a year or so ago. I need you to go stay there and find out who his visitors might have been.'

To go to London, now? John thought of Alys, alone in the midst of the court, and he realised he did not want to leave her so unprotected now. 'Now, Matthew? This is the busiest season at court.'

'And the busiest in London. We must move before his tracks are completely covered.' Matthew studied John carefully for a long, silent moment. 'You need have no fear for Lady Alys. She is well watched here and will come to no harm.'

'I owe her so much, owe her my life,' John said. 'I won't let her be caught in the middle of any vile plots here at court.'

'She won't be, unless she seeks it herself. She doesn't seem like a young lady who shrinks from danger.'

'She will help those who need it. I can't imagine she herself would be involved in any plots.'

Matthew shrugged. 'You never know how people will behave once they are in the midst of court. It is a strange place, John, you know that as well as I do. It changes people.'

'Not Alys,' John argued. Surely even the hard coldness of court could not change her kind heart.

'As you say. But she will be guarded in your absence, John, have no fear for her. With a fast horse, your errand should not take more than a few days.'

John nodded. He knew he could not refuse. 'Of course. I will be quick.'

'Very good. Now, it does grow late and you must depart at first light. You should seek your bed.'

'Aye. Goodnight to you, Matthew.'

As John rose and reached for the door latch, Matthew's soft voice called, 'Always remember, John—feelings must have no part in our work or we are done for.'

John could only nod. He made his way down the narrow stairs from Matthew's tower, but he didn't seek his own lodgings. He knew he wouldn't be able to sleep yet and he needed some air after the stuffiness of the palace, the long evening of merriment. He went out to the deserted gardens, breathing deeply of the cold river air as he strolled the pathway along the stone walls.

Around the corner, he came to a window high up, still lit despite the lateness of the hour. Shadows danced and flitted past, and he knew it was the maids' chamber. Was Alys in there, one of the ghostly dancing figures, laughing with the others?

He hoped she did laugh, that court did not frighten her. If only—if only he could be the one to make her smile, to protect her from all she didn't yet know, couldn't fathom about this new world she lived in. But he knew he could not.

Chapter Seventeen

'Holly and ivy, box and bay, put in the house for Christmas Day! Fa-la-la-la…'

Despite her preoccupation with thoughts of John, and his words of caution in the garden, Alys had to smile at the sound of the familiar song. Even the maidservants at Dunboyton sang it every year, as they bedecked the draughty old castle hall for Christmas. It was a comfort to hear it, to feel that a few small things stayed the same in the strange world of the court.

All the Maids of Honour, along with some of the Queen's Ladies of the Privy Chamber, had been assigned to decorate the Great Hall for that night's feast. Long tables were covered with holly, ivy, mistletoe and evergreen boughs, and every colour of ribbon and spangle. Under the strict eye of Mistress Jones, they were supposed to work efficiently to turn them into Christmas decorations to be hung by the pages from the beams and mantels of the hall.

But *efficiency* didn't seem to be the order of the day. Most of the ladies sang as they worked, leaping up to do a dance or twirl around with ribbons like wild Morris Dancers at a fair.

Alys laughed at their antics. For the first time since arriving at court, she didn't feel quite so uncertain. Christmas was Christmas everywhere, after all, whether at Greenwich or Dunboyton, and she knew what to do. Wind evergreen boughs together and tie them with ribbon. It was almost automatic.

She held up the wreath she had just finished and tweaked the bow a bit. She remembered such wreaths made at Dunboyton every year, with greenery she had gathered with her mother. And, later that night, she had glimpsed her parents embracing under the newly made kissing boughs. The thought made her smile, yet it also evoked a deep, bittersweet sadness. Even in that lonely place, her parents had never been alone when they had each other. Would she ever know such a thing?

An image of John flashed in her mind, the look on his face as he warned her of danger. What had he meant? She hardly knew what to think of him now, what to do.

She shook away the thoughts and reached for two bent wire hoops, binding them into a sphere as she remembered her mother doing. She chose the darkest, glossiest loops of holly and ivy from the table, twining them around the wires and tying them off with streamers of crimson ribbon.

'Are you making a kissing bough, Alys?' Ellen asked teasingly.

Alys glanced at her new friend across the table and smiled. Ellen was laughing, as usual, chatting with all the ladies around her, yet Alys wondered if she was feeling ill. Her cheeks were very pink, her eyes too bright.

'My mother taught me how to make them when I was a child. She said her mother taught her.'

Ellen held up her own wreath. 'How lovely it must be to have a kind mother like that.'

Alys wondered about Ellen's own family. She knew Ellen's brother was in some sort of trouble no one spoke about and her father wished her to marry someone wealthy. But what of her mother? Her home? 'She was the best of mothers, and I miss her very much. My father says she could not live without her warm sunshine. But she did teach me a great deal about Christmas decorations.'

Ellen's mouth opened in a shocked little 'o'. 'Alys, I am sorry! I didn't mind to remind you of any painful losses, not today.'

'It's not painful now. I have wonderful memories of her. Like making kissing boughs!'

'Was your mother not Spanish?' one of the other ladies asked, a tinge of suspicion in her voice. 'Do they even celebrate Christmas there?'

'Of course they do,' Alys answered quickly. 'And my mother was quite young when she came here.'

'How fascinatingly exotic.' Ellen sighed. 'I would so love to travel, to see something beyond England. I am not surprised your mother pined for the sun on such grey days as this.'

'You must marry an ambassador, then, Ellen,' another lady said, unfurling a spool of silver ribbon in the air. 'One who will carry you away from here!'

Ellen laughed. 'Where is he, then? Mayhap your kissing bough will bring him to me, Alys?'

Alys held up her completed bough, a sphere of greenery and red ribbon that fluttered enticingly. 'My mother did say if you stand beneath it and close your eyes, you will have a vision of your future husband.'

'I shall test it, then!' one of the Maids said. She snatched the bough from Alys's hands and held it high above her own head, squeezing her eyes shut. 'Nay, it works not. I see only darkness!'

Alys laughed and took it back. 'It needs mistletoe.'

Ellen offered a dark branch, heavy with pearly white berries. 'Try this one.'

Alys threaded it through the centre of the sphere, fastening it with the bows. She wondered if John might see it and kiss her beneath the greenery, if they might have a flash of clarity between them. But she shook her head even as the hope came to her. She could not afford such foolish thoughts.

'Who would you want to see beneath the kissing bough, Alys?' Ellen whispered.

Alys felt her cheeks turn warm, as if she had been caught in her thoughts. 'No one at all, I fear.'

'Really? No one at court has caught your eye?' Ellen said with a knowing little smile. 'Everyone has their little admirations, even though the Queen forbids us to take them seriously. There must be someone you think is handsome?'

'Of course. There are many handsome men at court.'

'Perhaps Lord Merton?'

Alys gave a startled laugh. 'Lord Merton? He is *your* admirer, surely.'

'But he seems to like you.' Ellen held up a length of green ribbon as if to admire it. 'Or maybe someone younger? Sir John Huntley is very good looking, though sadly his estate is in disorder.'

Alys swallowed hard and stared down at her work.

She feared she had not yet entirely learned courtly dissembling. 'I think no one could deny he is handsome, whatever his estate.'

'Very true,' Ellen said with a sigh. ''Tis sad he has left court, then.'

Shocked, Alys looked up. 'Left court?' He had left again, with no word to her?

'That's right. No guessing as to where, though. Or how long till he returns. Can you hand me that piece of holly there?'

Alys handed her the greenery, but she felt as if she did so in a dreamy haze. If John was indeed gone, where was he? Why had he left so soon after warning her of danger?

There was a sudden burst of noise at the end of the hall as a group of men burst through the doors, led by Lord Merton, who seemed intent on living up to his role as Lord of Misrule in an outrageous purple-and-green doublet with padded shoulders and five feathers in his cap. They trailed with them the cold of the day outside and their hearty greetings made all the Maids giggle and blush.

Alys was glad of the distraction and smiled at them as well. Better than worrying about John, who was the most maddening, inexplicable man ever.

'Lady Ellen,' Lord Merton called as he strode down the hall, followed by his entourage. 'You ladies should join us outside. We are going skating today.'

Ellen frowned down at her pile of ribbons, but a smile threatened to break through. 'Some of us must work, Lord Merton, and cannot be frolicking all day.'

'You shouldn't be so harsh, my lady, I vow,' Sir Walter Terrence said with a laugh. 'We are not merely frolicking. Her Majesty bids us to seek out a fine Yule log this afternoon. We could use the artistic advice of you lovely ladies.'

'Perhaps then we should go with you,' Ellen said. 'You cannot be trusted to find the right one. Alys, ladies, will you come?'

Most of the ladies clamoured with excited 'ayes', but Alys had another idea. If most of the courtiers were to be gone from the palace, perhaps she could mount a small search for clues in the mystery of John and his sudden disappearances? She shivered at the thought, fearful and excited all at the same time. It would be good to *do* something, no matter how far-fetched, rather than just worry and wonder.

'I don't care for the cold,' she answered. 'I think I shall stay here by the fire.'

Ellen gave her a worried glance. 'Do you feel unwell, Alys? Mayhap I should stay here with you.'

'Nay, you must go and enjoy the day,' Alys answered. 'I am quite well, but I will be content here alone for a while.'

'Aye,' Ellen said with a nod. 'It does sometimes feel too crowded here, does it not? Like a beehive, always buzzing.'

That was exactly what Alys had thought when she first arrived at the palace—it was a beehive, always busy, always noisy. And she needed quiet to venture out. 'I will make sure the decorations are all arranged.'

'Well, if you are sure…' Ellen said.

Alys climbed atop a stool to reach up and tie some of the ribbon loops, pretending to be most intent on her task as the others left. Once they were gone, taking their laughter and chatter with them, the hall seemed hauntingly silent.

She couldn't stop wondering about John's departure from court. Where had he really gone? Would he return? Was he safe? Her worries wouldn't stop whirling in her mind. Before she quite realised what she was doing, she climbed down from her stool and hurried out of the hall.

The corridors were crowded, but only with servants hurrying about their tasks. The Queen was closeted with her Privy Council and would see no one for hours, so most of the courtiers were out riding or seeing to their own business. No one paid any attention to Alys as she made her way through the maze of the palace. She asked a maid scrubbing at one of the fireplace grates where Sir John might be lodged. The girl giggled, but pointed her in its direction.

The chamber was at the end of long, narrow, distant corridor. She was able to find it thanks to the tapestry the maid described hanging nearby, but she wasn't sure if she could ever find it again.

She looked both ways and, seeing no one nearby, tried the door latch. To her surprise, it turned easily under her hand, unlocked. That did not bode well for any secrets being found inside, but she had come thus far already.

Alys cautiously eased the door open, carefully listening for any sound, any sign of movement. Only once she was sure she was alone did she slip inside.

It was a tiny chamber, more like a closet wedged into the layers of walls, but John had it to himself, which had to be a mark of some royal favour. The furniture was plain but of good, serviceable quality, a narrow bed draped in green and white, a desk and chair, a carved clothes chest, a looking glass above a washstand.

Alys wasn't sure where a true spy would start, or if she would even know what she was looking for if she found it. She opened the clothing chest at the foot of the bed and poked through the garments neatly folded there. They smelled of John, of that clean, almost lemon scent, and she quickly closed the lid on it. She found nothing unusual there, even when she felt around the bottom of the chest to see if there was a false bottom. She did not notice when her sleeve caught on the hinge of a box.

She glanced through the books and papers piled on the desk. There were a few documents in Spanish, but they all seemed to be about shipping manifests. It could be a code, of course, but she would need longer to even start to decipher such a thing. The books were all the usual things a gentleman would have, poetry and philosophy.

She felt most foolish as she slipped out of the chamber and hurried back through the corridors, blindly searching for the shelter of the maids' dormitory. She went down several wrong corridors into unfamiliar-looking chambers. She did long to know John's secrets, but surely such knowledge would do her no good unless he told her himself. Unless he trusted her.

Her thoughts had her so distracted, she became hopelessly lost again and stumbled into a pantry before she found the right staircase. At least, she thought, the halls were silent and there was no one to see her confused state.

Except for one. To Alys's surprise, Ellen was already in the maids' chamber, lying alone on her bed, her bright pink-velvet skirts puffed around her like flower petals. She lay there so very still that for an instant Alys was afraid she had swooned.

She hurried closer, winding her way past all the clothes chests and tumbled books and possessions on the floor. 'Ellen? Are you unwell? What is amiss?'

Ellen rolled over to face her. Her eyes were red-rimmed, as if she had been crying, her cheeks pale. 'Oh, Alys, there you are. I did wonder. You were not in the gallery when I looked.'

'I thought you would be out all day with the others. What is wrong?'

'Nothing at all. It was just very dull, as everything is at court.' Ellen sat up against her bolsters and gave Alys a bright smile, a smile too brittle. 'Tell me more about your home. Dunboyton, is it?'

Alys was startled by the sudden change of topic. She sat down carefully at the end of the bed. 'My home is much more dull than court. It is far from anywhere and the castle is very old. Very cold and lonely.' That was all true, but she also remembered the beauties of Dunboyton, missed it every night as she fell asleep. She didn't know how to talk about that 'But the sea is more beautiful than anything else I have ever seen. So changeable, sometimes grey and stormy, sometimes as blue as a sapphire. I like to walk along the cliffs above the waves every day.'

'It sounds lovely. Did your mother take you there when you were a child?'

'She did. We often went walking together.'

'She must have been interesting. I grew up in my grandmother's house after my mother died, I don't remember her at all.'

'I am sorry, Ellen. I do miss my mother so much, but at least I have memories of her.'

'And she was Spanish?'

'Her parents were and she still spoke the language and remembered some of the old traditions. She still had brothers in Spain. She said maybe one day we would travel back to Seville together and eat the oranges there that taste like the sun itself.'

'Like the sun.' Ellen leaned back on her bolsters with a deep sigh. She stared up at Alys with a strangely intent expression. 'Tell me, Alys. Was your mother of the—the old faith?'

That was dangerous talk indeed. Startled, Alys glanced over her shoulder to make sure they were alone. 'The—old faith? I do not know. I was still fairly young when she died, she never spoke to me about such matters. My father keeps an Anglican chaplain, but I admit he has never seemed deeply devout to me.'

Ellen nodded and seemed satisfied with such an answer. 'That is as it should be. We can't be responsible for everything our parents do, can we? Now, tell me, what shall I wear tonight for the banquet? I am so tired of those silver sleeves, I was thinking something red…'

John was weary and travel-stained as he made his way to his Greenwich chamber. London had been a frustrating experience. The landlady at Peter's lodgings had loved to talk, would talk for hours, days, if encouraged, which was always useful. Yet it took twice as long to sort out the wheat from the chaff of her gossip.

Peter, or at least a man much resembling him, had indeed stayed there and had greeted many visitors to his rooms, they came and went every day. There had been ladies, at least two, in hooded cloaks so she could not see their faces, as well as men speaking some strange language. She declared, though, that she was not one to mix in her lodgers' business, as long as they paid their rent.

He went to taverns and shops nearby. No one was willing to speak openly of anything to do with the Spanish, but John knew how to discover things deeply buried, even without the speaker's knowledge they had given it away.

Peter had squired a lady around when he was there and seemed most infatuated with her.

He made his way up the back stairs of the palace to his chamber. It was growing dark outside; he had to get ready for the night's Christmas revels. He would much rather have an evening of reading by the fire than dancing, but there was no choice.

He thought of those few, precious evenings in Ireland with Alys, sitting by the fire, talking and laughing. How he ached for such a thing now, it seemed like a distant paradise.

He took off his dusty cloak and unbuttoned his doublet before he sat down to pull off his riding boots. As he tossed them aside, his gaze fell on the stack of books and papers on his desk. They were not as he left them, in their careful piles, the titles carefully organised.

He hurried over to sort through them. Nothing was missing at all, even in the hidden desk drawer where he kept his coin. He never left any papers of importance in the chamber when he wasn't there, just as he seldom left the door locked. It would only attract suspicion.

But even an unlocked door seemed to have attracted some attention. He looked through the rest of his things, his travelling cases and boxes. On the hinge of one trunk, he found his one clue, a small silver-satin bow.

Who had been going through his things? A lady? No matter who it was, they would be sorry indeed when he found them.

Chapter Eighteen

'Round your foreheads garlands twine, drown sorrow in a cup of wine, and let us all be merry!'

Even Alys, still unsettled by her search of John's room and her encounter with Ellen, had to smile as the whole, vast great hall rang with song. It was obvious the entire court had already been drowning their sorrows in the Queen's fine malmsey wine. The tables were littered with the remains of the lavish feast, with goblets spilling their last red drops on to the white tablecloths, the dogs fighting over bones under the tables and the musicians playing louder and louder.

The decorations the ladies had made were wound round the fireplace mantels and hung from the ceiling beams, crowning tapestries and framing the carvings of the goddess of plenty and her bounty on the plastered walls. The Queen looked like the goddess herself, presiding over the feast of plenty. She sat atop her dais in a gown of purest white satin, trimmed in white fur and embroidered with a pattern of pearls and diamonds. She clapped and laughed at all the merriment, but Alys noticed that sometimes a pained spasm of something like sorrow crossed her painted face before she hid it again behind a smile.

Alys wondered how she could hide her own doubts and fears, if even the Queen could not entirely conceal hers. Queen Elizabeth mourned her old friend Lord Leicester and Alys longed to deny her own feelings for John, her longing for home in the midst of so much strangeness and uncertainty. Love was a painful thing, even at Christmas. Mayhap especially at Christmas.

Where *was* John? she wondered with a spasm of fear. Was he in danger somewhere? What could she do to help him? She feared there was nothing she could do, not unless he told her all. Not unless they could trust each other, as they had so instinctively in Ireland.

She took another sip of her wine and nearly spilled it on her own pale blue bodice as the doors to the hall burst open in a flurry of drums. Acrobats tumbled through, somersaulting in a blur of brilliantly coloured silks and spangles, tinkling with bells. They rolled between the tables, leaping up in dizzying leaps and twirls.

Behind them marched Lord Merton in his role as Lord of Misrule, fantastically attired in a multi-coloured cloak and tall hat crowned with scarlet plumes. He rattled a staff of bells as the acrobats swirled around him.

Ellen stiffened next to Alys and Alys shot her a curious glance. Ellen quickly smiled, but Alys could not forget her friend's strange reaction in the midst of such frantic merriment.

The Queen rose to her feet and waved her hand for silence. 'What do you seek here at my palace, sirrah?'

'I am the Queen's own Lord of Misrule! The High and Mighty Prince of Purpoole, Duke of Stapulia, Knight of the Most Heroical Order of the Helmet,' Lord Merton answered. 'I declare for this Yule that this is my kingdom, the realm of merriment.'

Queen Elizabeth laughed. 'The realm of chaos! Very well, my Lord of Misrule, let your reign begin. But pay heed, it will only last until Twelfth Night.'

Lord Merton bowed and strode to the Queen's dais to offer her his hand. He assisted her down the steps and between the tables. They made their way to a tall, velvet-cushioned chair set by the fireplace.

'How shall your reign begin?' the Queen asked.

'With the bringing in of the Yule log, of course.'

'As it should be. Ladies! To me!' the Queen called.

Alys followed Ellen and the others as they gathered around the Queen's chair, finding cushions and stools to sit on. The rest of the courtiers clustered behind them and Alys felt suddenly trapped. She wished John was there, but she was alone in the crowd.

Lord Merton waved his arms and the acrobats scattered to open the doors once more. They soon reappeared, bearing the Yule log on their shoulders, as long and heavy as one of the gilded ceiling beams. Greenery and garlands tied with fluttering red ribbons bedecked the sturdy oak.

'What then doth make the element so bright? The heavens are come down upon earth to live!' Lord Merton sang as the log was lowered into the fireplace. 'Who has the embers from last year to set the light?'

As one of the pages stepped forward with a torch to start the new fire, Lord Merton paraded around the crowd with his staff of bells. He sometimes stopped and twirled one of the ladies around, but when he came to Ellen she shook her head and turned away.

'Now,' Lord Merton said, 'I command those of you

whom the Queen calls on to tell your favourite Christmas memory.'

Queen Elizabeth laughed, the jewels of her gown glittering in the light. She looked younger in the shadows and flickering flames, her make-up a smooth mask, her smile wide. 'Who do you say shall go first, Lord of Misrule?'

'Your Majesty herself, of course.'

The Queen stared into the fire for a long moment and seemed very far away. 'I do remember the year I was summoned to Hampton Court by my father, old King Harry,' she said. 'His new Queen was Catherine Parr, who was very beautiful and kind, and who loved celebrating Christmas. There were dances and music, fine clothes, but also much reading of the new faith. I did learn so much from Queen Catherine that Yule season and it has stayed with me these many years.'

For a long moment, there was a heavy silence in the room, as if everyone remembered the dark days that followed the light of Queen Catherine. Then the Queen snapped her fingers as if to break the spell. 'What of you, Master Ambassador de Castelnau? How do you celebrate in Paris?'

Around the room went the thread of Christmas tales, from ambassador to earl to lady, until it came to Alys. 'What of my newest lady, then? Lady Alys Drury?' the Queen said. 'How do you celebrate the season in Ireland?'

Alys was shocked by the sudden sound of her own name and she felt her cheeks turn warm as everyone turned to look at her. She opened her mouth and to her embarrassment nothing came out.

'It must be wild there indeed,' Sir Walter Terrence said. 'Do you even have music?'

Alys laughed, her embarrassment broken by the absurdity. 'Of course we do. I learned to play the lute when I was a child. We decorate the halls there just as here and have feasting and dancing. It is too cold to stray far from the hearth.'

'Just like tonight,' Ellen said.

'But we do have our memories to keep us warm,' the Queen said wistfully. 'Well, Lord of Misrule, play your music again! We will have no sad faces this night, only merriment.'

Something startled Alys awake out of a dreamless sleep, something like a noise or movement. For a moment, she lay there perfectly still, a bit disoriented from being jolted from darkness to waking.

She blinked and sat up against her bolsters. She was not in her lonely chamber at Dunboyton, but in the crowded maids' dormitory at Greenwich. Usually the long, narrow space was full of chaos and noise, ladies dressing and laughing and quarrelling. Now, in the deepest darkness of night, all was silent. The ladies slept beneath their blankets, still and peaceful.

Except for one. The bed beside Alys's was empty. Ellen was gone, her quilts tossed back, her bolsters askew.

Alys sat up on the edge of her own bed and carefully studied the quiet room. No one moved at all. She waited a moment, in case Ellen had merely left the room for the privy and would soon return.

But she did not. Alys padded across the room to the window and climbed up on the clothes chest to peer outside. The moon cast the empty gardens in silver, like a statue. At first, she thought they were as quiet as the pal-

ace, but then she glimpsed a blur of movement along the
wall. A flash of light in the darkness, Ellen's red-gold
hair loose over her shoulders, Ellen wrapped in a light-
coloured fur. Her head was buried in her hands and she
seemed to be crying. No one else was around.

Alys quickly wrapped a shawl over her chemise and
stuffed her feet into her boots. Her heart beat quickly;
she knew she should not venture out of the palace, but
she couldn't leave Ellen alone. She ran down the stairs
and past the snoozing guards at the doors, out into the
garden. The wind hit her like an icy blast, catching at her
hair, but she pushed past it and soon found Ellen huddled by the wall. Her sobs racked her slender shoulders.

'Ellen, whatever is amiss?' Alys cried, running to her
friend's side. She took Ellen's arm and felt her shiver-
ing in the cold.

Ellen looked up, her eyes wide. At first she didn't
seem to see Alys there, but then she collapsed, falling
back against the wall. 'Oh, Alys,' she whispered hoarsely.
'I'm glad you found me. I was lost.'

'You lost your way from the palace?' Alys said, confused.

'Aye, so many things.' Ellen buried her face in her
hands. 'You are so lucky, Alys.'

'Lucky?' Alys managed to lead her towards the pathway. Ellen followed, as if she didn't know where she
went.

'To have a kind father and no siblings. You should go
back to him, you know. Away from this place. It is only
vipers here, you know.'

'It's all right now,' Alys murmured, completely confused. 'You are freezing. Come, let's find you some wine.'

Ellen went with her back to the maids' chamber and

let Alys pour some wine and wrap her in blankets. Ellen soon feel asleep, but Alys could not find slumber again at all. *Vipers*. Poor Ellen. What could be so wrong for her? And would the same snake soon come snapping for Alys, too?

Chapter Nineteen

The Great Hall was even more splendid than usual for the Queen's masked ball. Vast swathes of red-and-gold cloth were draped from the ceilings, forming a canopy above the dance floor that seemed to enclose them in some exotic tent. As the ladies processed into the hall, which was already lined with gentlemen in gold-and-silver masks that gleamed in the light, the Queen rose on her dais at the end of the room.

'Tonight, we shall dance a candle bransle, which was a favourite of the court for Christmas when I was a girl,' she announced. 'And I say we all must dance! No wallflowers this night.'

The Queen took one of her page's hands and climbed down the steps, moving among her courtiers as she matched people up, according to their masks. A gentleman with the visage of a Green Man went with a lady in a gown embroidered with ferns and leaves; two jesters in blue-and-green motley were matched. Alys reached up and felt the edge of her plain white mask, wondering if it meant she would be unmatched.

Or that she could wait for John to find her, though

she wasn't sure how she would know him with a mask and hooded cloak.

'My Lady Alys, would you do me the honour of partnering me for this dance?'

She spun around to see a man standing right behind her. He was tall and well muscled, but she knew it was not John. The beard was too pale below the edge of the elaborate gold mask, the doublet too stylish in its green-and-gold puffs. She thought it had to be Lord Merton and somehow the thought of taking his hand made her want to back away.

'I thought we were all meant to be anonymous tonight, sirrah,' she said, trying to be as light and teasing as she noticed were the other ladies, as they laughed with their partners and tried to guess their identities.

'I fear a lady of your beauty could never be unknown,' he answered. 'If I have offended…'

'Not at all. Surely such a compliment deserves a dance.'

Alys slowly took his offered hand and let him lead her into the forming dance set. They could not begin until the Queen took her place to lead the figures and Elizabeth was still strolling around the hall, matching up couples. Pages dashed around, lighting everyone's candles for the dance as the musicians tuned their instruments.

Alys studied the people gathered around her, the press of gilded masks and rich satins gleaming in the candlelight. It all made the scene so strange and mysterious, like something glimpsed in a dream. But she did not see John amid the crowd. Nor did she see Lady Ellen, though she had left the chamber before Alys did, in a distinctive autumnal-coloured gown.

The musicians launched into the lively music of the

old dance, one Alys only remembered from her child-hood. Luckily, most of the intricate steps began with the man and she could follow along easily. The man of each partner, his lighted candle held high in one hand, spun and hopped towards his lady, a series of intricate steps that ended in a low bow. The ladies then curtsied and danced to meet their partners, their skirts swaying around them.

Her partner took her hand to lead her in the turn and Alys thought he held her too tightly, peered at her too closely from behind the cover of his mask. She stumbled a little in another spin.

'You should take care, my lady,' he said. 'There is some danger in this hall for those who are unwary. For those who don't know the secrets.'

'The—the secrets of the dance?' she answered. She did not like the dark tone of his voice at all. She thought of Ellen and her vipers. Ellen had declared she must have been sleepwalking in the night and laughed Alys's concerns away, but those words haunted her.

'Any secrets, of course. They are not the fit province of ladies, anyway.'

'Then what is?'

'Dancing, of course.' He turned her again, a spin under his arm that took her too close to the candle's flame. 'Choose your dance partners, and your friends, ever wisely.'

They turned once more and he handed off the candle to her next partner. Fortunately he was a small, slim, leaping man, one with no strange menace behind his mask, and Alys laughed at his antics. They did their series of steps and she spun away to the next partner, and the next. As she turned again, she caught a glimpse of John at last, in the crowd of people at the edge of the room who did not dance. She knew it was him, despite the plain black mask he wore, the short cloak that shrouded his hair and shoulders.

But as she spun around yet again, her head whirling, she lost sight of him.

Her breath felt squeezed in her lungs, pinched by her new satin bodice, and her heart pounded so loudly she could hardly hear the music as it wound faster and faster. The lights of the dancers' candles seemed to flare in front of her eyes, blinding her. She felt like a wild bird, beating her wings against a cage, longing to soar free over the Galway cliffs again.

She wanted to be the innocent, unwary girl who had first met John again, wanted their strange, idyllic days at the abbey once more. Court was too confusing for one such as her.

She stumbled out of the patterns of the dance and fled the hot press of the great hall. She didn't know where she was going, she just wanted to hide and find herself again.

She ducked behind one of the sparkling tapestries and wedged herself into the small sanctuary space between the cloth and the panelled wall. She closed her eyes and let the muffled roar of the party rush over her. The contrast between the glittering, artificial party and her old life at Dunboyton was so sharp in that moment, so poignant, she almost cried for it.

'Cease this at once,' she whispered fiercely to herself. The old, practical, Irish Alys would never have been so sad.

Suddenly, the noise turned loud again as the tapestry was swept aside and Aly's eyes flew open. She was no longer alone in her sanctuary; John had followed her.

She had only a glimpse of his tall, lean figure, outlined by the torchlight, before the cloth dropped behind him and they were alone in their own dark little world.

He smelled like her John, of clean, light citrus and fine velvet, and he felt as she had felt him for so long in her dreams, warm and strong, a rock between her and what she feared. He was her Juan still in so many ways and yet also such a stranger, one who played games in this dangerous courtly world she could not yet fathom. Her instincts told her he was no villain, but she feared he was involved in something too complicated for her. She backed up until she felt the wall holding her up.

'Alys?' he said gently. 'Are you ill?'

'Nay, I…' She swayed dizzily. Maybe she *was* ill. She knew she was uncertain in her heart and she didn't like that feeling. She didn't know what to do when she was with him, but she knew she had to be brave now. 'It was so crowded, I could not quite breathe.'

'It's not like Galway, is it? No world could be as different. I do not wonder you had to step away.'

Alys nodded. He *did* understand, the way her homesickness warred with her curiosity, her fears. 'I feel I am always lost here,' she blurted out. 'That I never really know what is happening.'

His arms came around her, drawing her close to him, and at last she *did* feel safe, even as she wondered if he was the one she should fear the most. She rested her forehead against the soft velvet of his doublet and closed her eyes. For just an instant, she could pretend they were alone in Ireland again, in their quiet little room, with all the danger of the world closed outside the door.

She felt him kiss the top of her head and she tilted her

face up to his. His lips skimmed her brow, her cheek, lightly and sweetly.

At last, his lips touched hers again, and it was just as she remembered—hot and cold all at the same time, as consuming as a wave of the sea, washing over her and carrying her away. Once, twice, as if he too sought the memory of their kisses. And again, deeper, harder, hungrier, and she gasped for more.

That small sound against his lips made him groan and he drew her closer until there was not even a breath between them. Their bodies still fit together perfectly, as if they had always been meant to be just that way. As if nothing could tear them apart and in that moment nothing could.

Alys went up on the tips of her toes, her lips parting beneath his. His tongue lightly touched hers, tasting, testing, before he deepened the kiss and it was all she knew.

She wound her arms around his neck, feeling the soft silk of his hair between her fingers, holding on to him tight as if he would fly away from her again. But he was going nowhere now. Their kiss turned desperate, blurry with heat, and full of a need she didn't even know was there, hidden in her heart.

That need frightened her, yet she craved more and more of it. More of him. She wanted to be so close to him that everything else vanished for ever and yet she knew the world outside would not be left for ever. It would claim him again, as it had in Ireland.

She tore her lips away from his and backed away. 'John,' she gasped. 'What is this? What is happening?'

'I don't know, my dearest Alys,' he said, his voice rough. He rested his forehead against the wall beside her head, his breath ragged in her ear. 'I only know I have tried to deny it, to force it away, but it won't be gone. I have cursed myself for it.'

His words gave her a warm, thrilling feeling, all the way to her toes, yet it also scared her. 'John, will you not tell me what I have to fear here at court?'

He groaned. 'I cannot, Alys, not yet. I only—are you to accompany the Queen on her hunt tomorrow?'

'Yes, of course,' she said, bewildered. 'But why?'

'Stay close to me, promise me you will, and be most wary,' he said urgently. His hand sought hers in the shadows and held on to it tightly.

'I hope I am always wary. But how can I stay close to you when the court is near? The confusion of it all and if there is gossip…'

'Aye, I know it. Just be most careful. And meet with me tomorrow before the dancing? I will tell you more then.'

'I will meet you then.' Alys heard the music crash to an ending, the cheers of the dancers, and knew she had to return to the hall before she was missed. But she was most loathe to leave John, not now, with the taste of his kiss still on her lips and the feeling that she was near his truth now. 'You will not forget?'

'Nay, sweet Alys,' he said. Then he added, so softly she wasn't sure if she even heard him, 'I shall never leave you again.'

She slid out from behind the tapestry again and moved into the shifting, laughing crowd. Lord Merton, as Lord of Misrule, was directing the acrobats to tumble around the Queen's chair, making her laugh, and Alys was able to blend in as if she had not been gone. In truth, she knew she had only been behind that tapestry for a few moments, but it felt like years. As if the sparkling noise of the court was the dream and the quiet darkness with John's kiss the only reality.

'There you are!' she heard Ellen call and she turned to find her friend making her way through the crowd, a merry smile on her face. She held her feathered mask in her hand and waved it like a fan in the warm air. 'You quite vanished from the dance, Alys, are you well?'

'Very well,' Alys answered. 'I merely needed some air.'

'Of course.' Ellen's smile turned teasing. 'Many of the ladies require a breath of air when the Queen is distracted. Their suitors wait for it.'

Alys felt her cheeks turn warm. 'I have no suitor.'

'Certainly not! None of us do, on the orders of Her Majesty.' She leaned closer to whisper in Alys's ear, 'But we are young, who can fault us for enjoying a bit of admiration? We must only be very careful who we admire in return.'

Alys was confused. Did Ellen know about John? Or did she speak of something else entirely? Everyone here at court did speak in such codes, she feared she would never entirely learn it and wondered if she had missed something terribly dangerous. Just as John warned. 'I don't know what you mean.'

'Not everyone is who they claim to be,' Ellen whispered urgently. 'The Spanish might be defeated now, but they won't give up and some would aid them in such things. You never know what sympathies people truly hold. Who they really work for. Promise me you will be careful in the people you gift with your affection? So many men are dangerous, especially those who seem the most handsome, the most gallant.'

Alys could only nod, bewildered. 'I am always careful.'

'I know you are. And so am I. We must be.' Ellen's smile suddenly returned, as light and teasing as ever. 'Now, we must dance again, just once! The hunt begins early tomorrow...'

Chapter Twenty

As the long column of horses rode out from the palace stables for the Queen's hunt, Alys paused to wait for a moment at the crest of a hill and gazed back at the scene. She had hardly been able to sleep at all after the dancing, her head so a-whirl with John and Ellen's warnings that she needed the cold brush of the wind on her face to bring her back to the real world of the grey day. She had caught no glimpse of John that morning, so wondered how she could have obeyed his order to stay close. Yet it seemed there could be no danger with the Queen's guards all around.

The palace's red-brick towers and chimneys looked like a forest of stone against the pearl-grey sky and the clouds were beginning to rush together, as if it would begin to rain. Some of the ladies were already wondering if they should turn back, but the Queen, a majestic figure in green velvet perched on her pure white horse, the veil of her cap drawn down over her face, urged them onward.

The horses turned down the hill towards the Great Park. Its hills and meadows, no doubt lush and green in the summer, were a dry, stale brown now, streaked with veins of snow that had not yet melted. The bare trees stood like skeletons, frosted with ice at the tips like hard diamonds.

But Alys found she did not mind the bleak, cold landscape as some of the ladies did. The fresh wind against her cheeks, the clean country smells after the crowded corridors, felt wondrous. It made her think of home, of her long walks along the beach and to the abbey at Dunboyton, and the freedom of that place.

The freedom from confusion, as she always seemed to feel here.

The long column of riders came to a halt outside a gamekeeper's cottage, where the Queen's hounds would be released. Alys twisted around in her saddle to study the riders behind her, looking for John.

Ellen was a few riders behind her, her horse between those of her constant suitors, Sir Walter and Lord Merton. They laughed together and Ellen waved her crop in teasing menace towards Sir Walter. Ellen had said nothing else of her warnings about untrustworthy men. It was almost as if their strange little conversation at the dance had never happened.

Alys finally caught a glimpse of John, his head as usual above those courtiers around him, the plume of his cap waving in the cold wind. He gave her a small nod and then was lost to her sight again as the gamekeepers came out to make their formal greetings to the Queen.

The fox they were to chase was released, streaking away across the field as a russet blur against the brown and white of the grass, and the Queen shot off after him, her pack of hounds at her heels. Her speed and grace belied her years and she soon left everyone else behind.

Alys spurred her own horse to keep up. The courtiers

fanned out behind the Queen, an array of bright reds and winter greys against the sky, to cover the fields and woods in search of their prey.

Alys laughed as she urged her horse faster, the wind catching at her hat, rushing past her ears. John's horse galloped up beside hers and she caught a glimpse of his face. He smiled rakishly, the tension of the last few days vanished in joy at the moment.

'I'll race you!' she shouted to him.

He laughed and urged his horse faster, gaining on hers. Together, they leaped over a shallow ravine and Alys felt as if she was flying. Her doubts were all left behind in that moment.

The hounds set up a howl in the distance and the riders spun around to follow the barking. Alys, with John close behind, raced deeper into the woods, jumping lightly over ditches and fallen logs, off the lane into the trees. Her horse tossed its head, as if just as happy for the free moment as she was.

Alys laughed again as she pulled far ahead of John— just before a low-hanging branch snatched her hat from her head. She reined in her horse and tried to snatch it back.

It was only good fortune that made her move when she did, for suddenly there was a low, humming whine in the air next to her ear. An arrow, flying fast, thudded into her hat just above her hand. She screamed in shock and pulled back, her horse starting up in fear.

John leaped down from his own horse and dragged her out of her own saddle in what felt like only one movement. He carried her to the ground, his own body covering hers as his eyes scanned the horizon for threats.

Alys was frozen with shock, her mind whirling as

she tried to process what had just happened. 'Was it a gamekeeper in the wrong place?' she whispered. 'Or— or someone looking for the Queen?'

'I don't know,' he said grimly. 'I see no one nearby now. We have to get back to the others.'

He leaped lightly to his feet, reaching out to help her stand. She feared her legs were trembling too much to carry her far, but John lifted her into his own saddle. He gathered her horse's reins before he climbed up behind her and led them both out of the woods towards the Queen's noisy party as quickly as he could. He said nothing, but Alys could see the darkness in his eyes, the hard set of his jaw.

'John, what is happening?' she whispered urgently. 'Is this what you warned me about?'

He shook his head. 'Just remember, Alys—stay close to me and always be wary. I promise I will keep you safe now.'

Her throat felt dry, aching, but she nodded. Despite everything they had been through, she *did* feel safe with him now. She only wished he trusted her enough to tell her what was happening at court, what the real dangers were. The wind caught at her loosened hair and she shivered as she remembered her lost hat.

It could have been so much more lost in that moment. Alys was determined to find out what was going on. If John wouldn't tell her, she would just have to find some other means. But she refused to be afraid at every moment any longer.

God's breath, but could nothing go right that day?

The shooter lowered their bow and crouched down behind the tree to watch from a distance. The ignorant Irish girl had no idea what she was meddling with at court. She had got in the way much too often.

No one *wanted* to be rid of her. She was surely too pretty for that. But sometimes obstacles had to be swept aside, ruthlessly and quickly, before it was too late. If only King Philip had followed such advice, the terrible blunders of the Armada could have been avoided and the Spanish would be here now.

There was no time for bitterness now, despite the gall of disappointment. The next chance for Spain would be a better one, an unexpected strike that would leave Elizabeth and her traitorous friends helpless to defend themselves.

Just like the Irish girl. She was lucky that time. They had been given faulty information. Next time would be very different.

Chapter Twenty-One

'Alys! Is that you? Where are you going?'

Caught. Alys pivoted on the wooden step and glanced up the staircase, trying to smile as if she hadn't a care in the world and had a perfectly good reason for being in the wing of the castle that held John's chamber. She gave him her brightest smile and hoped it looked properly careless for court. 'I had a small errand for the Queen.'

He frowned and ran down the stairs to her side. 'Surely you should be resting after yesterday's hunt. You had quite a shock.'

'So the Queen said. She has surrounded herself with even more guards now, though she declares it must have surely been a foolish poacher.' She studied John's face, but his expression gave nothing away but concern. 'Do you agree?'

'It could very well be. We are examining a few possibilities.'

'Possibilities?' Could it be someone trying to kill the Queen, or one of her important advisers? Perhaps a Catholic taking revenge for the Armada? The possibilities truly were vast.

John smiled reassuringly. 'You need not fear, Alys. No harm can come to you here in the palace. But surely you should be resting.'

Resting was driving her to delirium, trying to read or sew or sleep in the midst of the maids'-room chaos. That was why she had come seeking John against all sense, to find some peace. But they should not be seen together. Any nugget of new gossip was like gold at court and reputations were fragile. 'There is no rest in the maids' chamber. They all leap about, practising their dancing all the time when they aren't quarrelling or crying.'

John laughed. 'I can see where peace would be impossible there.'

'Yes, I can't—well, I can't quite forget how it felt yesterday. It gives me terrible dreams. That arrow...' Her words choked off and she shuddered. Going from perfect laughter and happiness to such terror in only an instant had been horrifying.

John put his arm around her shoulders, warm and strong. His face was solemn as he looked down at her. 'Of course you cannot. To come so close to death makes all else look and feel strange, as if nightmares are all that can be true.'

Alys nodded. That was exactly how it felt—like real life had vanished and left only strangeness and fear in its place.

'Come sit in my chamber for a while,' he said. 'I promise there are no maids arguing and leaping about in La Volta there. You can have quiet for a while.'

Alys was quite tempted. She remembered his room from her ill-fated search and longed for its dim warmth, its silence. But was it safe for her to be alone with John again? Dared she trust herself with him?

'I—surely you were leaving on an errand?' she said.

'It can wait. You are more important. Come, sit down, Alys. You look rather pale.'

She did feel a little shaky. She took his arm and let him help her up the stairs to his chamber. It was just as she remembered, the sturdy furniture, the pile of books on the desk. Today the draperies were drawn back from the small window to let in the greyish daylight and a new blue rug was laid on the hearth. The bed, with its curtains drawn back, seemed to loom too large near her, drawing her imagination.

John found her a cushioned stool and went to pour out two goblets of wine. 'It is not the grandest chamber in the palace, I know,' he said lightly. 'I shall have to work harder to climb the ladder of favour. Mayhap buy some more elaborate doublets to catch the Queen's eye.'

Alys laughed as she took the goblet from him. To her surprise, he sprawled out on the floor beside her, his long legs stretched out on the rug. 'I think your doublets are perfect. I hope you never decide on as many slashings and silver buttons as men like Lord Merton.'

'Merton is said to be the height of courtly fashion.'

Alys thought of the man's towering plumes and gold-edged ruffs, and hoped that was not true. 'At home they would just call him a strutting peacock.'

'Do you miss your home?'

Alys sat back on her stool and sipped at her wine, thinking over his question. 'Sometimes I do. I'm used to hearing my own thoughts, following my own schedule, and that is impossible here. And I miss the sea.'

'And what do you like here at court? Anything at all?'

She liked *him*. Though she knew she could never say that aloud. 'I admit I do like the clothes. And the food.

Though soon I shall be so large from all the sugared wafers and spiced capons I won't be able to wear the clothes!'

John laughed. 'That cannot be true.'

'Perhaps not. All the running after errands up and down stairs balances everything quite nicely.' Alys studied the chamber as she finished her wine. It really was nice in there, peaceful, far from the maids and the rest of the court in their never-ending noise and movement. She wished she could just stay there with John, cocooned in their own quiet space, all dangers closed out just for a while.

Just as it had been at their old abbey dairy, their hiding place. But those cosy, intimate moments had been an illusion, with the fearful world right on their doorstep.

'What do you like about court, John?' she said.

John stretched sinuously, reaching up to run his fingers absentmindedly through his hair. It left it falling in unruly waves over his brow, so boyish and informal. It made him look different from the perfectly polished courtier, younger, lighter.

'The food,' he said. 'Especially those little apple tarts with cinnamon, the ones the cook makes look like little pastry flowers.'

Alys laughed. 'Is that all? Though I admit they *are* rather luscious.'

'Nay. I suppose I like court because I can do something, do things of use and import.'

Alys thought about what men did at home, farming and fishing and importing. 'Your estate is not of import?'

A frown flickered over his face. 'It could be. Once it was the greatest manor in the neighbourhood, a source of employment for dozens of servants and tenant farmers.

It was greatly neglected by my father. One day I will be able to restore it all, once I earn my way here.'

'I suppose I am trying to do the same thing here. To help my family. My father has served so long In Ireland, but now he needs a warmer, safer place for his retirement.'

'Did your mother like it in Ireland? It must have been quite different from Spain.'

'She did often speak of the sun. But she loved my father very much and he loved her. They made a happy home together, even if they might have longed for some place different.'

'My mother did not like Huntley at all and who could blame her? It was a miserable place with my father there. She lost much in her marriage.'

'But she had you. That must have given her some happiness, even if only for a while.'

'I do hope so.'

'You don't remember her at all?'

He shook his head. 'I wish I *had* known her. I like to think if she had lived longer, lived to see me grow up, I could have rescued her from her unhappiness. Given her the home she truly deserved.' He reached out to take the edge of her blue-silk skirt between his fingertips, studying it closer as if some secret was written in the fine fabric. 'Everyone deserves a home, do they not? A place where they belong. Yet too few are granted such a thing.'

Alys's heart ached at the sadness of his words, at the thought of families torn apart. Of John as a motherless boy, longing for warmth. Always searching, as she was, for a place to belong.

'Oh, John.' She slid down to sit beside him on the floor. He watched her closely, his eyes such a bright green, so full of swirling depths, like the sea itself. She felt as though she could fall into them and be lost, like plunging beneath the waves to find a whole new world.

He rolled to his side, reaching out to cradle her cheek with his palm. His long fingers slid into her hair, loosening it from its pins. He caressed the long strands, wrapping them around his wrist until they were bound together. Her lips parted on a sigh, but she couldn't move away, couldn't even look away from his gaze. She was lost. He cupped his other hand to the back of her head and drew her closer.

Her eyes closed tightly as he kissed her, as his lips sought hers with a hunger she had never known before. As if he longed for her, only her, as a starving man granted his one life-giving wish, and she responded with her whole heart.

She moaned softly and as her lips parted his tongue pressed forward, seeking hers. He tasted of wine and of that dark sweetness she had learned was only his. It was more intoxicating, more wonderful than anything else she had ever known.

He groaned, and their tongues touched and tangled, all artifice washed away in the ocean of sheer need. Come what may, ruin or wonder, none of it mattered when they were together.

Through that shimmering, blurry haze of need and tenderness she felt his fingers comb through her hair, pushing away the last of the pins as he spread the dark curtain over her shoulders. His lips slid from hers and he buried his face in her hair, in the curve of her neck.

'Sweet Alys, my angel,' he whispered. 'You are so beautiful.'

'Not as beautiful as you,' she murmured. She reached

for him as she laid back on the rug, pulling him on top of her so she could kiss him again, could press her hungry lips to his smooth-shaven cheek, his strong jaw, his throat, where the lifeblood beat so frantically. She unbuttoned his doublet, clumsily slipping the carved buttons free from the velvet, desperate to feel his warm skin. He tasted wondrous, of the sun and the winter wind and wine, and she wanted all of him. She wanted to hold him so close she became a part of him and neither of them were ever lonely again.

He whispered hoarse, incoherent words as his lips trailed down her neck to the lace edge of her bodice, his tongue swirling in the hollow at its base, as if their lifeblood could meet there. He kissed the soft slope of her breast, pushed high by her fashionable bodice. She gasped at the waves of pleasure that followed his mouth, the touch of his hands on her bare skin.

She drove her fingers into his hair, holding him close as he dotted a ribbon of kisses along the line of her bodice. 'I want to see you, Alys.'

She nodded, mutely arching her back so he could loosen her bodice lacings. The stiffened silk fell away with her thin chemise and he drew it aside until she was revealed to him.

For a moment, as he studied her silently, she held her breath. No man had ever seen her thus before and she longed for him to think her beautiful. She had felt so certain, so safe, only a moment ago. Now she felt so—shy.

She tried to draw her chemise up over her again, but his hand stopped her. 'Alys, you are so perfect. Perfect,' he said.

She laughed happily and drew him back down to her.

His lips closed over her aching nipple, caressing, drawing, until she moaned in delight.

Her eyes fluttered closed. She pushed his unfastened doublet off his shoulders until he shrugged it away. She wrapped her arms around him, her palms sliding along the groove of his spine, feeling the muscle tension of his shoulders beneath the thin linen of his shirt. It was still not nearly enough.

She wanted him in every way there could be, every way she had heard about among the maidservants. She wanted only him and the need burned like a bonfire.

'Please, John,' she whispered, throwing every ladylike caution away. 'Make love to me.'

He stared down at her, raising himself to his elbows on either side of her. His green eyes were shadowed with a flaming desire that matched hers, a lust that was out of control. But there was also a cold shard of caution and that she did not want. She couldn't bear for him to draw away from her now. Not when they had come so far to find each other again.

'Alys,' he said roughly. 'Have you ever—been with a man before?'

She shook her head, feeling a blush stain her cheeks.

'Angel.' He rolled away to sit up beside her, but he still held on to her hand. She saw the gold ring glint on his finger, the ring she had worn on the voyage to England which gave her courage. 'It will hurt the first time. And you know there could be—consequences. There are ways we can prevent it, but they are not certain.'

Alys swallowed hard, as she remembered whispered tales of court ladies who had tried to hide their secret pregnancies and been found out and cast out of court. But surely she was more clever than they? And she had

John beside her. 'I know,' she said. 'But I also know I want you. Do you not want me?'

'Want you?' He ran his hand roughly through his hair. 'I have wanted you ever since I opened my eyes after the shipwreck to see an angel.'

'Then we are right to have this.' She stood up, filled with a new confidence, a new joy. John was here with her, when once she had thought she had lost him for ever. Even if it was just for this one time, she wanted to be with him completely. She reached for the ties at her waist and fumbled with her heavy skirt, but she was shaking so much she merely knotted the tapes.

'Let me help,' he said gently. He rose to her side, his long fingers reaching out to deftly untie the knots. Her overskirt, her embroidered petticoats, all fell away like a cloud. He finished unlacing her bodice and untying the points of her sleeves, and she found herself standing in only her chemise, her stockings and shoes.

He slid down until he knelt at her feet. Gently, slowly, he removed first one shoe, then the other, running his thumb in a soft caress over the sensitive curve of her ankle. His palm flattened and slid along her calf, the bend of her knee, slowly, softly, until she could barely breathe.

He reached the hem of her chemise and lifted it up until he revealed her blue-satin garters, the bare skin of her thigh above. His fingertips traced that line where skin met silk and she thought she might snap from the tension of anticipation. The core of her womanhood felt so damp, so heavy with a need she had never known before.

At last, at last, he touched her *there* and she cried out. Her knees buckled beneath her with the jolt of hot pleasure. He caught her in his arms and carried her to his waiting bed.

He reached down to draw back the bedclothes before he laid her down amidst the linens. As she propped herself on the bolsters to watch, he pulled off his shirt, revealing his bare chest to her at last, just as she had imagined in too many fevered dreams. He was such a contrast of shadows and the golden glow of his skin. He was lean from exercise and a life lived outdoors, powerful and also beautiful.

She found she could not look away from him. He was truly a wondrous sight, the most handsome she had ever seen. He leaned on to the bed, bracing his palms on the mattress to either side of her, holding her a willing captive. His head lowered, his mouth capturing hers in a passionate kiss. There was no doubt or fear now, only the knowledge that for this moment he was hers, as she was his. A moment that was meant to be ever since the sea gave him to her.

He broke their kiss only to unfasten his breeches. Her legs fell apart and he eased between them, his body pressed close to hers. His manhood, which she had only seen before in drawings and thought a fearsome thing, was heavy and hard, hot against her. She wrapped her thighs around his hips, arching up against him, trying to feel yet more of him, all of him. His naked skin against hers made her cry out with pleasure.

His moans answered hers, his mouth trailing away from hers to press a soft kiss to the sensitive hollow just below her ear. 'I am sorry, my angel,' he whispered.

She nodded, closing her eyes as she felt him reach between their bodies. He gently pressed her legs further apart and she braced her feet flat to the mattress as his fingers slid inside of her, testing. Then his manhood followed, sliding slowly, ever so slowly, against her damp folds. She tightened her jaw against the stretching, burning sensation, her shoulders tensing.

'I'm sorry,' he whispered again, his whole body held taut above her.

He drove forward and she felt a tearing deep inside, a flash of lightning-quick pain. She tried to hold back her cry, but it escaped her lips.

''Tis all right now,' he murmured. His body went perfectly still against hers. His breath rushed against her skin, as if he held his power tightly leashed. 'It will fade now, Alys, I promise. I will make it better.'

He was right, it *was* fading. As he lay still, their bodies joined, she felt the pain slowly fade away, leaving only a tiny curl of pleasure low in her belly. She ran her hands down his back, feeling the hot, sweat-damp skin over his lean muscles, pressing him closer to her.

He pulled back slowly and drove forward again, a bit deeper, and that pleasure unfurled. Every movement of his body against hers, every moan and sigh, drove that pleasure higher, like a bonfire. It blinded her with its brilliant light, that hot spark of pure joy.

They moved together, faster and faster, reaching for that sun. He suddenly arched above her, shouting out her name as he pulled out of her.

Alys hardly noticed. Those sparks had blown into an enormous explosion of red-and-blue flames that threatened to consume her from within.

Then everything fell into darkness. When she opened her eyes again, she found herself collapsed on the rumpled bedclothes, John beside her.

His arm was close around her waist, holding her tightly. His eyes were closed, his breath laboured as if he too had felt that wondrous, devastating explosion of joy.

'John…' she whispered.

'Shh…' he said, not opening his eyes. He just pulled her closer, until she was curled against him. 'Just rest for a moment, Alys my angel.'

She closed her eyes again, resting her head on his shoulder as she felt the chilly air of the room beyond their bed brush over her damp skin. She would happily sleep for a moment, lay down all her worries and just stay here in his arms. She could happily do that for ever and ever.

John held Alys as she slept, listening to her soft breath, feeling her stir against him as the day slipped onward and evening gathered closer. They would have to part very soon, but he couldn't let her go. Not yet. That hour with her had been the greatest of his life and he feared he would never know it again.

Soon, all too soon, he would have to let her go; their magical hour would end.

But it had been magical indeed and that was more than he ever thought he could have in the coldness of life. His sweet angel, his Alys, had been a gift in his lonely life twice now, a gift he did not deserve. He had never imagined he could feel this way about a lady, about anything. But the gift had come at a most complicated moment. He now had to keep her safe as well as do his task.

He drew her closer, pressing a gentle kiss to her forehead. She murmured, her soft brow wrinkling in a frown, as if he interrupted a sweet dream.

'It grows late,' he whispered.

'Too cold to get out of bed,' she answered and burrowed closer to him under the blankets.

'I would love nothing more than to stay here with you

for days,' he said and he truly did. The peaceful moments he found with her were the sweetest ever. 'And for nights.'

'That sounds delightful,' she said. 'But I am sure we would be missed long before that.' She touched his cheek gently, tracing his features lightly with her fingertips. He caught her fingertip between his lips, making her giggle.

'I should take you back to your chamber,' he said reluctantly.

She gave a sad little nod. She rolled away from him, sitting on the edge of the bed to reach for her discarded chemise and skirts. John thought the curve of her back was so wondrously beautiful, so pale and elegant as the length of her glossy dark hair draped over her shoulder.

He sat up behind her, kissing the soft, vulnerable nape of her neck. She shivered and curled back against him as he wrapped his arms around her, holding her close. They sat there, bound together in silence, in that one perfect moment that was out of time, out of the dangers of the courtly world, and belonged only to the two of them.

'I must go,' she whispered. 'I told Ellen I would be at the banquet tonight.'

John hated to let her go out in a crowd such as that, vulnerable to the danger that always lurked around the Queen, as it had in the woods. But she was not alone now. He was always with her, even when she might not think it. Even when she came to hate him, as she surely would one day all too soon.

'Be careful tonight, Alys angel,' he said. 'Always be wary.'

She glanced back at him over her shoulder, a small frown on her brow. 'I am always careful. What do you think will happen tonight?'

'Nothing, I hope.' He drew her close to him again for one more soft kiss. 'Just be careful.'

She wrapped her arms around him and hugged him back, her head nestled on his shoulder as if she had always been just there. As if she was meant to be just there. 'I will be careful, John, if you will also.'

He gave her a grin, one of the careless smiles that always disarmed and distracted. It did not this time, for her frown deepened. 'I will be careful, too, Alys. I always am.'

She just held on to him even tighter, and he admitted—he had never felt more at peace in his life.

Until he knew he had to let her go. He reached down to help her gather her clothes—and he froze when he saw that her sleeve had a bow missing. A silver-satin bow.

Chapter Twenty-Two

Later that night, alone as he prepared for the night's revels, John turned the silver-satin bow between his fingers and envisioned the place where it should have been on Alys's sleeve. It had been *Alys* who came into his chamber and searched his things. Alys who put herself into danger here at court, playing a game she could not understand.

But that had to end now. He had seen too many people hurt, even killed, by messing in courtly schemes. He would never see Alys one of them. His gentle, beautiful Alys—she was too good for that world and for him. He had used her badly.

It would be so hard, to refuse that brightness she brought into every day when she was near, to turn away that glimpse of something good in his cold life. But he cared about her too much to selfishly hold on to her, no matter how much he longed to.

She deserved better than him, than the life he led. He had to end it now, no matter how much it hurt him.

'Wassail, wassail all over the town, our bowl it is white and our ale it is brown! A wassailing bowl we'll drink to thee…'

Alys laughed with the other ladies as they made their way along the gallery to the Queen's gift-giving and fireworks in the Great Hall. She worried she must look utterly silly, the way she had been smiling all afternoon as they got ready for the party, but she couldn't help herself. That small, warm bit of happiness she hid deep in her heart couldn't be repressed.

She'd had little sleep. Even after she left John and crept back into the maids' chamber, even after dinner and reading with the Queen, she had laid in her own bed and pressed her face to the pillow to keep from laughing at the delicious memories.

She was surely now a fallen woman. But wickedness felt as if it was entirely worth it. Even now she seemed to float on a fluffy cloud of delightful secrets.

They moved through the open doors into the Great Hall to take their places around the Queen's dais. The room seemed transformed into a treasure cave, sparkling with the gifts laid out on the long tables. Jewels, gilded salt cellars and goblets, bolts of satin and velvet and pelts of fine fur, all sparkled in the torchlight. But even such riches couldn't hold Alys's attention as she searched the gathered faces for John.

At first she could not see him, the crowd was packed so thickly, but then she glimpsed him with a group of men at the other side of the room. Her stomach lurched in a sudden jolt of pure excitement. Everything in her cried out to run to him, to throw her arms around him and kiss him. But the glittering crowd was there, watching, always watching, hoping for a scrap of gossip.

Alys bit her lip to keep from smiling and slowed her steps to a near-crawl as she passed him. She hoped desperately he would see her and come to speak to her, give her some sign that their time together meant as much to him as it had to her.

He *did* see her and he smiled, but it was not the joyful grin she had hoped for. It was quick, tight, vanishing in an instant.

He excused himself from his friends and made his way through the crowd to her side. His hand pressed hers fleetingly, hidden by the heavy folds of her satin skirt.

How very handsome he looked that night, the glossy dark waves of his hair brushed back to reveal the amethyst drop in his ear, the austere angles of his face. The gold embroidery on the high collar of his purple-velvet doublet set off his sun-tinged skin perfectly and he was every inch the stylish, sophisticated courtier.

Yet Alys preferred him as he was earlier, when they were alone in his chamber, with his hair rumpled and his eyes heavy-lidded with sated passion.

His smile then had been so different than it was now.

'Lady Alys,' he said quietly. 'How lovely you look this evening.'

'Th-thank you, Sir John,' she managed to say, though her throat had gone dry.

'Can you meet me later?' he whispered quickly. 'Here in the Great Hall, perhaps over by that tapestry, when everyone is outside for the fireworks.'

Only moments ago Alys would have been overjoyed at such an invitation. Now she wasn't so sure. 'Of course.'

He nodded and turned to melt back into the crowd, quickly lost to her sight. Alys felt a touch on her sleeve and she spun around to find Ellen watching her with a sympathetic smile.

'Is anything amiss, Alys?' she asked.

'Nay,' Alys answered brightly. 'Not a thing.'

* * *

All the courtiers crowded close to the stone parapets, bundled in warm furs and velvet cloaks against the icy wind that blew off the river and passing goblets of warm, spiced wine between them. There was much laughter and exultation over the success of their gifts to the Queen and the fineness of hers to them. The tables of the Great Hall were piled high with jewels, lengths of brocade and satins, feathered fans with ivory handles, exotic wines, and silver plate.

Alys automatically smiled and laughed with the others, but she was watchful, tense. John had not yet reappeared at the party and soon she would have to find him in the Great Hall. She sipped at her wine, trying to pretend she was not searching through the crowd for him. She could see little beyond the press of people. She drew her new embroidered shawl closer, a Christmas gift from her father that made her feel closer to him that night.

The black sky suddenly exploded above them, a crackling, glittering shower of red and white and green fireworks. A long waterfall of blue star-like lights followed, showering down on the gardens below. It was wondrously beautiful and for an instant Alys was pulled out of her worries at the beauty. It seemed to ignite a spark of hope in her own heart, hope for the future. She whirled around, longing to find John so she could share that hope with him.

Everyone else seemed enraptured by the fireworks, their faces turned upward. Alys slipped away from the other maids as their attention was on the sky. She hurried back into the palace and down a spiral staircase to the gallery.

She found him in the Great Hall, waiting near the tapestry where they had once hidden at a dance. The memory of that night overcame her and she lifted her skirts to dash to him, longing to feel that kiss again, to be reassured. He caught her by her arms and held her close.

'Alys—angel,' he said, and for an instant she thought he *would* kiss her. But instead his touch slid down her silk sleeves to hold her hands in his. He held her away from him.

Alys stared up at him, bewildered. His jaw was tight, his sea-green eyes darkened. 'What is amiss?' she whispered.

'I'm sorry,' he said hoarsely. 'Very sorry, my angel. I should never have let things go so far between us.'

She shook her head in hurt confusion. He still held her hands, they still stood so close together, but she sensed he was very far away from her. It felt as if a cold storm wind rushed between them, pushing them apart.

'What—things?' she stammered. She felt like a fool again—she had let him into her heart twice now, only to have him shatter it.

'I have work I must finish and I was selfish to involve you in any way,' he said. 'I should have seen that after the day of the hunt. I was wrong, very wrong to behave thus. I put you in danger again and I am sorry, Alys. I cannot do that again.'

'We both wanted this!' she cried. She took a stumbling step towards him, but he backed away. He was so distant from her and she couldn't reach him. 'Whatever the danger is, it doesn't matter. We have faced danger before.'

'Of course it matters! I made an irresponsible mistake. It must end here.'

'End?' Alys felt as if ice trickled down her spine, numbing her, making her feel entirely removed from the scene. If only it was not so terribly real, the shattering of her fragile hopes.

'I have work to do here at court and I've let myself be distracted from it,' he said coldly, not looking at her. It was as if they were suddenly strangers. 'You have your own duties. I wouldn't bring you trouble with the Queen, Alys, that would be poor repayment for all you have done for me.'

'I care not for that, John,' she protested. She didn't understand. Surely what they had, what they could have, was what mattered? Perhaps they could not be together then, but in the future...

The numbness faded and she felt instead the prickle of hot tears. Angry, confused tears she impatiently dashed away.

She had thought, ever since Dunboyton, they had a rare connection and was sure he felt the same. But now he watched her so coldly, so distant. She didn't know what could be happening, unless...

'You prefer someone else,' she whispered. So many of the ladies in their chamber cried over men who had changed their romantic allegiances. 'One of the other maids.' Someone more sophisticated, who could help him restore his home as she could not.

He frowned, but did not deny her words. 'I am sorry,' was all he said again. 'It is not that, but—this.' He held up a small silver-satin bow, and with a shock Alys realised it was from her own sleeve. The one she had to mend after she foolishly went to search John's rooms.

'I—I did not mean...' she stammered.

'I know you did not,' he answered tersely. 'You play a dangerous game here at court, Alys, one you cannot understand. It is my life, though, and I can't let you be a part of it. You should go back to your safe maids' chamber and forget playing at spies. I cannot help you now.'

Alys spun around, dashing away from him before her shameful tears could fall. She would never show him, or anyone, the dreadful, stabbing pain he caused her by pushing her away so suddenly. The shame she felt at taking a step so terribly wrong.

Alys didn't even know where she was running, she just knew she had to get away. She had been wrong, so wrong, about John, about so many things. She rushed past the laughing crowds of people in the Great Hall, trying to keep her head high, a smile pasted on her lips. She would *not* cry. She was a Drury, and a de Vargas. She would not crumble now.

No matter how much her heart ached.

'Lady Alys!' she heard one of the other maids call out and she froze. Her escape was utterly blocked and she feared that even a word might crumble the fragile shell she had gathered around herself.

But she had no choice. She had to answer.

Alys turned to see one of the youngest maids, the pretty, slightly silly Mistress Danton, hurrying towards her through the crowd, a confused expression on her dimpled face.

'Lady Alys, Her Majesty seeks a letter from her chamber, which she forgot to sign earlier and which is now needed most urgently.' Mistress Danton sighed and shook her head. 'Why it is now so urgent, I do not know, but it must be found. She said Lady Ellen would know where it is, but I cannot find her at all. I do not know what to do!'

'Shall I fetch the letter, then?' Alys asked, glad of an errand, a purpose. A chance to escape the crowd. 'I am sure I could find it without too much trouble.'

Mistress Danton's face crumpled in relief. 'Oh, thank you, Lady Alys! It is sealed with green wax.'

'I will go at once.' Alys hurried out the doors of the hall. The corridors were icy cold away from the crowds and the roaring fireplaces, and Alys shivered as she drew her new shawl closer around her shoulders. There was silence along with the chill, blessed quiet where the painful emotions swirling in her mind could grow still and she could numb herself.

She dashed up the stairs and through the ghostly empty Privy Chamber. There were a few guards there, but one slept and snored, and the others played at dice. They paid no heed to Alys as she rushed past them.

In the Queen's bedchamber, the candles were already lit for her return and the bedclothes folded back to wait for the Queen's return. All was as it should be.

But Alys found she was not alone in the chamber. Ellen was already at the Queen's desk, along with a man whose back was turned to Alys. They were sorting hurriedly through the royal documents and Ellen looked distraught.

'We haven't much time,' she said. 'They will return soon and if they find Sir Matthew's report…'

'Do not grow hysterical now, Ellen,' the man growled and Alys recognised Lord Merton's voice. 'You knew what could happen when you agreed to receive Master Peter's letters. You cannot grow pale now.'

Alys gasped and spun around to flee, to summon the guards. She could hardly believe it—her friend, a traitor! But there it was, right in front of her. She called out.

'Nay, stop her!' Lord Merton cried as Alys ran for the door, her shawl tumbling from her shoulders. She didn't get more than a few steps when there was a flurry of heavy, running footsteps and a strong arm caught her around her waist and jerked her off her feet. A gloved hand clamped over her mouth, smothering her cries.

Alys twisted in Merton's iron grip, panic rising up in her like a cold, drowning wave. She bit down hard on the suffocating hand, penetrating leather and nicking skin. The metallic tang of blood almost made her gag.

'God's teeth!' Merton shouted.

'Let her go,' Ellen cried, a tinge of panic to her voice. 'She has done nothing, she isn't part of this.'

'She is now,' Merton said. 'Shall I finish her?'

'Nay!'

'Not here,' another man said and Alys recognised Sir Walter. What conspiracy was this, then? What was happening between those three? 'That would have the whole palace down on us if her body was found in the Queen's own chamber. Besides, she might know something. Wasn't her mother Spanish?'

'You can't kill her!' Ellen sobbed. 'Let her go.'

'You know we can't do that,' Merton said and shouted out when Alys managed to bite down again. 'Z'wounds, but she is a vixen!'

'Must I do everything? Here, hold her down so I can bind her,' Sir Walter said.

'I said leave her alone!' Ellen cried. 'This cannot go on any more. Let her go!'

There was a terrible sound, as if a series of slaps, and Alys heard Ellen fall to the floor. There was silence from her then, but Alys had little time to fear for her. She herself was roughly pushed to the floor and a gag knotted over her mouth. Her heavy satin skirts weighed her down, but she managed to kick the man trying to bind her squarely in the chest as he tried to tie her feet.

'Enough of that,' Merton growled and she glimpsed a gloved fist flying towards her. There was no time even for fear. A burst of pain, fiery and sharp, exploded in her jaw, then she fell deep into a cold darkness.

What had he done?

John moved through the crowd, bowing and smiling at their greetings as if nothing in the world was amiss, even as his chest ached physically at the memory of Alys's pale, shocked face as she ran from him. He had wanted with all his strength to run after her, to grab her up in his arms and never let her go. But he knew he could not. He had vowed to focus on his work again, to let her move on with her life and find true happiness, as she deserved. He had done what was right, he was sure of that. Why, then, was it such agony?

Doubt was certainly not a sensation he was familiar with. He could never succeed in his dangerous work if he ever doubted a step. Yet now it tugged at him with its sharp, cold fingers. In trying to do what was best, had he fatally wounded them both?

He studied the crowd around him, but Alys was not there. Surely she should have returned to the party long before? After all that had happened…

A lady bumped into him and apologised in a flustered flurry. He looked down, half-hoping it would be Alys, but it was a Mistress Danton, tiny and golden, her eyes wide and confused.

'Can I be of some help, Mistress Danton?' he asked.

'Oh, Sir John! I am looking for Lady Alys Drury—have you seen her? She went to fetch a paper for Her Majesty from her chamber and has not returned. The Queen is asking for her. I cannot find her anywhere.'

John frowned, a tiny, cold prickle of unease forming in his mind. Alys, of course, could be in any number of places, perfectly safe. Yet he could not quite shake away the feeling that all was not right, a sense that had always served him well in his work.

'I will go search the Privy Chamber, Mistress Danton, and ask if the guards have seen her,' he said. 'You ask in the kitchens.'

She nodded and he left her to dodge around the now-drunken revellers, making his way out of the crowds and up the empty staircase to the Queen's quarters. He scowled at the lack of guards everywhere, even as he came near the Privy Chamber. Had they been given a small respite, perhaps a ration of ale to celebrate the holiday? Or was something more sinister afoot?

He wrapped his fingers around the hilt of his dagger and made his way carefully through the empty room. The darkness of the usually crowded chamber felt ominous and he could hear nothing in the echoing silence. The empty throne lurked, shadowy, on its dais.

Even the Queen's own chamber, usually so inaccessible to normal mortals, was empty. A few flickering candles and a low-burning fire in the grate was all that illuminated the cave-like space. The papers on the desk were disarranged, some of them tumbled to the floor.

And lying there in their midst was a lady huddled in her white skirts, perfectly still.

'Alys!' John called in a rush of cold fear. He dashed to the woman's side and knelt down, reaching out to touch her throat. A thin, thready pulse of life beat there, but he saw it was not Alys. It was Lady Ellen, her golden hair tumbling down, her face bruised.

She blinked, as if slowly coming back to consciousness, and let out a low sob. 'Oh, Sir John! Thank God you have come. They have taken her! It is my fault, I never meant for this to happen. My brother said…'

John sat back on his heels, going very still. The old, cold battle instinct was strong in him again, that tense, ominous feeling that came before the clash of steel, the blood and death. 'They have taken who?'

'Alys, of course,' Ellen sobbed. 'Oh, please! You must find her and quickly.'

Chapter Twenty-Three

Alys slowly came awake, as if she was swimming up from some dark depth towards a tiny, distant spot of star-like light. Her whole body ached and everything in her screamed to fall back into the painless dark. But she knew she could not. She had to fight onward to that light and grab on to it.

She forced her eyes open and the sudden light made her head throb as if it would split open. She made herself breathe slowly, carefully, until she could see straight again.

She was not in her chamber at Dunboyton, or even at the maids' room at Greenwich, but somewhere she had never seen before, some place strange and rather fearsome. She was lying on a dirt floor, a thatched ceiling above her, shadows shifting all around to reveal a small, bare space.

Then she remembered it all, in a hot, dream-like rush. The Queen's bedchamber, Ellen and those two men going through the Queen's papers. Being hit, falling, that darkness.

But where was she now and, more important—where

were *they*? What did they want of her? She had obviously caught them in some treasonous act. Whatever it was, she refused to surrender to them. She was a Drury, she would fight.

As the cold, painful waves of her headache receded a bit, she was able to push herself up and examine her surroundings more closely. It seemed to be a cottage, somewhat similar to the abbey dairy she had once shared with John. There was no furniture except for a travelling trunk, draped with a blanket. The window spaces were covered over with boards.

She could hear the whine of the winter wind outside, sweeping around the walls. And something else, something that sounded like the blur of angry voices. A heavy silence fell amid the pounding hooves of a horse departing and, before Alys could react, the door flew open and heavy, booted footsteps pounded across the dirt floor. A hard hand grabbed her arm and yanked her up painfully, loosening her bonds with quick, jerky movements.

She spun around and saw it was Lord Merton, his face red with fury as he stared down at her. His over-fashionable doublet was torn, the sleeve stained with blood, and she remembered how he had knocked Ellen to the floor before driving his fist into her own jaw.

Alys felt fury wash over, sweeping away fear. 'How dare you!' she screamed. 'Traitor!'

Merton scowled, grabbing her by the shoulders and shaking her until her teeth rattled. Her head felt like it would explode under the onslaught, but she managed to twist hard under his grasp and wrench herself away. She had to get away from this man, no matter what.

He snatched at her again and she ducked away as she

slapped out at him. Her nails scratched in a bright red arc down his cheek.

'Witch!' he shouted. He grabbed her arm again, nearly yanking it from its socket, and she scratched him with her other hand at the same time kicking out at his leg. She landed a lucky blow and he fell back with a curse. She took the advantage and ran as fast as she could, ducking out of the cottage and into the freezing night. She had no idea where she was, where she was going, but she kept running.

Her breath ached in her lungs, her stomach lurching with fear as she dodged around the dark hulks of trees. She could barely hear anything, her heart was pounding so loudly, but Lord Merton let out a roar behind her, driving her onward.

'Come back here!' he shouted. 'You will only die in the darkness, you stupid witch.' He tripped over one of the fallen logs she had clambered across, giving her more of an advantage in distance, despite her skirts and her dancing slippers.

Then she came to a fork in the pathways and for an instant she was baffled, not knowing which way to turn. A tree was at her back, a stout old oak, and she suddenly remembered when she would sometimes climb trees at the abbey at home, much to her mother's distress. She could go high then, in the monks' old orchard; could she do it now?

She quickly tucked up her heavy skirts and jumped up to the lowest branch of the tree. She strained to pull herself up, ignoring the way the bark scratched at her palms, and grabbed the next branch up and the next. Her hands slid on the icy wood, but she kept pulling herself upward, not daring to think of anything else.

She could not look at the ground, could not listen to Merton's shouted threats as he found her and circled the base of her sanctuary tree. She just had to keep going up. She felt the tip of his sword catch at her stocking, making her leg sting, but in the next instance she was out of his reach.

At last she reached a vee in the stout trunk and wrapped her arms around it tightly as the wind caught at her hair. She closed her eyes and made herself picture John. Not his cold expression as he told her they could not be, but his smile by their fire in Ireland, his kiss, the touch of his hand. His laughter. Surely he would come for her, even if he was angry. Surely he cared enough to do that. Didn't he?

She prayed harder than she ever had in her life that it was so.

Help me, she begged silently. *Find me!*

He had to find Alys, and soon, before those villains could hurt her. Ellen's sobbing confession had told him they would stop at nothing to achieve their goals of seeing Queen Elizabeth overthrown. Anyone who got in their way would pay a terrible price.

He urged his horse faster through the night, paying no heed to the cold wind that caught at his cloak, to the lights of the palace behind him. Finding her was all that mattered; Alys was all that ever mattered. He loved her, he could see that now so very clearly, and he had been foolish to try to deny that. He had thought he could leave her behind in Ireland, that it was best for her, and she had come to him again anyway. She was a great gift and he had been a fool to deny that at all.

He had to tell her that, before it was all too late.

He followed the tracks left in the dusting of snow on the ground. Surely no one else had come this way that night. Ellen could not remember where their abandoned cottage lair was, but she remembered the river nearby, the woods behind them.

The thought of his Alys out there in the cold night, frightened and unsure, made him feel a burning anger he had forgotten was within him. The years of fighting in the Low Countries, of spying on the Spanish and living on their hellish ships, had meant he had had to freeze any feelings. To put up a shield of ice in order to do his tasks. That work, bringing down England's enemies and restoring his own family honour, was all that mattered.

But now—now a burning fury swept away the ice and he knew if he was to find Alys, it had to be defeated.

He urged his horse down a narrow track between the trees, scanning the night around him for any flash of movement. He thought of Alys's sweet smile, the way her head rested on his shoulder. His beautiful, sweet saviour. She had not left him on that beach to die and he would never leave her now. She had made him dare to think of a future, a *real* future, as he never had before. A home, a family—an end to frozen loneliness.

And now she had been snatched away from him, just as he had found her again. But he would save her and make her kidnappers pay so dearly for daring to hurt her. That was all that mattered now.

At last, he noticed something in the blank darkness, a snap of light between the trees. He reined in his horse and left it concealed behind the branches. He drew his sword from its scabbard and crept silently forward, following that light. He found himself in a small clearing, a ramshackle cottage at its centre. The walls looked so crooked he wondered they had not collapsed, but a horse stood nearby and he could hear the echo of incoherent shouts. As he watched, narrow-eyed, the door flew open and Alys ran through, closely followed by Lord Merton.

The man's ridiculous slashed and padded doublet was torn, his hat lost and his hair standing on end. His face was a bright red as he bellowed for Alys to stop, but she disappeared between the trees. Merton followed, crashing like a bull, and John followed silently on light feet, silently willing Alys to run faster and faster.

She did give a very good chase, he thought with pride as he tracked them through the woods. Her light footsteps in the snow were far ahead of Merton's and the man kept bellowing like a wounded bull. But they eluded his sight.

Until he heard a woman's scream, breaking through that eerie, glass-like night stillness. Holding to the hilt of his sword, John followed that sound to a crossroads in the pathway. A most astonishing sight met his gaze. Alys was up in a tree whose base Lord Merton stalked, shouting and waving his sword. Alys was very high up; John saw his Irish warrior lady perched on a stout branch beyond reach of Merton's prodding sword. She screamed down at him as she dodged his stabs, her words snatched away by the icy wind, but her furious tone most clear.

'Merton!' John shouted, holding his own sword out in challenge as he stepped towards the tree. 'If you are intent on a fight, here I am. Cease bullying defenceless ladies. Lady Ellen has told her tale and you shall never escape.'

Merton swung around, his face distorted by red fury. His sword arced away from Alys, towards John—just as he wished. 'Defenceless? The wench stabbed me! I should have known a traitor to our Spanish cause would come for her. You shall both burn in hell.'

'Not yet, I think,' John said, calmly swinging his sword around in a slow circle.

'John!' Alys cried, the fear behind her bravery making her voice crack.

John struggled to hold on to the icy distance of his battle haze. It threatened to break at that sob in her voice. He could not lose control now, not until he knew she was safe. 'Hold on very tightly, Alys. It won't be much longer.'

'John, please, be careful,' she cried.

With an incoherent shout, Merton dived towards John, his sword waving wildly. John's own blade shot up and the two points of steel met with a deafening clang. He felt the impact of it through his whole body, but he recovered quickly, freeing his sword with a deft twirl.

His opponent's blood was obviously burning hot and his attacks were wild with fury. John had to find his footing on the slippery, frozen ground and he spun away to deflect another blow. When Merton faltered, John leaped forward with a series of quick, light strokes to press his advantage.

Merton stabbed out at him, nearly catching his shoulder, but John managed to drive him back to the shadow of the looming trees. Merton stumbled and fell back against one of the snow-dusted trunks. With a roar, he tried to drive his sword up into John's chest, but it was neatly sidestepped. The tip of Merton's blade did catch his shoulder, though, with a startling sting. John spun around and drove his own blade neatly through Merton's padded sleeve, pinning him to the trunk of Alys's tree.

Merton roared and ripped his sleeve free to drive forward again. But then the man did something John could never have expected in all his years of battle. He turned and ran, crashing through the trees like a wounded bear.

John ran after him, following the man's twisted, almost blinded path as he made his way towards the river. John wondered if Merton had a boat there, or if he was merely crazed. His own shoulder ached and he could feel blood seeping through his doublet, seeming to freeze in the cold night, but he hardly noticed. He kept running, chasing after the coward who had fled from their fight. The villain who had dared to hurt Alys.

They broke free from the line of trees to the half-frozen river. Merton ran to the very bank itself, his boots sliding. He glanced back and saw John gaining on him, and plunged ahead on to the river itself.

The ice, though, was only at the water's edge, and with a terrible cracking sound, he plunged into the water below. His head surfaced briefly and a terrible, shrill scream split the night.

'I can't swim! Help me,' Merton cried. 'Help me…'

John carefully crept closer to the river, watching for the tides as they swept past, carrying chunks of ice. He was lighter than Merton, leaner, and he walked lighter. The man's screams were pitiful and, even knowing of what he had done, John felt compelled to help him if he could. Merton had to pay for his crimes, but not like this. He held out his sword towards the man's flailing arms, but the river was sweeping him away.

'Catch on to the blade!' John shouted. 'I can pull you out.'

Merton's hand flailed for that small lifeline, but he was now much too far away. The river wanted to claim her own victim now. Merton sank below the water and couldn't be seen any longer at all.

John fell back on to his heels, exhausted and saddened by all that had happened that night. But he knew he had to keep moving. His own tasks were not finished and the most important one lay before him.

He made his way back to the turning of the pathway, and found that Alys had climbed down her sanctuary tree. She stumbled into his arms, sobbing, and he caught her close.

'I hoped you would come for me,' Alys sobbed against his shoulder. 'I hoped you did not mean it when you sent me away.'

John held her close, kissing her over and over, feeling her precious warmth in his arms. The past seemed gone in that moment, washed away. Alys was with him, safe in his embrace, and he knew he couldn't ever let her go again. He had done it twice. He did not have the strength to do it a third time. 'My love,' he whispered. 'My brave, brave love. I am so very sorry I ever hurt you.'

'I fear I am not so brave.' She shuddered against him. 'I was so frightened. When I found out what he had done...'

'It is over now. You are safe. You will never be in such a place again, I promise.'

She looked up at him, her eyes wide and bruised in her pale face. 'But you are not! Your arm, look.'

In truth, John had barely noticed when Merton's sword had nicked his arm and he had forgotten it now. The cold wind, the relief in having Alys safe, it had all numbed him, sent him into almost a different world. 'It's only a small scratch. I can't even feel it now. Come, we must get you back to the warmth of the palace, before you catch the ague in this chill.'

'I am a bit cold,' she murmured, her tone full of surprise. 'I didn't even notice it before, but now I feel quite frozen through. How odd.'

She *did* look pale, he saw as he lifted her face up to his and examined her beloved features most carefully. Her lips were turning blue and her eyes were wide and startled. She swayed against him and he caught her up in his arms. He carried her towards his waiting horse, and her head drooped on to his shoulder. He had seen such things so often; the heat of battle carried men forward and when it was over they suddenly collapsed.

'We'll have you back to the palace in only a moment,' he said with a calm cheerfulness he was far from actually feeling. He could not let her see his own fear. 'With a warm fire and some of the Queen's own fine malmsey wine.'

'I feel quite well now,' she said, but her voice was faint, her head growing heavier on his shoulder. 'I don't even feel the wind.'

John carefully lifted her into his saddle and swung up behind her, turning his horse towards the palace even as he heard the Queen's soldiers thundering towards them. He would have to tell them everything, to account for his actions that night, but not yet. The most important thing was to see to Alys. *Please,* he begged silently. *Do not let her be ill.* Not when they had only just found each other again…

Chapter Twenty-Four

Alys lay on her side in her borrowed bed, staring out of the window at the river far below. The small private bed-chamber the Queen had given her when she was brought back to the palace after John rescued her was a comfortable one, with fine painted cloths lining the walls to keep out the cold and velvet bed hangings and quilts. A fire crackled merrily in the grate and there were piles of books and embroidery to keep her occupied.

But she saw none of it. She could only think about John, of the way he had come for her, saved her and held her close in the chilly darkness. How he had kissed her, as if he had not rejected her before and left her heart broken. Surely he did love her, as she loved him? Surely he saw that was all that truly mattered?

Yet she hadn't seen him in the days since. She wished she could know his thoughts now, know what would happen next.

'Alys, are you awake?' a voice whispered from the doorway.

Alys sat up, startled to see Ellen there. She had heard that Ellen was still at court, though her brother had been arrested in the countryside for his part in Merton's plot. Alys saw Ellen's face was still bruised, her eyes reddened as if she had been crying. She no longer wore courtly silks, but a plain grey-woollen gown, her golden hair drawn back under a cap.

'Ellen, how do you fare?' she asked gently. 'I have been so worried.'

Ellen smiled ruefully as she sat down on the stool next to the bed. 'You should not be worried about *me*, Alys. I betrayed you.'

'Only because you were forced to, I am sure,' Alys said. 'Lord Merton threatened your brother, did he not?'

Ellen hesitated before she answered. Keeping secrets was deeply ingrained at court. But then she shook her head and said, 'My brother worked with him. He was promised great riches once the Spanish were here. He knew Peter when they were boys, at a Catholic school for young Englishmen in the Low Countries, and I met him when he visited our home once. He was infatuated with me and often wrote to me. Merton thought I would be a good contact for Peter, to receive word of the Armada's progress. Merton, he—he knew my brother could not always be trusted to be discreet and he threatened me with my family's exposure if I did not do as he said.' She burst into tears, and buried her face in her hands. 'Now we are ruined anyway and I hurt you, my friend! Can you ever forgive me?'

Alys shook her head sadly. 'Oh, Ellen. Of course I can. You tried to help me in the end, tried to keep them from taking me away, and you were also hurt for it. We all must serve our families here when they are in danger, it seems, no matter what.'

She thought of her own father, far away at Dunboyton,

and her hopes of bringing him to England. Of John and all the danger he had faced for his own family's honour.

She pressed a handkerchief into Ellen's hand and Ellen gave her a weak smile. Alys remembered Ellen's offer of friendship when she first arrived at court, so alone and uncertain. 'What will you do now, Ellen?' she asked. 'Will you stay at court?'

Ellen shook her head. 'I cannot do that, not with my brother in disgrace. Sir Matthew Morgan has arranged for me to go to my father's cousin, Lady Everley, at her country estate. I will be out of the way there.'

'Sir Matthew?' Alys said, thinking of John's austere godfather, a man with many secrets behind his calm grey eyes. He did not seem like the sort to gallantly help a lady for naught.

'He thinks perhaps I might have an aptitude for codes that could prove—useful.'

Alys studied Ellen's face, worried for her friend. What would her future hold, in the power of a man such as Sir Matthew? 'I hope you will be most careful.'

Ellen flashed a smile that was almost like her old, brilliant self. 'You need have no worries about me. You should just enjoy yourself now! You are acclaimed a heroine at court, who saved the Queen from villains invading the royal bedchamber.'

Alys felt her cheeks turn warm with a blush and she pulled the blankets up around her shoulders as if to hide. 'I am hardly a heroine, just for getting snatched away.'

'But you saved the Queen from such a fate! You should relish it now. Surely you will be rewarded. Perhaps even with marriage.' Her smile turned teasing. 'Sir John has been hanging about in the corridor outside this chamber for days, questioning all the physicians most closely.'

A tiny flame of hope flickered to life deep in Alys's heart. He had been there, asking about her? He had not truly forgotten her?

'The Queen has said you were not to be allowed visitors, until today, in fear it would tire you,' Ellen said. 'But I have the feeling he might just be waiting now...'

She gave Alys one more smile and stood to leave the room. There was the low murmur of voices outside the door and, before Alys could even smooth her hair, John appeared at her bedside.

His hair was rumpled and a dark shadow of whiskers covered his jaw, as if he had neglected to shave in the last few days. He knelt down beside the bed and took her hand in his, studying her carefully with his sea-green eyes, as if to make sure she was truly there.

'Alys,' he said, 'you are well?'

She smiled at him, that hope that had touched her heart a moment ago flaming brighter. 'Very well, thanks to you. You came after me. I knew you would.'

'Alys, my angel,' he said hoarsely, bowing his head over her hand. 'Can you ever forgive me for hurting you? I thought it for the best that we parted, I thought that was the only way I could cease to hurt you.'

'Only you going away from me could hurt me, John.'

'I knew that once you were taken from me,' he said. 'I have never known such fear in my life. The thought that I would never see your sweet smile again, never touch your hand like this—I could not bear it.'

Alys laughed with joy. 'I feel the same, John. We are bound together, you and I. We have been ever since I found you on that beach.'

He smiled and it was like the summer sun coming

out, warming her heart. 'So we must go on saving each other?'

'For the rest of our lives, I hope.'

'Does that mean you will marry me, Alys? That you will stay with me even in a tumbledown pile like my house at Huntleyburg?'

Alys feared her heart would burst, it was so full. 'I would go with you anywhere at all, John, as long as we are together.'

'My angel,' he said and leaned closer to press his lips to hers in a warm kiss filled with the promise of all the days to come. 'I do love you.'

'As I love you.'

He kissed her hand. 'I have petitioned the Queen to hear us at the banquet tonight.'

Alys shivered with a touch of apprehension, remembering how the Queen had declared she did not like her ladies to wed. 'Will she give us permission?'

'If she does not, we may have to go live in the woods like Robin of the Hood,' he said. His words were light, teasing, but Alys knew him well now and she could hear the doubt behind them.

'If I have you, I have my home,' she said and clung tightly to him.

'Then wear this,' he said and took out the ring she had once worn all the way from Ireland and then lost. He slid it on to her finger, a solid promise between them. 'And remember we are always together, no matter what.'

'Are you sure you must do this, my lady?' Alys's maid Molly asked, fastening a pearl necklace around Alys's throat and straightening her lace ruff. 'You do look pale.'

Alys shook out the folds of her white satin gown,

trimmed with silver fox fur and embroidered with fine silver flowers. It was her best gown, saved for a most special occasion. 'I cannot miss any more of the festivities, can I, Molly? It's become so lonely in here.' And she had to see John again, to touch his hand and know they were bound together, come what may.

She quickly pinched her cheeks, hoping to look less pale, to look as if she hadn't a care in the world except to celebrate Christmas. She smiled at Molly and hurried out the door and along the corridors to the Great Hall, where crowds were gathering to await the Queen's arrival.

Alys marvelled at the beauty around her. The vast, dark hall had been transformed into a wintry forest. Hangings of white and silver draped from the ceiling beams, enclosing them in shimmering moonlight, and tall trees in silver pots lined the aisles. Pages also in white moved among the courtiers with trays of wine goblets and the musicians in their gallery played soft madrigals of love and summertime.

Unlike the real winter forest outside, the air was warm from the roaring fires and the crowds of velvet- and fur-clad people, who clustered around Alys as she appeared to exclaim over her adventures. She smiled and chatted with them, sipping at her wine, but all the time she searched for John's face in the crowd. She did not see him and a tiny, icy spot of worry touched her heart.

Suddenly, there was a loud herald of trumpets from the gallery and Queen Elizabeth appeared in the doorway, dazzling in black velvet with sleeves of cloth of gold, her red hair piled high and twined with gold-wrought leaves. On her arm was John.

Alys's heart beat quicker at the sight of him, so very handsome in a tawny-gold doublet trimmed with black ribbons and jet buttons, a topaz earring in his ear and a courtly smile on his face as he listened to the Queen. He did not seem worried at all; surely she should not either, Alys told herself.

The Queen mounted her white-draped dais, her golden train rippling behind her. She raised her hand and silence fell over the hall. 'We have much to celebrate tonight, methinks, after so many dangers have been turned aside and we have music and wine in abundance. We also have thanks to give. Lady Alys Drury, come forward!'

Alys folded her hands together to stop them from trembling and made her way forward. John met her at the foot of the dais and together they made their bows to the Queen.

'We owe you a great deal, Lady Alys, for the bravery you have shown in our defence,' Queen Elizabeth said. 'And, as it is the Yule season, we are given to dispensing gifts. What would be your wish?'

Alys glanced at John, who gave her a reassuring smile. 'Your Majesty's safety is a great gift indeed.'

The Queen waved the words away with her jewelled hand. She turned to John with a teasing arch of her brow. 'What would *you* gift such a heroine, Sir John?'

'I would give Lady Alys anything in my power, Your Majesty,' he answered with a bow.

'Hmm.' The Queen frowned as if she contemplated what to do next. 'Then we have a suggestion, provided that Lady Alys's excellent father agrees. He has served me long and well in Ireland and now we are minded to think of his retirement. He has been sent for and should arrive at court very soon.'

'Oh, Your Majesty, thank you so very much!' Alys

cried, her heart lifting at the thought that she would see her father again.

'If Sir William Drury agrees, then we shall have a wedding in the New Year,' Queen Elizabeth said. 'Sir John, we order you to marry Lady Alys, and make her mistress of your estate at Huntleyburg. Craftsmen and workers shall be sent there before your wedding to make it comfortable. What say you? Is this too onerous a task?'

Alys's hand tightened on John's and his fingers squeezed hers. This could not be real, she thought. It was another dream. She had just been given all she could ever desire! She looked up at John and saw her own hope and joy reflected in his green eyes.

It *was* real. She had her love.

'I would say I am most content with this, Your Majesty,' he said.

'And you, Lady Alys?' Queen Elizabeth said. 'Do you accept this as reward for your bravery?'

'I do, Your Majesty,' Alys whispered.

'Very good. Now, we must have a dance! Musicians, play a galliard,' the Queen commanded and swept off her dais to lead the dance.

Alys took John's arm and let him lead her to their own places in the figures. 'Is it true, then?' she said, holding his arm tightly so he could not slip away from her. Not now, so close to their dream coming true. 'We will marry and live at your home, and my father will come to England as well?'

'It seems so,' John said with a laugh. 'But are you truly sure you want to marry me, my angel, after all I have put you through? Will you be content as a country lady, away from the court?'

'I shall be the most content lady England ever saw,'

she said. 'I only ever wanted your heart, John, as you have mine.'

'And that you shall have, my lady, for the rest of our days. Now—may I have this dance?'

Alys laughed, and held on to his hand to twirl into the most merry Christmas dance she had ever known. A dance of truest love.

Epilogue

St James's Palace—springtime

'There, Alys. You look absolutely beautiful.' Ellen finished adjusting Alys's lace ruff and stepped back with a smile to examine her handiwork.

'If I look at all presentable, it will be thanks to you.' Alys laughed nervously, and twitched at her sleeve, white brocade shot with glittering silver thread and slashed to reveal fine silver satin beneath. 'I've never worn such a gown before.'

'The raw material for stylish beauty must be there first, of course,' Ellen answered. 'Now, go have a peek in the looking glass.'

Alys went to the precious polished glass the Queen had loaned them and peered cautiously into it. She almost gasped at what she saw, sure it could not be her. She wore her new gown of silver-and-white brocade and satin, trimmed with lace and pearl embroidery, a silver edge to her ruff and a train attached at her shoulders of deep blue velvet. Her dark hair was piled high and twined with pearls, and she wore her mother's pearl-and-diamond earrings. A new necklace of pearls, the gift of her father, shimmered at her throat.

'Oh, Ellen, you *have* done wonders! I do not look like myself at all.'

'It isn't every day a lady gets married and in the Queen's own chapel,' Ellen answered with a wistful smile. She seemed sad for a moment, but then she laughed and turned away to smooth her own blue-velvet skirts. 'We should hurry, or we'll be late. You cannot keep your handsome bridegroom waiting.'

Alys thought of John, her wonderful, handsome John, soon to be her own husband, and she laughed with the marvel of it all. 'Yes, let us hurry.'

Ellen led the way out of their dressing room and through the corridors to the Queen's great gallery, a long walkway with tall, sparkling windows on one side, looking out to the spring-green park, and fine tapestries lining the dark wood wall on the other. Alys's train wound behind her, until two little girls in gold brocade and crowned with flower wreaths hurried to pick it up. More girls walked before her, scattering rose petals as she walked. The courtiers who waited, a bouquet themselves in their bright satins, fell into procession behind her.

Alys had been wounded in the Queen's service and this was how Elizabeth rewarded her, with a wedding fit for a princess. Alys couldn't believe this was how the Queen lived every day, with people staring and processing behind her, everyone clad in their finest in her honour. It seemed amazing, for a while anyway, but Alys couldn't wait to depart. She and John were being sent to Paris for a royal mission, then would return to Huntleyburg to make their home there.

They moved down a covered outdoor walkway towards the royal chapel. The winter seemed truly gone now, the breeze from the park warm and scented with sweet flowers and greenery. The world seemed made entirely new with the sun. The dangers of the winter were far behind them at last.

Her father waited at the doorway for her, smiling as he held out his hand to her. He, too, wore white satin and blue velvet, a plumed cap on his greying head. He seemed to have regained so much of his health since he had returned to England and his smile was brighter now in his own new life.

'My dearest Alys,' he said, his voice thick with tears as he kissed her cheek. 'How beautiful you are. Just like your mother.'

Alys felt tears prickle at her own eyes. 'I am sure she watches us today.'

'Elena is always with us. She walks with us now.'

The doors opened, spilling out a great fanfare of music, and Alys took her father's arm to step inside. The royal chapel, where they said the Queen had knelt in prayer as the Armada advanced on her kingdom, was truly splendid. The gilded ceiling far above their heads, carved with Tudor roses and royal initials crowned, glittered in the light from the tall windows and the mosaic floor beneath their feet gleamed. The guests took their places in the tiered pews and Alys and her father processed towards the gold-and-white altar. In the gallery above their heads, the Queen herself watched the ceremony, a spring princess in pale green and silver.

But the only person Alys could see waited for her at the altar. John had never looked as splendid as he did in that moment, in blue velvet slashed and embroidered with gold, yet Alys saw only her Juan in his rough clothes and beard. The man who had opened the whole world to her, shown her that she had her own strength.

They had both been so lonely in their lives and now they would never be alone again. They would see the world together and make the rest of their lives something most splendid.

Her father gently placed her hand in John's and the Queen's own chaplain stepped forward to unite them.

John raised her hand to his lips for a gentle kiss. When he smiled at her, his beautiful eyes shone with tears and it made her want to cry with joy, too.

'My beautiful bride,' he said. ''Tis a lovely day for a wedding.'

'Oh, aye,' Alys answered. 'The most beautiful day of all…'

* * * * *

*If you enjoyed this story,
you won't want to miss these other
great reads from Amanda McCabe*

*THE RUNAWAY COUNTESS
RUNNING FROM SCANDAL
BETRAYED BY HIS KISS
THE DEMURE MISS MANNING*

Author Note

The Spanish Armada—*La Grande y Felicisima Armada*: 'The Great and Most Fortunate Navy'—was one of the most dramatic episodes of the reign of Elizabeth I and one of her defining moments. If it had succeeded, the future of England would have been very different indeed, but luckily the weather, the Spanish under-preparedness and the skill of the English navy were on the Queen's side. The mission to overthrow Elizabeth, re-establish Catholicism in England and stop English interference in the Spanish Low Countries was thwarted.

King Philip began preparing his invasion force as early as 1584, with big plans for his fleet to meet up with the Duke of Parma in the Low Countries, ferry his armies to England and invade. His first choice as commander was the experienced Marquis of Santa Cruz, but when Santa Cruz died Philip ordered the Duke of Medina Sedonia to take command of the fleet.

The Duke was an experienced warrior on land. But he had no naval background and no interest in leading the Armada, as the invasion fleet came to be called. He begged to be dismissed, but Philip ignored the request, as well as many other good pieces of advice about adequate supplies and modernising his ships.

After many delays the Armada set sail from Lisbon in April 1588. The fleet numbered over one-hundred-and-thirty ships, making it by far the greatest naval fleet of its age. According to Spanish records, over thirty thousand men sailed with the Armada, the vast majority of them soldiers. A closer look, however, reveals that this 'Invincible Armada' was not quite so well armed as it might have seemed. Many of the Spanish vessels were converted merchant ships, better suited to carrying cargo than engaging in warfare at sea. They were broad and heavy, and could not manoeuvre quickly under sail.

The English navy, recently modernised under the watch of Drake and Hawkins, was made up of sleek, fast ships, pared down and manoeuvrable. Naval tactics were evolving; it was still common for ships to come alongside each other and allow fighting men to engage in hand-to-hand combat. Advances in artillery were only just beginning to allow for more complex strategies and confrontations at sea. At this stage the English were far more adept at artillery and naval tactics than the Spanish, who were regarded as the best soldiers in Europe.

The Spanish plans called for the fleet to sail up the English Channel and rendezvous off Dover with the Duke of Parma, who headed the Spanish forces in the Netherlands. This in itself presented huge problems. Communications were slow and the logistical problems of a rendezvous at sea were immense.

Perhaps worst of all the problems faced by the Armada was Philip himself. The King insisted on controlling the details of the Armada's mission. He issued a steady stream of commands from his Palace of the Escorial, yet he seldom met with his commanders and he never allowed his experienced military leaders to evolve their own tactics. He did not listen to advice, which was a shame, for Philip had little military training and a poor grasp of naval matters. He firmly believed that God guided him and that therefore his mission would succeed.

A series of signal beacons atop hills along the English and Welsh coasts were manned. When the Spanish ships were at last sighted off The Lizard, on the nineteenth of July, 1588, the beacons were lit, speeding the news throughout the realm. The English ships slipped out of their harbour at Plymouth and under cover of darkness managed to get behind the Spanish fleet.

The Spanish sailed up the Channel in a crescent formation, with the troop transports in the centre. When the Spanish finally reached Calais they were met by a collection of English vessels under the command of Howard. Each fleet numbered about sixty warships, but the advantage of artillery and manoeuvrability was with the English.

Under cover of darkness the English set fire ships adrift, using the tide to carry the blazing vessels into the massed Spanish fleet. Although the Spanish were prepared for this tactic, and quickly slipped anchor, there were some losses and inevitable confusion.

On Monday July the twenty-ninth the two fleets met in battle off Gravelines. The English emerged victorious, although the Spanish losses were not great; only three ships were reported sunk, one captured and four more run aground. Nevertheless, the Duke of Medina Sedonia determined that the Armada must return to Spain. The English blocked the Channel, so the only route open was north, around the tip of Scotland and down the coast of Ireland.

Storms scattered the Spanish ships, resulting in heavy losses. By the time the tattered Armada regained Spain it had lost half its ships and three-quarters of its men, leaving a fascinating trove of maritime archaeological sites along the Irish coast—and myths of dark-eyed children born to Irish women and rescued Spanish sailors! In reality, most of them met fates far more grim and sad.

In England the victory was greeted as a sign of divine approval for the Protestant cause. The storms that scattered the Armada were seen as intervention by God. Services of thanks were held throughout the country and a commemorative medal was struck, with the words 'God blew and they were scattered' inscribed on it.

Come and visit me any time at ammandamccabe.com, where I always have historical info and fun stuff like deleted scenes!

If you'd like to read more about this fascinating and tragic event, here are a few sources I liked:

Robert Milne-Tyne, *Armada!*, 1988

Ken Douglas, *The Downfall of the Spanish Armada in Ireland*, 2009

Neil Hanson, *The Confident Hope of a Miracle: The True History of the Spanish Armada*, 2003

Laurence Flanagan, *Ireland's Armada Legacy*, 1988

James Hardiman, *The History of the Town and Country of Galway*, 1820

Colin Martin, *Shipwrecks of the Spanish Armada*, 2001

Garrett Mattingly, *The Armada*, 1959

I have come this far... I cannot give up now.

She sucked in a deep breath and reached for the huge
iron knocker. Still she hesitated, her fingers curled around
the cold metal. It felt stiff, as though it was rarely used.
She released it, nerves fluttering.

Before she could gather her courage again, a loud
bark followed by a sudden rush of feet had her spinning
on the spot. A pack of dogs, all colors and sizes, leaped
and woofed and panted around her. Heart in mouth, she
backed against the door, her bag clutched up to her chest
for protection. In desperation, she bent her leg at the knee
and drummed her heel against the door behind her.

After what felt like an hour, she heard the welcome
sound of bolts being drawn and the creak of hinges as the
door was opened.

Grace turned slowly. She looked up...and up. And
swallowed. Hard. A powerfully built man towered over

her, his face averted, only the left side visible. His dark brown hair was unfashionably long, his shoulders and chest broad and his expression—what she could see of it—grim.

"You're late," he growled. "You look too young to be a governess. I expected someone older."

Anticipation spiraled as the implications of the man's words sank in. If Lord Ravenwell was expecting a governess, why should it not be her? She was trained. If his lordship thought her suitable, she could stay. She would see Clara every day and could see for herself that her daughter was happy and loved.

The man's gaze lowered, and lingered. Grace glanced down and saw the muddy streaks upon her gray cloak.

"That was your dogs' fault," she pointed out indignantly.

The man grunted and stood aside, opening the door fully, gesturing to her to come in. Gathering her courage, Grace stepped past him, catching a whiff of fresh air and leather and the tang of shaving soap. She took two steps and froze.

On the left-hand side, a staircase rose to a half landing and then turned to climb across the back wall to a galleried landing that overlooked the hall on three sides. There, halfway up the second flight of stairs, a small face—eyes huge, mouth drooping—peered through the wooden balustrade. Grace's heart lurched.

Clara.

Don't miss
THE GOVERNESS'S SECRET BABY by Janice Preston,
available December 2016 wherever
Harlequin® Historical books and ebooks are sold.

www.Harlequin.com

HHEXP1116

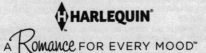

REQUEST YOUR FREE BOOKS!

✦HARLEQUIN®

ℋISTORICAL

Where love is timeless

2 FREE NOVELS PLUS 2 FREE GIFTS!

YES! Please send me 2 FREE Harlequin® Historical novels and my 2 FREE gifts (gifts are worth about $10). After receiving them, if I don't wish to receive any more books, I can return the shipping statement marked "cancel." If I don't cancel, I will receive 6 brand-new novels every month and be billed just $5.69 per book in the U.S. or $5.99 per book in Canada. That's a savings of at least 12% off the cover price! It's quite a bargain! Shipping and handling is just 50¢ per book in the U.S. and 75¢ per book in Canada.* I understand that accepting the 2 free books and gifts places me under no obligation to buy anything. I can always return a shipment and cancel at any time. Even if I never buy another book, the two free books and gifts are mine to keep forever.

246/349 HDN GH2Z

Name _____ (PLEASE PRINT) _____

Address _____ Apt. # _____

City _____ State/Prov. _____ Zip/Postal Code _____

Signature (if under 18, a parent or guardian must sign) _____

Mail to the **Reader Service:**
IN U.S.A.: P.O. Box 1867, Buffalo, NY 14240-1867
IN CANADA: P.O. Box 609, Fort Erie, Ontario L2A 5X3

Want to try two free books from another line?
Call 1-800-873-8635 or visit www.ReaderService.com.

* Terms and prices subject to change without notice. Prices do not include applicable taxes. Sales tax applicable in N.Y. Canadian residents will be charged applicable taxes. Offer not valid in Quebec. This offer is limited to one order per household. Not valid for current subscribers to Harlequin Historical books. All orders subject to credit approval. Credit or debit balances in a customer's account(s) may be offset by any other outstanding balance owed by or to the customer. Please allow 4 to 6 weeks for delivery. Offer available while quantities last.

Your Privacy—The Reader Service is committed to protecting your privacy. Our Privacy Policy is available online at www.ReaderService.com or upon request from the Reader Service.

We make a portion of our mailing list available to reputable third parties that offer products we believe may interest you. If you prefer that we not exchange your name with third parties, or if you wish to clarify or modify your communication preferences, please visit us at www.ReaderService.com/consumerschoice or write to us at Reader Service Preference Service, P.O. Box 9062, Buffalo, NY 14240-9062. Include your complete name and address.

HHI5